"John, I'm p

He sat back and looked at the bare wall opposite him. He was mistakenly caught in someone else's life. He had to be.

"Did you hear me?" Caroline Prater's voice, though soft, seemed to grate.

"I'm sorry." He turned to look at her. "What did you say?"

"I said I'm pregnant."

Uh-huh. Well. What did he do now? "I, uh, I'm sorry," he told her. "I don't really know what to say."

"I had to tell you. You have a right to know."

This was a right?

"Aren't you going to ask if it's yours?"

His eyes met hers. Their brown depths were as luminous as he remembered them. Her slim, strong, perfectly curved body was pretty impressive, but it was those eyes that had captivated him that cold December night in Kentucky. What, six weeks ago?

"I'm assuming you wouldn't be here if it wasn't."

Dear Reader,

Whether you've been to Shelter Valley before or find yourself here for a first visit—welcome! It's never too late to join us in this town—a home away from home for many readers around the world. Shelter Valley has become a place of refuge, of hope and happiness, of new beginnings, of strength through adversity, of *life*.

If you're here for the first time, don't worry. So is Caroline Prater. Join this intelligent but uneducated farm girl as she comes to town with a big heart…and some shocking secrets. You'll travel with her from her home in Kentucky, find a boardinghouse, meet the residents of Caroline's new town. And if you've been here before, I think you'll enjoy seeing the world of Shelter Valley through her eyes. You'll meet old friends and find out what they're up to, how they've fared since you saw them last. Pretty much everyone you've met in Shelter Valley appears in *Somebody's Baby*.

Don't let me give you the impression that this is going to be a lighthearted romp through town. It's not. Caroline and John and the rest of the Shelter Valley residents are living life—real life—with its ups and downs, its fears and hardships. They ask questions of themselves and each other, the same questions we all ask. Hard questions that don't always have answers. Certainly not easy answers…

So come to Shelter Valley! We're waiting. With refuge and hope, the promise of happiness, the possibility of new beginnings and—most of all—with the belief that love truly is the greatest thing of all.

Tara Taylor Quinn

I love to hear from my readers. You can reach me at P.O. Box 13584, Mesa, Arizona 85216 or through my Web site at www.tarataylorquinn.com.

TARA TAYLOR QUINN

SOMEBODY'S BABY

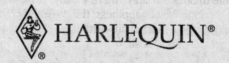

TORONTO • NEW YORK • LONDON
AMSTERDAM • PARIS • SYDNEY • HAMBURG
STOCKHOLM • ATHENS • TOKYO • MILAN • MADRID
PRAGUE • WARSAW • BUDAPEST • AUCKLAND

ISBN 0-373-71272-3

SOMEBODY'S BABY

Copyright © 2005 by Tara Taylor Quinn.

Printed in U.S.A.

For all the members of my family, blood and otherwise,
who manage to hang on through all my life's changes
and love me, regardless. Who accept my love for them,
regardless. You've shown me the real life strength of love—
a knowledge I now share with the world.

Books by Tara Taylor Quinn

HARLEQUIN SUPERROMANCE
567—YESTERDAY'S SECRETS
584—McGILLUS V. WRIGHT
600—DARE TO LOVE
624—NO CURE FOR LOVE
661—JACOB'S GIRLS
696—THE BIRTH MOTHER
729—ANOTHER MAN'S CHILD
750—SHOTGUN BABY
784—FATHER: UNKNOWN
817—THE HEART OF CHRISTMAS
836—HER SECRET, HIS CHILD
864—MY BABIES AND ME
943—BECCA'S BABY*
949—MY SISTER, MYSELF*
954—WHITE PICKET FENCES*
1027—JUST AROUND THE CORNER*
1057—THE SECRET SON
1087—THE SHERIFF OF SHELTER VALLEY*
1135—BORN IN THE VALLEY*
1171—FOR THE CHILDREN
1189—NOTHING SACRED*
1225—WHAT DADDY DOESN'T KNOW

HARLEQUIN SINGLE TITLE
SHELTERED IN HIS ARMS*

*Shelter Valley Stories

MIRA BOOKS
WHERE THE ROAD ENDS
STREET SMART
HIDDEN (coming in July 2005)

THE RESIDENTS OF SHELTER VALLEY

Will Parsons: Dean of Montford University.

Becca Parsons: Mayor of Shelter Valley, wife of Will.

Bethany Parsons: Daughter of Becca and Will.

Ben Sanders: Husband of Tory, cousin of Sam Montford.

Tory Sanders: Wife of Ben.

Alex Sanders: Daughter of Ben, stepdaughter of Tory.

Phyllis Christine Sanders: Daughter of Ben and Tory.

Randi Foster: Sister of Will Parsons, married to Zack Foster. Manages women's athletic department at Montford.

Zack Foster: Veterinarian. Husband of Randi.

Cassie Montford: Veterinarian. Married to Sam Montford.

Sam Montford: Descended from the founder of the town. Married to Cassie.

James Montford: Father of Sam, married to Carol.

Mariah Montford: Adopted daughter of Sam and Cassie.

Phyllis Sheffield: Psychologist. Prominent in psychology department at Montford. Married to Matt Sheffield.

Matt Sheffield: Married to Phyllis. Works in theater at Montford University.

Calvin and Clarissa Sheffield: Twin children of Phyllis and Matt.

Beth Richards: Found refuge for herself and her son after escaping abusive ex-husband. Married to Greg Richards.

Greg Richards: Sheriff of Shelter Valley. Married to Beth.

Bonnie Neilson: Sister of Greg. Runs local day care. Married to Keith Neilson.

Katie Neilson: Daughter of Bonnie and Keith.

Martha Moore: Friend of Becca Parsons. Married to David Cole Marks, minister.

Ellen Moore Hanaran: Martha's daughter, married to Aaron.

John Strickland: Architect. Widower. Originally from Chicago.

Caroline Prater: New to Shelter Valley…

CHAPTER ONE

"ARE YOU CRAZY, Ma? You've lived in Grainville your whole life!" Caroline Prater could hear her son clearly, even with the phone held at arm's length. "You can't just pack up and move across the country all by yourself! And where *is* Shelter Valley, anyway? I've never even heard of the place. This is nuts! I knew I should never have left home...."

"It's in Arizona, Jess." She moved the phone close enough to speak into the mouthpiece, but kept the earpiece as far from her head as she could.

Sitting on the front porch of the little white farmhouse she'd lived in for almost eighteen years, Caroline snuggled more deeply into her old winter coat and pushed gently against the ground with one booted foot, setting the aged rocker in motion—and waited for Jesse to slow down enough to be able to listen to her. At not quite thirty-five, she was far too young to have a son who was a freshman at Harvard.

And way too old to be in her current predicament.

"What about Gram and Papa? And Grandma and Grandpa? You can't just *leave* them...." Her parents. And Randy's. She shored up her defenses against the twinge of guilt as Jesse's words hit their mark. Randy's parents had taken his death hard. He'd been their only son. Seeing her seemed to make things worse. And they had four daughters in Grainville—four sons-in-law. They'd be fine.

But her parents… Caroline looked out over the slush-covered two-acre yard in front of the house. She was going to have to get out the plow to smooth the potholes in the two dirt paths that served as a driveway or she'd never get her little and embarrassingly old pickup out of the gate.

She was going to miss her parents terribly, especially her mother, but there were things about her parents—about her father—that Jesse didn't know. And something about her that no one knew.

"Why didn't you say anything when I was home at Christmas, Ma?"

"Because I hadn't made up my mind then."

"It was only a week ago!"

Their first Christmas without Randy had been hard on all of them. It was harder on Caroline than anyone knew. Not only had she just lost the man she'd loved since childhood, but she'd suddenly become far too aware that, other than Jesse, none of the family with whom she'd been surrounded all her life were actually related to her. That had never been an issue before.

Jesse went on for another five minutes, reminding her about her responsibilities to the small cattle farm she and Randy had worked for the nearly eighteen years they'd been married.

He was right about that.

And he talked about her friends. All women who were resigned, most of them happily, to living out the lives that had been mapped for them in Grainville since the day they were born. The girls she'd gone to school with who'd stayed in town after graduation were married, with high-school-aged children.

Her son reminded her how unsafe it was for a woman to travel alone these days. Since Randy was killed when the tractor he was riding had exploded last summer, Jesse had taken to warning her about everything. Mostly she only half listened—just in case he said something she needed to hear, although that wasn't usually the case. Who did he think had been taking care of her—and him—all his life?

"I can't believe you aren't listening to me!"

Taking off a mitten, she glanced at her nails. They'd need to be fixed before she dared leave this town. "I'm listening, Jess."

"No, you aren't." His tone was filled with disgust. "I'm just gonna have to come home."

"No, you aren't." She didn't raise her voice as she repeated his words back to him. She didn't need to; Jesse knew the tone.

At seventeen, Jesse Randall Prater, one of the youngest freshmen at Harvard, was intelligent beyond his years, and also emotionally young. She'd been living with his outbursts of frustration most of his life. And giving them the credibility they deserved—which was none.

He huffed. And then again.

As she stared down at the peeling wood floor of the porch, a strand of auburn hair fell forward over her shoulder. It was clean. And that was about all she could say for it. Panic filtered down from her throat to her stomach. She couldn't afford some fancy hair salon.

And she was never going to pass for anything other than what she was—an uneducated country bumpkin—if she showed up in Shelter Valley looking like this. Her clothes were all wrong. Old jeans. Homemade shirts. Her makeup, which she'd worn maybe three times in the past year, had come from the grocery store in town. And she didn't own a single pair of shoes that hadn't, at some time or other, been in contact with cow manure.

"I don't get it, Ma. There's something you aren't telling me, isn't there?"

Caroline tensed. Her smart boy was back. It was the moment she'd been waiting for. And dreading.

I'm prepared, she reminded herself. *Just do it like you practiced it last night. And the night before that. And the night before...*

"Yes, my new cell number, for one." She rattled it off. "If you need me for anything in the next week, until I get settled and perhaps have a more permanent number, you can reach me on that."

He repeated the number. "I'm glad you got a cell," he added. "You're there all by yourself, driving back and forth to town with no one at home to know if you made it okay. You need a cell phone. And with the extra field we planted last year, you can afford it."

"Jess, I'm moving."

He swore again. And in the space of a second switched from maturing young man to little boy. "You can't move, Ma! Grainville's our home!"

Perhaps, but she couldn't dwell on that. Not if she was going to be able to leave.

"It's a town with a house. A mostly empty house."

He was quiet again. Caroline, desperately needing to fill the silence, to tell him the rest of why she'd called, didn't know what to say. She'd forgotten all her well-rehearsed lines. Her little boy was hurting and she was trapped by life's circumstances and couldn't help him.

More trapped than anyone knew.

"So, what is it you aren't telling me?" His words, when they finally came, were soft, compassionate.

Caroline's recently rehearsed lines popped into her chaotic brain. "You know I'm adopted."

"Yeah. So?"

The phone wasn't the right way to do this. It was, however,

her best shot at getting through while standing her ground. An uneducated country woman, Caroline understood her role—to be accommodating and obedient. And fell into it all too easily.

"Jess? Hear me out, okay? Without judgment or commentary?"

A pause. Then he said, "Sorry—yeah, I'll listen."

"Remember when I told you last fall about going through all the boxes in the cellar?" That first month after he'd left for school she'd thought she was going to die. Had prayed to die. Newly widowed with her only child gone, she'd never felt so alone. Her life seemed pointless, as if it might as well be over. Burying herself in memories, sorting them, preserving them, had been her only way to stay alive.

"Yeah. You sent me that comic Dad drew in high school." Randy had only been dead a couple of months before Jesse left for college. But the rift between him and the boy who looked so much like him had been in place long before that. They'd just been so completely different....

"I took some things to Gram one day, too, some old pictures. And after seeing them, she brought up a box from her cellar and gave it to me."

"What was in it?"

Caroline gave a shove against the ground, scraped the almost threadbare fabric of her jeans with one finger, willing her queasy stomach to calm. "She wouldn't tell me, wouldn't let me look until I got home, wouldn't talk about it at all. It was little—an old stationery box." It had pink roses all over it. Caroline couldn't imagine her mother ever having written a letter on a piece of paper covered with pink roses.

"So what was in it?" Jesse's voice was quiet now. But it still sounded as though he was waiting to take charge.

"A letter. And a ring."

Glancing at the bare hand growing pink with cold, Caroline studied the ring she'd worn since that day—although normally, when she was with other people, it was on a chain around her neck.

"It's the most beautiful piece of jewelry I've ever seen," she told her son. "A sapphire. Set in gold."

"Where'd it come from?" Jesse asked. And then, before she could answer, he burst out, "If it's so great, why did Gram have it stuffed away in some old box in the basement?"

"The letter—and ring—were from my birth mother." Caroline blinked as her eyes blurred, still staring at that ring. Jesse was going to think her a fool. Her father—and Randy's—would surely agree with him. And maybe she was.

Still…

"Who was she? Some teenager who got knocked up?"

"Jesse Randall Prater!" Caroline's cold cheeks burned, every nerve beneath her skin tensing. Did her son think of her with that same disrespect?

And if so, God help her, what would he think of her now?

"Well, isn't that why you had me, Ma? Because you knew what it felt like to be given away and you couldn't bear to do that to anyone else?"

She'd forgotten he knew that. It wasn't a part of her life that she talked about—it wasn't part of the reason she normally gave. But once, when Jesse had been about fourteen, and his father had taken his own insecurities out on his son, leaving the child feeling insignificant and unwanted, she'd told him her secret. That she hadn't just kept him because she'd loved his father and wanted to get married. Or because his maternal grandparents, who'd never been able to have children of their own, were fully supportive of their sixteen-year-old pregnant daughter, offering to help wherever they could to make it possible for her to keep her child. She'd kept him because she didn't ever want him to feel unworthy of life's basic necessities—food, shelter and unconditional love.

She'd never, for one second, regretted the decision. But there were times when being Jesse's mother hurt. A lot.

"I'm sorry, Ma." The apology came after only a minute of silence. She'd have waited ten if that was what it took. "You're just freaking me out with all this going-away stuff."

Jesse was scared. So was she. Terrified.

"My birth mother was well into her forties when she had me. My father was in his early fifties. She'd gone through menopause. They thought pregnancy was impossible."

"Wow," Jesse said softly. "You'd think, being that old, they'd have been able to provide for a kid."

Pulling both knees to her chest, Caroline laid her head on them, the worn denim soft against her cheeks as she gazed out at the yard that had barely changed since she'd moved there at seventeen. The old red maple tree was bigger. But it had already been huge. They'd put up a new fence ten years before. And the mailbox had been replaced when the old one was knocked down by a snowplow when Jesse was still a toddler.

"They did provide for one," she told her son. "They just couldn't manage two."

"Two!" His voice cracked. "You're a twin?" She almost smiled. It hadn't taken long for her genius son to figure *that* out.

"Yes."

She really should go inside where it was warm. But it was so empty. Unless she counted the memories that wouldn't leave her alone.

"Cool! Two Mas." He sounded like he was grinning. Caroline was grateful for the diversion, even knowing it would be short-lived. "Wait. Was the other kid a girl or a boy?"

"A girl."

"Were you identical?"

"No." Not that the letter had said one way or the other. Caroline had found out for herself, from pictures in newspaper articles on the Internet about her very successful twin. Her mother had given her the box at the end of September and within a week she'd joined a couple of Internet tracking services and had a folder on her computer filled with information.

"Damn!" Jesse said, quickly adding, "Uh, darn—sorry, Ma."

"You're a freshman in college, Jess," Caroline said, walking over to the porch rail, wondering how many more years it would stand up to Kentucky's weather. "Certainly old enough to make your own vocabulary choices."

"It's just so fantastic." His voice was more that of her intense little boy than the man he was quickly becoming. "I wonder how they chose which one of you to keep."

"Birth order," she told him. "They kept the first. I was born second."

Silence fell on the line.

"This had to be pretty hard on you, huh?" he asked a moment later. "Here I am, going on like some kind of jerk, not even thinking how this must've made you feel. Being the one given away and all."

"It's okay, Jess," she told him, hoping that someday the words would be true. "I've always known I was given away."

"Yeah, but knowing that one was kept—"

A chill swept through Caroline. She brushed some twigs off the top of the chipped porch rail and wrapped her arms around her midriff.

"And there I go again, putting my foot right in it," Jesse said, bringing a slow grin to his mother's face.

"So…does this, uh, talk about Shelter whatever have to do with the letter?"

"Yes." With the thumb of her left hand she reached for the sapphire on her ring finger. According to the letter from Caroline's birth mother, her twin had been given a ring, too. An opal. Apparently their mother had liked jewelry. "Her name is Phyllis Langford Sheffield. She's a professor of Psychology at Montford University in Shelter Valley."

"She married?"

"Yes. To a man named Matt Sheffield, Fine Arts Technical Coordinator at Montford." She wasn't too sure about her brother-in-law. She'd found an article about him, too. A disturbing one. Several years before Mr. Sheffield had taken the job at Montford, he'd been charged with statutory rape and sentenced to prison. He'd allegedly impregnated one of his students. That was a piece of news she was definitely *not* going to share with her son.

"They have any kids?"

"Two." She thought of the grainy newspaper photo she had in her wallet. "Twins. A boy and a girl. They're three."

"Damn!" Jesse said again. "Must run in the genes, huh?"

Her heart gave a little flip at his mention of genetics. "Yeah."

"Okay, I can see why a trip to Shelter Valley's important," Jesse said, almost magnanimously. "I'll be home for spring recess the last week of March. We can go then."

Pulling open the buttons on her coat, Caroline went inside, letting the screen door fall shut behind her. Randy had bought her year-round windows for the door a few Christmases ago, so she could leave the big old wooden door open, even in winter, and see out into the yard.

"I'm moving to Shelter Valley, Jess. This weekend."

"No way, Ma! You can't! You're being ridiculous. I get it about wanting to see your sister. Hell, I even get that you're feeling lonely, what with Dad dying and me gone almost right after, but you can't just up and move! What about the farm?"

"I'm going to hang on to it for a while. At least until I see how I like Shelter Valley. It's all paid for and the taxes are practically nothing…."

"We have cattle, Ma," Jesse said, as though speaking to a child. "They aren't just gonna wait around to see how you like life on the other side of the country. And we sure as hell can't afford to pay someone to look after them for us."

Us. It sounded so good. Too good. Because it wasn't true anymore. Jesse was off starting a life of his own. And Caroline had her own life to tend to. Whether she wanted to or not. She had some consequences to pay.

"I sold the cattle."

"You *what?*"

Even with the phone at arm's length, she could hear Jesse's yelp. She'd wanted to talk to him about the cattle—had thought he deserved to be a part of the decision—but she knew he'd talk her out of selling. And going.

And sister aside, she had to go. There was more reason to go to Shelter Valley than she could tell her son. He'd have to know eventually, her saner side kept reminding her.

But there was only so much she could handle at a time. And right now, that didn't include Jesse's likely reaction to her other news.

"I sold the cattle to give me enough money to live off until I get settled."

"I can't believe this!" He was sighing and whining and groaning all at once. "How do you expect to support yourself?" he asked. "You never even graduated from high school!"

"I got my equivalency years ago, you know that."

"And that'll get you a great career for sure," he said sarcastically.

In the tiny kitchen she'd lived in her entire adult life, Caroline poured a cup of coffee into her favorite mug, careful to miss the chipped part of the rim as she took a gulp.

"I'm planning to enroll in college," she said quietly, trying to control the fear and the doubts clutching at her heart. There was no one else on earth she'd have dared tell. "The semester doesn't start for another two weeks."

"You have to apply, Ma." Jesse's voice was equally soft. And loving.

"I did."

"And?"

"I've been accepted, Jess."

This time the silence was almost unbearable. With a shaking hand, Caroline lifted the mug again, took another sip of coffee that had been kept too hot by the old warming plate she'd been using with the old metal pot since high school. And burned her mouth.

She poured the stuff out. She shouldn't be drinking it, anyway. Not for the next eight months, at least. Although she'd drunk coffee when she'd been pregnant with Jesse.

"Congratulations, Ma." The pride in Jesse's voice was her undoing.

"AH, MERI, HERE I AM AGAIN…"

With an embarrassed look, John Strickland slid into the bubbling spa in his professionally landscaped private and walled yard. He leaned back and closed his eyes. It wasn't late, just dark. He'd had a long day. But his inner vision wasn't restful. Meri was there, her memory filling his mind. She was dressed in his favorite red gown, diamonds glittering at her throat and wrist, laughing.

And then not.

Now the glittering came from the lights of the fire truck,

police cars, the ambulance. Meri was lying inside the ambulance, wearing the red gown. But she wasn't laughing.

"Breathe," he said aloud. "Breathe." He could almost feel her struggle for air.

And then he opened his eyes. As long as he opened his eyes, she'd still be breathing.

"I know I promised we'd quit meeting like this." His words fell into the not-quite-freezing Shelter Valley January night, becoming part of the air around him, floating aimlessly in space. Just as he was.

"I'm supposed to be at dinner at Will's," he told his wife, as he imagined her sitting across from him. "Instead, here I am again, forgoing life to sit and talk to a dead woman."

A cold breeze wafted over the water. And his face.

"I need a drink."

He hoped to God his neighbors couldn't hear him over the bubbling water. Not that there was much chance anyone would be lounging around a backyard in what, for Shelter Valley, was considered a major cold front. Any time you could see your breath, it made the news.

"I'm still traveling more than you liked." He squinted at the empty space across from him, an idiot who was weak and disappointing himself even as he gave in to the overwhelming need to connect with the woman who'd left his life more than six years before.

He wiped at a trickle of sweat making its way from his forehead down between his eyes.

"Business is good. Finished another signature Strickland design last week."

The water was hot, but it didn't warm the blood in his veins. Nothing was going to do that. He'd resigned himself to the truth.

He hadn't told Meri about the capitol building dedication

he'd attended in Kentucky the first week of December. Hadn't talked to her at all over the holidays, keeping his promise to her—and to himself.

"I'm still working on my own," he reported aloud. "I have to commission some of the menial stuff, but I've been able to hang tough and not give in to the pressure to commercialize the Strickland trademark."

She'd cautioned him about that often. Said the world would be better off with fewer Strickland buildings if the ones it had were pure Strickland and not some watered-down version.

He currently had a small office in Shelter Valley with draftspeople and clerical staff, and another in Chicago. Most of his work he did out of his home.

"I have two state capitol buildings coming up in the next year. One on the East Coast, one on the West."

She'd want the details. So, as his butt turned numb, buffeted by jets while he sat on a cement bench, John gave them to her.

His backyard was really quite something. On one side was an arboretum shaded by a couple of olive trees that he'd paid a bundle to have brought in mature. From there, desert landscaping stones led down to a brick divider and then grass lush and green enough to have been on a tournament golf course. The grass led around to the wall in the back, where flowering bougainvillea climbed randomly, covering every available inch. In front of the grass was a negative-edge pool that appeared to be fed by a waterfall from the big boulder that flanked it. Off to the right was a gazebo with wet bar and stools and a gas barbecue. He'd had them put in when he bought the house.

He'd never used them.

"I broke off my engagement." He'd meant to tell her that

right off. But he'd needed some time alone with Meri before he brought another woman between them. Even if it was only to tell her there was no other woman between them.

John took a deep breath, ducked under the water, blew out the breath and came up for air. Pushing the hair off his forehead, he blinked and sat on the other side of the spa. There was still time to get inside, take a quick shower and get over to Will's before Becca served dinner. He could make some excuse for having missed the appetizer and drinks portion of the evening.

"I've tried, Meri." The pain and hopelessness in his voice scared him. Glancing at the star-filled blackness above him, he searched, as he had countless times, for some sign that he was being heard. That there was meaning to his existence, guidance from something stronger than his weak and pathetic self. "I just don't know how to live without you."

Oh, he had his moments. Times when his mind was preoccupied with other things and he actually behaved like a fully functioning, relatively normal human being. But they were only moments.

"I hurt Lauren."

But not as much as he would've hurt her if he'd married her and then remained committed to Meredith.

"You'd have liked her." John had liked her.

Pressure built in his head. He was getting too hot. He'd move inside. Soon. Get himself a drink. And maybe throw a frozen dinner in the microwave. Though he was relatively skilled in the kitchen, he didn't feel like cooking. Too much trouble for too little benefit.

"Martha Moore got married."

She was the first woman John had dated after Meri's death. He'd had a lot of talks with his wife about that. The day he'd met Martha. Whenever he'd passed her on the street. After the time—the only time—he'd been intimate with her.

And on the night last year, when he'd heard that the young woman who'd been raped in Shelter Valley was Martha's nineteen-year-old daughter, Ellen.

"Shot a thirty on the back nine today. Not my best, but still under par."

The spa, operating on an automatic timer, shut off. John got out, cooling off while he walked over to push the button again, then slid back into the dark depths, watching as his body slowly disappeared from sight. He needed a little more time before he rejoined the living.

Even if it was in name only.

He fought the urge to close his eyes and rest. He couldn't risk picking up the inner vision where it had left off. He wasn't going to let Meri stop breathing.

CHAPTER TWO

IT TOOK HER two and a half days to get to the Arizona border. And another five and a half hours to reach Shelter Valley. Or, at any rate, to take the turnoff for the town she couldn't wait to see. She passed Wal-Mart. Remembered reading about the kidnapping and subsequent rape that had taken place nearby the year before.

Felt again the tug at her heart as she pictured the town ahead, almost as though these people were already part of her. She wondered if Phyllis knew the girl who'd been raped. Or if John Strickland did...

That was when Caroline yanked the car onto a deserted-looking dirt track, turned off the ten-year-old half-size pickup with its brand-new locking bed cover—under which she'd packed most of her cherished possessions and the few articles of clothing she'd thought the least offensive—and sat.

Was it legal to sit on the side of the road in a nonemergency situation in Arizona? That was something she could check as soon as she got settled someplace and was able to hook up her computer. The cobbled-together piece of equipment was buckled into the seat next to her. Next to Jesse, that machine was the most important thing in the world to her. Though she'd had different versions of it through the years as various parts grew obsolete and were replaced, either using funds saved from egg money or by begging the library to give her cast-offs, the computer had long been her very best friend. Many times, it had felt like her only friend.

But soon she was going to be dealing with more than just a screen she could manage at will. Up ahead were real people.

And at least one of them wasn't going to be happy to see her. With a hand on her stomach, Caroline reached for her journal, a companion she referred to often and turned to the page she hadn't read since the night she'd made the entry.

Saturday, January 1, 2005

I took the test today. It told me what I already knew....

With a finger marking the page, she closed the book. She'd written those words only a week ago. But there were more. Another entry she hadn't dared to look back on.

She reached for the sapphire ring she'd put on a chain around her neck before leaving Grainville. It was there, hidden beneath her blouse, reminding her who she was.

She wasted a few minutes staring out over the unusual plants scattered across the desert to her right. She'd come this far. She could do this. Continue on, into town. Face whatever waited there. Begin her new life.

She deserved the chance.

Straightening her shoulders, Caroline opened the book again, flipped back several pages.

And forced herself to read.

Monday, November 22, 2004

I want to die. It would be so much more expedient to die. I went from being a child to being Randy's wife and Jesse's mom and now, suddenly, unexpectedly, I'm nei-

ther. Who am I, then? I ask and ask, and find there are no answers. And more frightening yet, I ask my heart who I want to be—and still can't find answers.

I've been married. Given it all I had. Imagined Randy and me in our eighties on the porch swing, smiling and trying to listen through our respective hearing aids to Jesse's grandchildren playing around the vibrant flower beds set off by a lush green yard. In this vision, the swing is treated birch, soft and supple, the porch floor solid oak. The house newly painted pristine white with forest-green shutters. And the porch rail strong enough to withstand any kind of weather.

Just like my real porch rail, my visions are chipped and faded, and any possibility of having them come true is lost forever. I will never, no matter what, grow old with Jesse's father and, with him, watch Jesse's grandchildren at play.

And what else do I have to offer? How can I change my future? I have no money. And no training that would allow me to make money. I can run the farm by myself for now, but even I know I won't always be able to do that.

My heart is empty. There is no joy. No excitement or anticipation. I've lived my best years and

Oh, God, what am I going to do?

Tears fell on the page, bringing Caroline out of that heartache and into the present. She held her breath, the sobs threatening to break free. She wasn't going to lose control now. She just couldn't.

She could turn the page. Travel to Frankfort, Kentucky. To the dedication of a building that had been designed by a Shelter Valley architect, and the political gathering that had been part of the proceedings. She could read what happened next.

Instead, Caroline hid the book in her glove compartment. It would be safe there. Safe from harm. And she would be safe from it.

Starting the truck, thanking it silently for cooperating on the first turn of the key, Caroline backed so slowly she barely kicked up any dust. She clunked the old vehicle into gear and drove toward Shelter Valley.

Before she could worry about starting college at the age of almost thirty-five, or coming face-to-face with a twin sister she'd never met, before she looked for a new home, or a bed to sleep in that night, she had something else to do.

Some news to deliver.

The town came into view. A streetlight glistened. Houses dotted the side of the road, growing more dense, and she saw her first Shelter Valley citizen, an older woman, carrying a plastic grocery bag, walking a dog without a leash. Her stomach fluttered with comfort. And then panic.

She thought she might throw up. She hadn't thrown up in years.

She watched for Mojave Street. And promised herself that whatever lay ahead, whatever his response, she could accept it.

She pulled into the driveway. Knocked on the door. Waited. Knocked again. And eventually returned to her truck. What did she do now? Every single time she'd imagined the beginning of her new life, this stop had been first—as though nothing else could happen until it was done.

It was stupid to sit there. He might not be home for days. Or maybe he'd be back in an hour.

The journal in her glove compartment drew her, as though the answer to her current dilemma lay in the revelations she'd decided to avoid.

Ignoring the impulse, she waited another half hour. Reached for the key in the ignition. And ended up at the glove compartment instead.

Wednesday, December 1, 2004

> *I read an article this morning and I can't think of anything else. An architect from Shelter Valley is going to be in Frankfort this weekend to dedicate a building he designed. His name is John Strickland. I read in an old Shelter Valley newspaper last week that Will Parsons hired an architect named John Strickland to design the new classroom building at Montford University. Will's the president of Montford. He hired Phyllis!*
>
> *Oh, God, I know I'm crazy, but I have to go! This man might actually know my twin sister!*

JOHN SHOT ONE HELL of a game of golf Saturday afternoon. Probably one of his best. Meredith would have teased him about his bragging. And later, she would've congratulated him with a kiss filled with pride—and a passion that never seemed to lose its urgency. He congratulated himself instead with a mug of beer at the bar, joining the other guys who didn't have wives and children to hurry home to. There were three of them that afternoon. John and two men whose wives had taken their children to the zoo in Phoenix to do research on a school project involving apes.

Sometimes, as much as he loved the peace and sense of home he found in Shelter Valley, John hated the place.

Trying to concentrate on positive thoughts, he pulled his Cadillac into the driveway of his two-year-old ranch-style custom home to find someone there ahead of him. It was a testimony to the state of his mind—of his life—that the surprise visitor brought a tinge of anticipation. For the next few moments, anyway, he wasn't going to be home alone trying to find ways to entertain himself during the remaining hours until the world once again became a workplace full of challenging issues and busy people. People demanding the kind of interaction he was capable of delivering…

A particularly telling testimony, considering the fact that the vehicle in his driveway probably belonged to the new yard guy. He'd never seen the old and rusty pickup before.

Parking to the side of the truck in the double driveway, he got out and approached just as the driver's window was lowering.

"Can I help y—"

The last word stuck in his throat. The driver wasn't his landscaper. It wasn't even a guy.

The woman stepped down from her truck. She was wearing jeans, a blue turtleneck, a worn-looking thickly knitted beige cardigan and the same brown leather boots she'd had on the first time he met her. She held out a hand with freshly polished nails. "John? I don't know if you remember me. I'm Caroline Prater."

He remembered.

"Caroline, hi." Fresh from the golf course, he wanted to shower and change out of the golf slacks and slightly sticky sweater he was wearing. The sun was shining as brightly as usual from clear blue skies. And although the temperature was only about sixty degrees, it had been hot out on the golf course.

"You don't seem pleased to see me, and I don't blame—"

"No!" He cut her off. Took her hand. It was as rough as he remembered. Working hands, she'd said. Something about that had touched him. "I'm just surprised. Kentucky's a long way off."

"And Shelter Valley is a very small town," she added with a nervous smile. He remembered that about her, too. Her air of uncertainty. As though she wasn't quite sure she was worth the space she took up but was going to occupy it anyway.

Neither of them spoke after that.

"Uh…do you want to come in?" he asked a moment later. Why was she there? Surely not to see him. He'd never given her any indication that he'd expected to see her again.

Of course, with the way she'd vanished while he'd still been sleeping off the bottle of wine he'd bought them at dinner and then drunk most of himself, she hadn't given him a chance to actually say as much.

Though he rarely used the front entrance himself, he walked her up to the door and unlocked it.

"So what brings you to Shelter Valley?" He hoped the question wasn't as bald as it felt scraping past his throat. She'd passed him in the hall, leaving a brief lily-of-the-valley scent in her wake. Her shampoo, if he remembered correctly.

"I've been accepted at Montford," she told him with a hesitant grin. "I start school in another week."

Oh. Well, good then. She had a reason for being here. Other than him. She'd mentioned, that night in Kentucky, that she'd already applied to college; she'd been unable to attend after high school because she'd married young. Caroline seemed to consider that a pretty big deal. He'd felt a little sorry for her over it.

"Can I get you something to drink? A beer? Or a glass of wine?" More relaxed now, John walked over to the wet bar dividing his formal living room from the dining room he'd never used.

"Do you have a diet soda?"

While she perched on the very edge of one end of the sectional couch, he grabbed a glass, filling it with ice. "You look different," he said, smiling, deciding this might not be such a bad turn of events. Maybe she'd join him for dinner.

They could catch up like old friends, though they hardly knew each other. He could wish her luck with her new scholastic endeavor, and then, if they ever ran into each other in town, they could smile and say hi without some residual awkwardness hanging between them.

Her smile was tenuous. John poured the drink, then carried it over to her, wondering if she'd be able to unclasp the hands in her lap long enough to take hold of it.

"It's your hair," he said.

"I…had it shaped. And conditioned." She took the glass. But not before he noticed how badly her hand was shaking.

He'd never met anyone like her. One minute confident enough to walk up to a total stranger at a political gathering and introduce herself, and then the next, so insecure she barely allowed herself to breathe.

"You left it long, though," he said, returning to the bar for a can of beer. He didn't usually drink more than one on any given day, but what the hell. He was still recovering from his vigil with Meri the other night.

"Yeah." She took a sip. Sort of. He wasn't sure any liquid actually passed her lips.

"I like it."

"Thanks."

"These days so many women keep their hair short." Meredith had been one of them.

"It's easier to deal with."

That was what Meri had said.

"I like it long."

"Thanks."

She sipped again. John took a seat and did the same. She watched him openly—yet said nothing.

"Did you want something from me?" he finally asked.

"No!"

Well, that was clear.

"I…just…"

For the first time since she'd arrived, she wouldn't meet his gaze. Frowning, John sat forward. He'd thought dinner would be nice, but not if it was going to get complicated. He just didn't have what it took to deal with complicated.

Hell, based on the way he'd broken his promise to himself and run back to his memories of Meredith the other night, he didn't have what it took to deal with living.

"Well, it was nice of you to stop by." He hadn't really intended the words but was relieved when he heard them. Yes, better just to end this and get on with the boring evening ahead. There were no surprises in boring.

"John, I'm pregnant."

He sat back, the half-empty can of beer resting on his lap, loosely cupped by both hands, and looked at the bare wall opposite him. He was mistakenly caught in someone else's life.

"Did you hear me?" The woman's voice, though soft, seemed to grate.

"I'm sorry." He turned to look at her. "What did you say?" The beer can was soothingly cool to the touch. He lifted it, drank. And kept drinking until it was empty.

"I said I'm pregnant."

Uh-huh. Well. What did he do now? The beer was gone. He crushed the can between his fingers, just to confirm that.

"I, uh, I'm sorry," he said. "I've never been in this position before. I don't really know what to say."

Mostly, he didn't know how to make sure he didn't *feel*.

"I had to tell you," she said. "You have a right to know."

This was a right?

"Aren't you going to ask if it's yours?"

His eyes met hers. Their green depths were as luminous as he remembered them. Her slim, strong, perfectly curved body was pretty impressive, but it was those eyes that had captivated him that cold December night in Kentucky. What, six weeks ago?

"I'm assuming you wouldn't be here if it wasn't."

He couldn't breathe properly. The cords in his neck tightened; his skin was hot. He wanted her out of his house. Now.

He wanted her never to have arrived. He wanted never to have met her.

"I could be lying. Or I could have done this on purpose, to trap you. I orchestrated our meeting, after all. I could've had a carefully thought-out plan—you know, the lonely widow trying to get out of a tiny little town that's suffocating her."

Some small part of him that was outside, watching the horrific scene unfold, could almost have smiled—if he hadn't been so terrified.

"Yes." He looked her straight in the eye. "You could have."

"I didn't."

"I didn't think you had. You aren't the artificial type."

She nodded, her lips tremulous as she lifted the still-full glass with a shaking hand. He hoped she didn't spill the drink. He didn't think he was up to standing at the moment, let alone going for paper towels.

He'd never felt so awkward in his own home. Or helpless. Lost, yes. Hopeless, yes. But not this.

There were things he should be saying. He just had no idea what they were. He sat there watching her, drawing a complete blank.

"I'm not here to ask anything from you," she said, after excruciating seconds had turned into even more excruciating minutes.

He appreciated that. John passed the remains of the beer can back and forth between his palms. Her focus followed the movement.

"I just had to tell you."

It was the second time she'd said that.

She stood, set the glass on the low, square wood table in front of the sectional. "I guess I'll go, then. Thanks for seeing me."

He was suddenly looking at her back.

"Wait!" John didn't move. He couldn't.

"What?" Her eyes were wide.

"Can you come back? Sit down? It seems like we should talk."

"Okay."

She sat.

She wasn't a bad-looking woman. Different than he was used to. She didn't wear makeup. And her clothes were baggy and without any discernible style. But they were clean. And she wore them with a curious and understated grace that was no less powerful for its unobtrusiveness.

"You're pregnant." John found himself back at the beginning.

"Yes."

"With…my baby." The words were so completely foreign to him that he felt stupid saying them.

"Yes."

Her hand slid down to cradle her stomach.

Oh, God.

She had a baby in there.

His chest cramped as he tried to draw in a breath.

His baby.

He jumped up. Tripped over the table. Threw away his beer can and missed the trash bucket. Leaving the can crumpled on the hardwood floor, he pulled another from the mini refrigerator behind the bar. Popped the lid and drank.

He looked over at her. Tried to figure out his next move. What was right. And best.

All he wanted to do was run. As far as he could.

"I have to take responsibility." The words came of their own volition, but as soon as he said them, he knew they were right.

"No, you don't. Really. I'll be fine. I have plans. A little money put aside. I wasn't just talking when I said I don't want anything from you. I really mean it."

The sincerity in her eyes was unmistakable. An open sincerity that was all the more remarkable because of its contrast to her usually unrevealing expression.

"I'm sure you do," he said. "But you misunderstood. I don't have to take responsibility because of you, I have to do it because of *me*. The point is not negotiable. As you said earlier, I have rights."

Her chin dropped to her chest.

"Is there another man in the picture?"

"No!" That brought her head up. She looked horrified by the very idea.

He shrugged. "You could've met someone between then and now."

"In six weeks? Over the holidays? In Grainville, Kentucky?" She shook her head with a self-deprecating laugh. "I haven't met anyone new in my hometown in years! And certainly not a male in my age bracket."

He wasn't sorry to hear that. It uncomplicated things a bit.

And then, suddenly, he was hit with a thousand complications at once. Everyone in this town knew him. Would know about this. He was going to have a baby to consider. In his home—at least part-time. In his life.

While he stood there, his mind wandered to the Little League field he'd become familiar with when he'd been friends with Martha Moore. Her only son, Tim, was one of the town's best hitters.

Would he have a son?

Or a daughter?

He felt a pain that was harsh and physical. He'd said good-bye to this moment six years ago. And before that, had imagined it. He and Meredith holding each other. She had tears in her eyes. He'd touch her belly reverently. They'd kiss....

"John? Are you okay?"

No. He wasn't okay. John wasn't sure how much longer he'd be able to stand there without climbing out of his skin.

"What are your plans?" he asked. "Do you have a place to stay?"

Anger flooded through his pores. But he didn't want to lash out at her.

"I have a computer printout of possibilities. Shelter Valley appears to be a lot like Grainville in that there are plenty of people with big houses who are willing to rent out a room."

He nodded. "There are a couple of boardinghouses, too."

"I saw that. They're more expensive. And really, for now, one room's all I need." She shrugged. Smiled a sad kind of smile. "It's not like I have much stuff."

"Did you sell your house?"

"No."

He let out a relieved breath. That would have made everything so final.

"My folks are going to take care of the farm for the rest of the year. I'll decide what to do after that."

After the baby came.

"Do they know?"

"About the baby?"

What else could there possibly be? John nodded.

"No. My enrolling in college was enough for them to digest."

He frowned, leaning against the bar as he sipped on the remainder of his beer. "Didn't they wonder why you came so far just to go to school?"

If, when she'd first appeared, his mind had been functioning, it would've occurred to him to wonder the same thing.

Caroline glanced up at him and then immediately away, and John tensed.

"I…spend a lot of time on the Internet—checking out different places."

Eyes narrowed, John studied her. She'd told him she was pregnant, looking him straight in the eye. And now she wouldn't look at him at all. Was there another reason she was here? Something her parents knew that he didn't? Something she didn't want him to know?

He guessed that if there was, it had to do with him.

And she *had* been pretty forward about their meeting.

"You told me you couldn't get pregnant," he remembered suddenly, straightening.

She nodded, looked at him fully. "I hadn't had a period since my husband died last summer. The doctor said it wasn't all that unusual. My system had simply shut down because of the stress. He said it might start back up again. And it might not. In any case, at the time, as far as I knew, it wasn't working. Chances were pretty slim that it would choose to resume normal activity again a day or two before I met you."

Her face was dark red when she finished. But during those words her gaze had never wavered.

John crushed his second beer can. Tossed it in the direction of the garbage pail. Thought about taking himself out to the golf course to beat the hell out of some balls.

He felt strangely like crying, something he hadn't done since the night his beloved wife had died in his arms.

"Do you have a cell phone?" he asked. "Some way I can reach you?"

Caroline fumbled in her homemade purse for a scrap of

paper and scribbled the number on it. Then she rose and handed it to him.

He set it on the bar. "Thanks."

She headed for the door.

"I'll be in touch," he said.

He thought she nodded. Hoped to God she wasn't crying. And couldn't wait to hear the door shut behind her.

He didn't breathe much easier after it happened. Her news lingered. He was going to be a father. With a woman he barely knew.

He, who was no longer capable of caring about a living human being, was going to be a father.

John had to get out. Go somewhere. Find an escape.

He made it to the window in time to see Caroline drive off.

The sun was still shining.

CHAPTER THREE

CAROLINE TOOK the first room she looked at. Her landlord, Mrs. Bea Howard, reminded her of old Mrs. Thomaswhite who ran the bakery back home in Grainville. With graying hair and wrinkled hands, she was plump, cheerful and seemed to know everything there was to know about everyone in town. A good source, Caroline surmised, for stories about her sister.

And someone to stay away from, in case she revealed more of herself than she wanted anyone to know.

The room was fairly small. The predominant piece of furniture was an old-fashioned four-poster bed that stood a good three-and-a-half-feet off the ground and boasted a down-filled homemade granny-square quilt in all the colors of the rainbow. There was a long dresser with a white lace runner, six drawers and a full-size mirror, plus a nightstand that had a lamp bright enough to read by. There was also a closet in which she could store the few belongings she'd brought with her. Best of all was the desk along the far wall directly beneath a window that looked out over the quiet street. Behind the desk was a high-speed Internet hook up. And a plug. Her computer could be up and running by nightfall.

There was no room for Jesse's old bassinet, waiting at home in Grainville.

Mrs. Howard lived alone but had two other tenants—both

of them single women who worked at Montford and had not yet returned from visiting family over the holidays. Caroline handed over first and last month's rent and didn't ask if Mrs. Howard allowed children.

Monday morning, after a sporadic night's rest accompanied by a couple of long nocturnal visits with her computer, Caroline quickly showered in the bathroom she shared with the other tenants—both women she had yet to meet—pulled on her daily attire of loose-fitting jeans, sweater and boots. Then she grabbed the instructions she'd printed off an Internet map service to get to Montford University. Craning her neck, she absorbed every impression of Shelter Valley that she could process. Harmon Hardware looked like a slightly smaller, and equally old, rendition of Jim's Hardware back home and the Valley Diner a larger, more modern place than the diner cum pub in Grainville. Weber's Department Store had a display of baby equipment in the window.

With butterflies swarming in her stomach, she made the last turn into the university parking lot. Large old buildings lay before her amid a breathtaking expanse of perfectly green lawns broken up with the occasional cement table and bench. While the place was currently deserted, she could envision students sitting at those tables, enjoying the sunshine while they grabbed a quick lunch or studied. She imagined couples huddled together on the benches, having private conversations. She counted at least three cement-mounted swings on white latticework gazebos—a far cry from the splintery version that hung on her porch at home.

It was only the second week in January, still the semester break, so there was little chance that her sister was anywhere in the vicinity. But as she filled out the necessary papers, retrieved required signatures, met with the proper people to register for her college classes, Caroline strained for a glimpse of a not too tall, fairly thin redhead with green eyes and an opal on her finger.

"Here you go, ma'am—this is your copy." The skinny young dark-haired man behind the counter at the registrar's office smiled almost condescendingly as he handed Caroline a copy of her first-ever college schedule.

"Classes start on the nineteenth. A week from Wednesday."

"Thank you." She smiled back, not because she appreciated his making her feel like an incompetent dinosaur, but because she'd seen the schedule. Relaxing for the first time in months, she almost skipped out into the Shelter Valley, fifty-degree sunshine. Right there on the first line, it guaranteed that she'd meet her sister. Along with a couple of required freshman courses and two English classes, Caroline had been admitted to Phyllis's Introduction to Psychology.

CAROLINE HAD BEEN in town three days. She'd spent much of the past twenty-four hours staring at her meager wardrobe, hot with humiliation at the prospect of sitting in class with eighteen-year-olds, looking like a bumpkin off the farm. But she'd need most of the cattle money for rent, and panicked at the thought of spending any more of her little nest egg from Randy's life insurance than she had to—even at a secondhand store. She had no idea how long that money would have to last.

And there was a baby to think about....

For once the Internet produced no solution. Tuesday afternoon, sitting at her desk in a room that was spotlessly tidy in spite of the cramped quarters, with paper stacked neatly on the floor beneath the desk, and all the other supplies she'd brought from home beside her, Caroline didn't know whether to cry or get angry. Web site after Web site was only confirming what she already knew. Her appearance was wildly out-of-date. She could pull her hair up into a ponytail—a fashionable clip would cost a couple of dollars—but after that…

Even if she was lucky enough to find more fashionable clothes at a secondhand store, she'd have to spend fifty dollars or more to update herself, and that fifty dollars could go toward the coming doctor's bills.

A tinny rendition of Beethoven's Fifth sounded and she jumped, looking around to figure out where the sound was coming from. Then she remembered the cell phone in the drawstring bag she'd made out of one of Randy's old shirts a couple of years before.

Only three people had that number. Her mother. Her son. And John Strickland.

Scrambling for the phone, her fingers tangled in the rope threaded through a casing at the top of the purse, holding it closed. If it was Jesse, she didn't want to miss his call. Talking to her son made her happier than anything else on earth.

And if it was her mom—if there were more problems with her dad…

The number on the display had a Shelter Valley area code.

She answered it anyway.

"Caroline? This is John Strickland." Even on the phone, his voice sounded just as she remembered it.

"Oh. Hi."

"Am I bothering you?"

Her hands were shaking, her stomach queasy. Did that count? "No."

"I'd like to see you."

Glancing around her room with desperate eyes, Caroline said, "Why?"

"To talk."

She didn't want to talk to him. She'd done her duty where he was concerned. He made her uncomfortable. Unsure of herself. Around John Strickland, pregnant Caroline Prater felt like an idiot.

She heard herself saying, "Okay."

"Would you like to go for dinner? We could drive down to Phoenix."

She'd driven through Phoenix on her way to Shelter Valley. She'd told herself she'd go back to explore as soon as she could afford the gas: Which wouldn't be until she had a better idea of how much having this baby was going to cost.

Growing warm with embarrassment, Caroline said. "I was planning to eat here." Board was included with the room.

"Can't you let me take you out? I'd like to. My treat."

She opened her mouth to deliver an adamant *no,* turned away from the bed where she'd dropped her bag and caught the trapped look in her eyes in the mirror attached to the dresser across from her.

"You don't owe me anything," she said.

"I know you really believe that, and maybe that's why I really want to."

Hot again, she sat down. "I'm not…um…that woman you were with in December. She was just…" Caroline swallowed. Silence hung on the line. "I was—it was my first Christmas without Randy…um, my husband…and, well I don't usually act like that."

"I'm not sure what you're trying to tell me."

"I'm not interested in you—like that." Her palms were sweaty with the effort of asserting herself. This was all so new to Caroline, a woman who'd spent the first thirty-four years of her life trying to fit in by giving in. Who'd grown up in a small town where people still defined a woman's worth by how happy she made her husband.

He didn't say anything, and Caroline half hoped he'd decided against dinner. Or ever talking to her again. Except that might be difficult considering the circumstances.

"I can't go on a date." ·

John sighed—which sounded as if it was accompanied by a slight chuckle. "Caroline, you are unlike anyone I've ever met."

Was that a good or bad thing?

"We need to talk. I need to eat. You've already spent at least some money on a test to diagnose a condition for which I am half-responsible. I can pay back my half with tonight's meal. From there on, hopefully, we'll have reached some other arrangement."

"I told you, I don't want anything from you. This is *my*…situation. I'll deal with it."

"The child is mine." There was a certain hardness to his voice now. "I *will* share in the responsibility."

Caroline sighed, too. She didn't mean to—at least not out loud. But he was right; there was no way of avoiding a conversation between the two of them.

God, what a mess.

"Okay, do you want me to meet you somewhere? Or I can drive to your house."

"Call me old-fashioned, but I'd rather pick you up." John's deep voice brought peace even while his words frightened her. "What's your address?"

She didn't want to give it to him. Didn't want to give anyone more information about her than necessary. She had too many secrets.

In a voice that was thick with tangled emotions, Caroline gave John her address.

"I've done a lot of thinking in the past couple of days."

They were having dinner at a somewhat dark restaurant off the I-10 freeway in Ahwautukee, a suburb, John had explained, in south Phoenix. This was the first bit of personal conversation he'd offered.

"I can imagine," she told him, studying the dinner salad she'd ordered and had only picked at. Across from her in the maroon leather booth, he was finishing off a cup of potato soup. He'd dressed casually, in jeans and a beige pullover with slip-on casual leather shoes.

She'd never been out with a man with slip-on casual leather shoes.

At least in Phoenix, with all the Old West cowboy overtones, she didn't feel so out of place in her boots. And her blue jeans, faded flower blouse and brown cardigan were clean.

He glanced over. "Would you like to wait until after dinner to talk?"

The drive had been spent on a horticulture lesson about desert cacti and other flowering plants—much more information than she'd already learned from the Internet.

"No, this is fine." Anything not to prolong the evening.

Nodding, he set down his spoon. "It occurred to me that I need to tell you some things about myself so you can understand what I have to say."

Caroline took a bite of lettuce and cucumber. The baby that had yet to make itself physically known in any way other than through a little queasiness and two solid lines on a home pregnancy test, needed sustenance.

There were quite a few patrons in the restaurant, which, she'd been glad to note, had a varied but not too expensive menu. And the booths were far enough apart, private enough with pillars and high backs between them, to allow for intimate conversation.

Still, she would've been more comfortable in a fast-food hamburger joint.

"Other than determining that we were both unattached in December—and because of that, lonely going into the holidays—we never broached any information about our romantic lives."

Glancing up at him, Caroline nodded, uncomfortable with the direction he seemed to be taking. His dark eyes were open and sincere.

Would her baby's eyes be that brown? Jesse had green eyes like hers.

"I'm a widower."

"Oh." And when surprise didn't seem an appropriate response, she said, "I'm sorry." She paused, then added, "So am I. A widow, I mean." Her fork hung suspended in midair, clasped in fingers that were holding it so tightly the metal was leaving indentations in her skin.

Her widowhood certainly wasn't a secret. She just felt so vulnerable, talking about it.

Forearms resting on the table, he toyed with his fork. "How long's it been for you?"

"Six months." And she hadn't slept more than a couple of hours at a time since.

"Six years here."

She wanted to ask him if it got any easier, but couldn't get that intimate.

"Sometimes it feels like it's only been six months," he continued, staring down at the fork he still fingered.

The man's lost look drew Caroline's sympathy. "What happened?"

He raised his head and then lowered it again. "Car accident."

"Was she alone?" Randy had been. And visions of him lying there hurt, frightened, needing her, haunted her daily.

He shook his head, dark brown hair falling over his forehead as his gaze met hers. "We were in a cab in New York, coming from a Broadway show."

Oh, God. She'd never been to New York. Or to a play, for

that matter, if you didn't include the elementary-school variety. But she could imagine being on vacation, having fun, completely unsuspecting of the tragedy that would occur.

"She lived for a couple of hours," he continued. The food was taking too long to get there. Caroline wanted the interruption more for him than for herself.

"I begged her to hold on. All the time we were in the ambulance, trying to maneuver through Manhattan traffic, I pleaded with her to breathe."

Caroline had a feeling the woman would have done everything in her power to honor this man's request.

"What was her name?"

"Meredith." His eyes grew vacant, and Caroline had a pretty good idea he'd fallen into what she'd come to know as the dark abyss. A place where lost lives and broken dreams waited to taunt those left behind.

"My husband's name was Randy."

He blinked, an expression of compassion and understanding replacing the emptiness. "Was he sick?"

She shook her head. Not unless you counted a lack of self-esteem and the resultant relationship with a bottle. "Tractor accident on our farm."

"How old was he?"

"Same as me. Thirty-four."

"Meredith was thirty-one. We were planning to have kids," he said, more to himself than to her. "She was an investment broker and wanted to build a clientele so she could work from home and be able to stay with the babies."

An investment broker. And Caroline had never finished high school.

"You sure don't expect to lose a spouse in your early thirties." The words sounded inane to her, but she didn't know what else to say.

"Here we go, folks. Sorry this took so long." The young man who'd taken their order appeared at their booth, carrying two plates of salmon and steamed vegetables. Caroline sat back, napkin on her lap as he placed the food before her. Other than that night in Frankfort, she'd never eaten anywhere fancier than the diner in Grainville. And was scared to death that she'd forget some of the rules of etiquette she'd learned on the Internet so she could educate her son. There wasn't a lot of opportunity for practice with proper forks and bread plates on a farm like hers. She and Randy had never even owned a set of matching silverware.

She was, however, thankful to have had the interruption before John could ask the next obvious question—about her and Randy's plans for a family. She had a feeling John assumed she had no family, since she'd told him, in December, that she lived alone.

And to have a child old enough to leave home, she'd've had to be pregnant at sixteen.

John was quiet while he ate, other than to inquire politely about the suitability of her food. And to make sure she had everything she needed. Caroline felt relieved; not only was she spared the worry of where conversation might lead, but the food was so much more luxurious than anything she'd ever tasted before that she was completely engrossed in enjoying it.

She looked longingly at the desert menu as it was presented, but declined. She was stuffed.

"Shall we go?" He laid a couple of twenties on the table and stood, then gestured for her to pass in front of him. And suddenly, Caroline wanted to stay. At least in the restaurant there were other people around, the possibility of interruption.

BACK IN THE CAR she waited for him to say whatever he'd taken her to dinner to say. Obviously something about the baby. And she steeled herself to listen with an open mind. The child growing in her body was half his. It was a point she couldn't argue.

"This is a lovely car," she ventured when it appeared that they might be making the hour-long trip back to Shelter Valley in complete silence.

"Thanks."

"What kind is it?"

"A Cadillac."

That would explain why she'd never been in anything like it. The plush leather seats were contoured and adjustable in a variety of ways. And she didn't even try to decipher what all the buttons and lights and controls on the dash were for. But if she wasn't mistaken, that screen above the radio was one of those computerized map things she'd read about on a pop-up on the Internet last winter.

If she wasn't so afraid of looking like a fool, she might've asked him about it.

He kept up his end of the conversation after that, mostly telling her about life in Arizona. He talked about the summer heat. And the wildlife. Scorpions and black widow spiders. She didn't need to be afraid of scorpions, he said. While they were ugly, only the really small kind was lethal enough to make you sick—and then, only if you were already vulnerable. With all the others, their sting hurt and could cause temporary numbness in the affected limb, but there was no lasting damage.

"Don't worry," she assured him, with a slight smile in the darkness. "You can't live on a farm and be afraid of spiders. I learned to use a fly swatter long before I learned to read and write."

He grinned over at her, then quickly returned his attention to the highway. "I'll bet you're pretty good with a rifle, too, huh?"

"Mmm-hmm." When she had to be.

"I've never fired one."

As far as she knew, he was the first man she'd ever met who'd never fired a gun.

"We had a bear on our property once," she told him, more to direct the conversation away from things he might bring up than because she really wanted to share her past with him. She never knew if what she said would make her seem too strange to someone like him.

"Randy was in town getting seed and the bear came right up to the barn. I saw him out there getting close to my hen-house and I didn't even think." Without egg money she'd have had no groceries. "I just grabbed the gun and marched outside—as if that black bear was going to see me as some kind of threat and head back the way he'd come."

She'd been young then. And still sure that life had happily-ever-after in store for her.

"What did you do?" His eyes were wide, revealed by the light from the dash as he stole another glance.

"When I realized he wasn't nearly as impressed by me as I'd expected him to be, I did the only thing I could do, cocked the gun and brought it to my shoulder."

"You shot a bear?"

For a second there, hearing the incredulity in his voice, she wished she had.

"No, I aimed for the ground by his feet. And then on either side of him."

"You scared him off."

Well, yes, but… "It was stupid, really. He could just as easily have gotten angry and attacked."

John shook his head, grinning, one hand on the wheel and

the other resting casually over the armrest next to him. "Is there anything you're afraid of, woman?" Somehow the admiration hadn't disappeared from his tone.

Which was why she just shrugged and looked out into the night. She couldn't bear to tell him that right now—with him, in Shelter Valley, at Montford—there was very little that *didn't* scare her.

"HERE'S THE THING," John said when he pulled up in front of her house.

Hand on the door handle, thankful that she'd made it through the evening without whatever horrible conversation she imagined he wanted, Caroline turned, every muscle tense and waiting.

"I loved my wife."

She nodded. That much was obvious.

"Too much, probably."

She turned away from the door handle, facing the car's interior. "How can you love someone too much?"

He'd shut off the engine, leaving them in darkness except for the light coming from the streetlamp half a block away and the dim glow from the front window of Mrs. Howard's house.

"I can't love anyone else."

Ironically, with those words, Caroline relaxed. "You're trying to warn me not to get any crazy ideas."

His head cocked slightly to the side, John shrugged. "It wasn't so much a warning as an explanation. I don't want you to think it's you…."

"John." She almost laid her hand on his arm, and restrained herself just in time. Grainville familiarities might not be recognized here. "You have nothing to worry about from me. I meant it when I said I wanted nothing from you. Nothing.

I married once, for a lifetime. And found out that fate had other ideas in mind. There was nothing I could do—it was out of my hands. I can't go through that again."

"You warning *me* off?" he asked, with a wry grin.

"Just explaining."

Leaning back against the corner of the door, he was quiet for a moment. "I'm not afraid of the commitment," he said. "Not afraid of loving again. I just can't get beyond *her*."

"Have you tried?"

"I was engaged to the women's softball coach at Montford until a week before I came to Kentucky."

No wonder he'd seemed as emotionally raw as she'd been, so needy and yet willing to settle for nothing but escape.

"What happened?"

"I couldn't let go of Meredith."

"Do you have to?" she asked, frowning. Randy would always be part of her, no matter what. They'd spent nineteen years together.

"I...talk to her."

She talked to Randy, too, but hadn't thought the habit would last for years—just until she got used to living alone. "About what?"

"Everything," he said, his voice soft. "I shot a hole-in-one over Thanksgiving, playing in a tournament with some of Shelter Valley's best golfers. The only person I even considered telling was Meredith. Not Lauren."

For one absurd second, Caroline was jealous of a dead woman.

CHAPTER FOUR

PHYLLIS LANGFORD SHEFFIELD COULDN'T stop herself from taking one last backward glance as she accompanied her closest friend, Tory Sanders, down the walk of Tory's small home. Their neighborhood was perfectly safe, featuring quiet stucco houses with desert landscaping in the yards.

"Let's just do this block," she said, her feet moving in place as she geared up for the jog Tory had planned for them.

Tory's soft blue eyes glinted with an unusual confidence as she, too, glanced back at the house. "There are only eight houses on this street," she said, grinning. "You gotta establish a rhythm and get into the groove if you're going to tolerate jogging." She'd taken both of them shopping the previous day for top-of-the-line running shoes, leggings and soft cotton zip-up jackets. Phyllis's was black. Tory's was pink, which complemented her short dark hair and expertly lined eyes.

Bouncing some more, Phyllis nodded. "A groove. Okay…" She didn't move from her spot.

"They're going to be fine," Tory said gently, with the strange mixture of neediness and confidence that had first drawn Phyllis to the younger sister of her murdered best friend. "Alex is great with all the kids. You know that."

Alex. The eleven-year-old adopted daughter of Tory's husband, Ben. The little girl had been abused by her biological father and mother and come to live with Ben, her stepfather, at about the same time Tory—also an abused child and then abused wife—had found refuge in Shelter Valley. If all went well, Tory would soon be adopting Alex. "I know," Phyllis said. She was ready to head up the street. Really. As soon as her feet felt warm. "But she's never been left alone with my two," she said, on the off chance Tory hadn't already heard Phyllis's worries on that score. The jogging was Tory's idea— to help Phyllis keep off the weight she'd had trouble losing after having her twins two and a half years before.

"But she *has* been alone with Chrissie," Tory reminded her. Chrissie—Phyllis Christine—was the four-year-old daughter Tory and Ben had together. "Calvin and Clarissa won't be a problem for her," she added. "They're just like their mother, too analytical for their own good sometimes, but practically perfect in every way. They'll have Alex reading to them the entire time we're gone."

"Unless Chrissie gets bored…" Tory's daughter was at that age.

"As long as she's sitting in her big sister's lap, she'll be completely content." Tory started jogging slowly down the sidewalk. "Come on, we aren't going to be away very long…"

"I HAD A LETTER from Brad." Doing as she'd been told, Phyllis concentrated on the rhythm of her breathing in conjunction with the sound of her feet hitting the pavement. So far, jogging still felt like an endurance contest. Only Tory—the sister she'd never had—could've managed to get her to do this.

"Why would your jerk of an ex-husband be writing to you after all this time?" Tory, not even a little out of breath, glanced over. "When did it come?"

Phyllis moved aside to avoid a parked car as the two women jogged side by side along the road. "Yesterday."

"What did he want?"

"He made a pie-in-the-sky investment when we were married—had to do with satellites." She paused to breathe. "During the divorce…he got his broker to claim a potential value for it that far exceeded its worth at the time." More breath. In and out. She had to think about the rhythm of her feet against the pavement. That was here and now. "The judge allowed the value to stand…. Brad magnanimously gave that investment to me in exchange for our more liquid assets."

It smarted even to talk about those days.

"And in an effort to keep the peace, you let him get away with it."

By now, Tory knew all the sordid details of Phyllis's marriage to her egotistical, unfaithful and completely selfish first husband.

"I was fighting for my self-esteem. Money paled in comparison."

"And part of you hoped that if you were generous and cooperative, he'd suddenly realize that your intelligence wasn't a threat to him and he'd find you desirable again."

"Which only goes to show that I wasn't nearly as smart as he thought I was," Phyllis said, slowing as they approached a corner with a stoplight. The blue sky above, glistening with sunshine that gave a cheery brightness to everything around them, reminded Phyllis that none of it mattered anymore. She was a different woman than the one who'd gained weight after her husband's numerous affairs and the emotional torment he'd caused her. Married to a man she adored, working in a job she loved, mothering the two most precious children ever and jogging with the sweetest friend a woman could want in sixty-degree weather on the second Wednesday in January, she bore absolutely no resemblance to that other Phyllis at all.

Except that occasionally, like now, she still felt the sting.

"So why was he writing to you?"

She'd known Tory would get back to that.

"The worthless investment suddenly become a windfall?"

"As a matter of fact—" Phyllis jogged across the deserted street beside Tory "—it did. Apparently I'm sitting on a quarter of a million dollars, minus taxes."

Tory stopped in the middle of the street. "A quarter of a million dollars?"

"Before taxes." Phyllis met her friend's incredulous stare before grabbing her arm and pulling her to the opposite corner.

"And why do I get the feeling that Brad wasn't writing out of the goodness of his heart to tell you about this?"

"Maybe because you know what he's like," Phyllis said with a humorless chuckle.

"He wants part of it," Tory guessed, walking now as they approached her road again.

"He wants all of it. The original investment was his, and his name's still on some of the documents. I didn't think it was worth the couple of hundred dollars it would cost in legal fees to have it changed."

"What does Matt say about all this?"

"I haven't told him yet…."

JOHN HAD DECIDED to stay away from her. On the golf course early Wednesday morning with Will Parsons and Matt Sheffield, he'd spent the entire front nine feeling guilty and given up his usual first-place ranking for last. The back nine had gone better. In the guilt department at least. When the baby was born, he'd do his part. Until then, he had nothing to contribute. He certainly didn't owe Caroline Prater anything.

He'd come in last on the back nine, as well.

She picked up her cell on the first ring. And agreed to take a walk in the desert with him before dinner. He hadn't even tried to talk her into sharing another meal. Finishing up early at the office on Wednesday afternoon, knowing he'd be working late that night, John stopped at home only long enough to put on his jeans and walking shoes. Then he picked her up at Mrs. Howard's place before she could change her mind.

"Are you sure it's safe out here?" she asked when he stopped the Cadillac on a dirt path Will had shown him. As a kid, Will had roamed this desert as though it were a ball field in the middle of town. It hadn't taken John an hour to fall prey to its wonder.

"Safe how?" he asked, looking over at the woman who was still such a stranger to him. And had his baby growing inside her. "As in, are we going to get mugged, or robbed by a gold-panning squatter, or taken captive by an Indian warrior?"

"Indian warrior?" Caroline asked with an arched brow. "I was talking about the nonhuman variety of danger." Her boots barely made a sound as she trod slowly down the path that led to a rocky ledge. It overlooked a surprisingly green ravine up ahead.

Careful to keep enough distance between them so he wouldn't be inhaling the fresh lilac scent of her hair—he supposed it was the kind of shampoo she used—John shoved his hands into his jeans pockets and shrugged. "Yeah, the desert can be dangerous, but not if you're careful."

She slowed, glanced over her shoulder at him. "So those javelina I read about on the Internet, are they around here? Or only up in the mountains?"

"They're here," John said, focusing on both sides of the path—playing a game of name that plant. Cholla. Prickly pear. Palo verde. It was either that or look at her nicely rounded butt moving back and forth in those threadbare jeans. "But javelinas usually stay out of sight. Mostly you want to watch for rattlesnakes. As long as you don't step on one, they'll leave you alone. And you never, ever, want to be out here without water. Something as simple as a sprained ankle could leave you out in the desert for hours or days."

Her step picked up again. "I'm guessing you've got water in that pack thing you're carrying?"

"Yep." The leather pack had been a Christmas gift from Becca and Will two years before. "A bottle for each of us. And a first-aid kit, too. I go with the theory that if I have one, I won't need it."

"Good theory."

John enjoyed the silence that fell as they continued their walk. Maybe on the way back he'd point out some of the different varieties of Arizona desert plants they were passing. For now, he was feeling more peaceful than he had in days.

As long as he didn't think about that body ahead of him— and the life it was hiding. Then he felt the need to unbutton his long-sleeved corduroy shirt and let in some air.

They reached the rock Will had shown him that first day and sat, not quite touching, facing the ravine.

"Did you know that saguaro are only found here in Arizona, Mexico and a few places in New Mexico?" she asked, staring out. He had known that, but wasn't familiar with many of the other facts she regaled him with during the next ten minutes. And he'd spent the past couple of years making a point of picking up information on one new plant a month.

"How do you know all this stuff?" John finally asked.

She shrugged, her ponytail sliding up and down her back with the movement. "The Internet."

He should've guessed. She'd found a college that way, too. And Caroline seemed like the kind of person who'd make it her business to find out everything there was to know about whatever she was doing.

Including having a baby?

"We have to talk about it, you know," he said, glancing at his watch. They couldn't keep meeting like this—casually chatting, getting to know each other. They had to get on with business. It was the only reason he'd called her.

There was no marked difference in her, just a changed energy in the air around them. She said nothing.

So, fine. Probably easier like this. Just state his facts, come up with a plan that was agreeable to both of them and go their separate ways.

"Have you chosen a doctor yet?"

Head turned away from him, she appeared to be taking in the desert beyond the rocky hill that descended down to green bush and wild grass below them.

"Really," she said, her voice small, "you don't have to do this."

"Do what?" he asked, although he knew.

"Be involved."

"I'm as responsible for this predicament as you are." The words weren't news to him; he just hadn't confronted them head-on until that point. "There is no way I can go on with my life as usual while yours is being turned upside down."

"It's not a predicament."

He didn't know what he'd expected her to say. But it hadn't been that. They had real issues to discuss here.

"Sorry."

She turned, her green eyes narrowed and filled with a fire he hadn't seen there before. "We're talking about a person here, a child's life. *My* child's life. He or she is not and will never be a predicament to me."

"Okay…"

"Just because I didn't choose to have a baby—or choose the father, for that matter—does not mean this pregnancy is any less valid than one I'd planned and hoped for. Because the life that results will be just as valid."

He had the most incredible urge to pull her toward him, kiss her forehead, rub her back. He sat on his hands. "True." The temperature was only sixty-three degrees, but in the sun, John was starting to sweat. The breeze coming over the ravine was a relief. With the sudden tightness in his chest, he was finding it a little hard to breathe.

He waited to see if she had anything more to say. And then, when it appeared she didn't, he told her, "All the more reason for me to be involved."

He heard her sigh. And felt it, too. "Look." She turned on the rock until she was facing him. "You're right. Part of the reason I came here was so you could be involved in this baby's life if you chose. He deserves a father just like everyone else. Deserves to know his biological father if you're interested in having him know you." She wasn't even stopping for air. "So, after he's born, if you want to be involved, we'll set up whatever visitations you need. But until then, this is just about me and the job my body has to do."

"I disagree." *Shut up!* his mind screamed. She'd just given him exactly the out he needed. And wanted. "There'll be costs. And hardships as you find it more difficult to do certain things. For instance, what if you have to take your computer in for repair? Once you get further along, you won't be allowed to lift heavy things."

He was winging it. And afraid that was exactly how it sounded. Why the hell had this suddenly become so important? Just because she'd told him no?

He'd never been a man who had a problem with women in authority.

"Don't believe everything you hear, Strickland," she said, her tone reminding him of the friendly woman he'd known so briefly that weekend between Thanksgiving and Christmas. Very different from the self-conscious though still capable Caroline she'd been since arriving in Shelter Valley. "Kentucky women come from strong stock. Goodness, if they had to slow down the whole time they were pregnant, their families and farms would be in trouble. A small farm doesn't run itself, you know."

An iguana—a desert lizard—scooted by an inch from John's shoe. Caroline watched it go.

"They're kind of cute," she said as it scurried away. "I read that they're good to have around your yard at home because they eat crickets."

"And other bugs," John agreed. He didn't want to talk about desert plants or wildlife anymore.

"Listen, Caroline," he said, not even sure what she'd be listening to. Compelled by an uneasy feeling inside, he continued anyway. "As you say, that baby you're carrying is as real as any other child conceived. He's also my flesh and blood, and I'm not the type of man who can turn away from that responsibility. I don't even *want* to." He was surprised to find that much was true. "I'd like to be around to hear that first heartbeat. Or at least some of the heartbeats. I want to hear what the doctor has to say about his size and growth and overall health. I want to see the ultrasound that might tell us if he's a boy or a girl."

God, he couldn't breathe. And he didn't know how in hell he was going to make any of this happen. Or follow through on it. They were discussing a new life. And his world revolved around the memory of a dead woman.

"Okay."

He blinked. Stared at her. And then down into the ravine. He loved the browns and golds of the desert. But sometimes that green just looked so good. Cool and peaceful and…breathing.

"Really?"

She nodded. "You're his father. I have no right to deny you access to his life. As long as you understand that except where it's absolutely necessary, you have no role in *my* life."

That was that. Much easier than he'd expected.

Then why did he feel so…out of his league? Why did he feel he wanted to start running and not stop until he collapsed on the ground?

Meredith should be here. Spending the next months with him. Learning it all with him.

But she wasn't. The pain of that was almost unbearable. As he'd known it would be. When he'd lost Meredith, he'd vowed never to have children. She'd been too much a part of that dream.

And now here he was, having a child with a woman he barely knew.

He should resent Caroline.

But he didn't.

"CAN I ASK YOU something?"

Caroline glanced over at him, her auburn hair glinting in the light from the setting sun. "I guess."

John didn't know how it had happened, but they'd been there for over an hour. Sometimes talking. A lot of the time lost in their own thoughts. There was so much to discuss, so many decisions to make. But he didn't really feel like doing these things. And, perhaps, neither did she.

He pulled out the bottles of water, opened one and handed it to her before taking a long swig from his own.

"Why did you react so strongly when I referred to the pregnancy as a predicament?"

She took a small sip of water. Recapped the bottle. Held it with both hands on the rock between her knees. He wasn't used to spending time with women who didn't wear makeup and was surprised by how much he liked the freshness of her natural beauty when she turned toward him.

"Have you ever looked in the mirror and wondered where you belonged?"

"No, I don't think so," John said slowly, watching her.

"Or considered the idea that your life was worth less than the lives of those around you?"

"No." He'd had the usual teenage insecurities, of course. But his parents had always encouraged him to believe that the world was his to do with what he could. He'd been dreaming big his whole life.

Until the dream came crashing down.

"I have," she said.

And although he didn't want to know, he had to ask. "Why?"

She wasn't going to tell him. He'd overstepped the boundaries she'd set less than an hour before. Her chin was set, her eyes showing very little of the emotion that he suspected must be roiling around inside her.

And then her mouth softened, her eyes focusing on the distance, perhaps a farther distance than the vista spread before them.

"For starters, I was an only child," she began. "On a farm out in the country in Kentucky. That in itself is very isolating. And no matter what I did, I never fit in. Not at home with my folks. And not at school, either. I was different from everyone else. Saw the world differently. When it came time to make decisions, my opinions were almost always opposite to my parents'. Things that mattered to me didn't seem to concern them, and a lot of the time, the reverse was true."

Caroline pulled her feet up on the rock, the worn, rounded toes of her brown leather boots hanging over the edge. Arms wrapped around her knees, she shifted back slightly. John wondered what she was thinking.

"I had this insatiable need to *know*. Not what other people in town were doing, or who was marrying whom, but why the sun rose and how. And where air came from. I wanted to know who was in national office and I cared about every major decision out of Washington." Her grin was a little sad. "My poor parents. They were worried about having enough fertilizer for the field and finding ways to make the equipment last another year while I went on about global warming. I'm sure I drove them crazy."

Mesmerized, John didn't move. He didn't want to do anything that might remind her he was still there, make her aware that she was opening up to him after just telling him he could play no part in her personal life. He didn't want to lose this glimpse of her.

When he'd first met Caroline Prater he'd found her an interesting enigma. And—not that he allowed himself to dwell on that night—she'd been a pretty decent lover, as well. Now he was just plain intrigued. He'd never known anyone with so many facets. All of them different. And all of them sparkling in their own way.

"Anyhow, one day when I was about seven, I yelled at my mother in a fit of frustration, telling her I couldn't possibly be her kid because she didn't care that a popular hamburger chain—I'd only eaten out twice in my life and both times it had been there—was being accused of stealing characters from my favorite television show, *H.R. Pufnstuf.*"

A quick grin accompanied her words before her focus turned once again to the desert. "You can imagine how surprised I was—and how little I suddenly cared about the company's ad campaign—when my mother yelled back that I *wasn't* her child. I was adopted."

Shit. What a way to tell a seven-year-old kid something as earth-shattering as that. John didn't know what he could possibly say that would make any difference. So he said nothing.

"I'd already been considering that I'd been planted in Grainville by aliens." She laid her cheek on top of her knee. "From that point on, I quit fighting. I'd already been rejected by one set of parents. What would happen if the second set decided I was too much trouble?"

John, not detecting even a note of self-pity in her tone, wondered for a split second what it would've been like if he'd met her at a different time. Say fifteen years before, when they were both starting out.

He had a feeling he'd have liked her. A lot.

"I spent the next ten years of my life feeling like I didn't belong anywhere. In a town as small as Grainville, where everyone belongs to everyone else, feeling that way wasn't easy."

He wondered what had happened to her at seventeen to change that but didn't ask.

She stood up, brushed herself off, gave a shaky laugh. "Sorry, I didn't mean to go on like that," she said, heading back the way they'd come. "Put it down to overprotectiveness. I just don't want any child of mine feeling that way. Not if I can help it."

Propelled by something he didn't dare analyze, John caught up to her, grabbing her hand only long enough to pull her to a stop. She turned, facing him. "I may not have chosen these circumstances," he said, his eyes locked with hers. "But that baby will always know I love him and want him in my life."

Tears pooled in her eyes before she blinked them away, nodded and began walking again.

"NOT TO KEEP HARPING on it, but I'd really like to know what you're planning to do about medical care," John said as they sped down the highway toward Shelter Valley. Caroline had said that Bea Howard served dinner at five-thirty sharp and they'd stayed longer in the desert than he'd intended.

"I've called the clinic in Shelter Valley. The obstetrician there can take me."

"Do you have insurance?" She didn't answer immediately and he continued. "Because under my insurance, the baby will be covered completely, but the pregnancy won't. I'm prepared to handle that with cash."

"That won't be necessary."

"Caroline," John said, taking his eyes from the road for just a second and glimpsing the bland look on her face, "we've already established that I'm going to carry at least half the burden over the next seven or so months. Obviously we can't divvy up the physical challenges, so I'll have to do my share on a more, shall we say, *detached* level. Expenses would fall nicely into that category."

"Okay."

Another glance showed him that her expression hadn't changed. More than ever, he wanted to know what went on behind that unrevealing look. He suspected it was the result of a lifetime spent hiding her curiosities and opinions.

In any event, there was nothing for him to do about it.

"So, when's the first appointment?"

"I haven't made it yet."

"I'd like to be there."

And at the instant shake of her head, he quickly added, "Not for the examination part." He didn't want to embarrass her. "Just to sit in on the talk with the doctor afterward."

She hesitated too long. "Okay."

"You'll let me know as soon as you have an appointment?"

he pushed, not sure whether she'd acquiesced or was merely placating him.

"I'm hoping to get in sometime during the next week, before school starts."

Okay, then, she'd meant it. Good. They were getting somewhere. "I can go any day but tomorrow."

"Fine."

"A large group of us are going to Phoenix tomorrow," he explained when it occurred to him that she might think he was putting her off for a golf date or an appointment at work. "One of our young women is a witness in a court case and Shelter Valley plans to be there in full support."

"Ellen Moore's rape case," she said so softly he almost didn't hear her. "I'm glad you're all going."

Having just come off the ramp from the freeway, John kept his foot on the brake and stared. "How did you know about that?"

"It was in the papers," she said. "There was a lot of coverage, probably because someone rich and powerful is involved. Anyway, I've been following the story on the Internet and knew it was set for trial."

And she remembered the date? Impressive. John's heart was pumping a little faster than normal as he pulled into town. He couldn't afford to feel anything for this woman. Especially considering the responsibilities they were going to be sharing for the next eighteen years. Raising a child would be hard enough without personal tension between them.

But damn, it wasn't fair that a woman as intelligent and pretty and downright interesting as Caroline Prater—a woman almost thirty-five years of age—was still so desperate for a place to belong that she was developing bonds with people she'd never even met.

CHAPTER FIVE

SHELTER VALLEY WAS probably quieter on that second Thursday in January than any of the other days Caroline had been there. But as she walked downtown midafternoon, learning her way around, window-shopping for things she might never be able to afford, she certainly felt as though the town was drained of life. She didn't need to turn her head to catch a glimpse of her sister or any of the other people she knew only from grainy newspaper photos. The town's mayor, Becca Parsons, and her husband, Will, who was the president of Montford University. Or Cassie Montford, the vet who'd been in the news with her innovative pet-therapy program. Caroline had followed the story avidly, as Phyllis had collaborated with Cassie in the therapy portion of the program.

There was no point in thinking the dark-haired woman on the corner was Bonnie Nielson, owner of the local day care, who'd made various Arizona newspapers because she'd developed a nationally known program for children and seniors together.

Today Caroline didn't have any chance of running into Beth Richards, wife of the local sheriff, Greg. She'd read an article about Beth when, as a fugitive, she'd turned state's evidence in Texas on a cult she'd inadvertently been part of with her ex-husband. Nor was she going to see Martha Marks or her new husband, preacher David Cole Marks. Ellen's mother and the minister who'd helped track down her rapist would undoubtedly be sitting on either side of her in that courtroom in Phoenix.

With a hand on her still-flat stomach, Caroline smiled at an older woman who was entering into Weber's Department Store and decided she should head home. If the online version of the Phoenix newspaper was going to report Ellen's trial—and she suspected it would, since it involved some of Phoenix's most powerful men and the breakup of a large prostitution ring—the link would probably be up before her fellow townspeople returned home.

SHE HAD TO REFRESH her browser a couple of times, but before dinner that evening, and after her weekly call to her mother from the cell phone that didn't charge extra for long-distance, Caroline was watching a video of the first day of jury selection online. Of course the clip was only a couple of minutes long. But it was enough to give a sense of being involved in something that meant so much to the people she was hoping would someday accept her as one of their own. The accompanying news story was fairly detailed, painting a courtroom picture that was both heartbreaking and inspiring.

Later that evening, she turned to her journal.

Thursday, January 13, 2005

> *I wish I could've been there today! I saw all the Shelter Valley people outside the courthouse. Apparently the news reporter thought the town's collective support noteworthy. It was just a glimpse and yet it affected me so deeply I can't quite get away from the feeling. They were like one huge supportive family. In the clip I managed to see, Matt Sheffield, my sister's husband, was*

holding Randi and Zack Foster's son, Billy. Randi is Will Parsons' youngest sister. I recently saw the little boy in a photo in the Shelter Valley paper. He'd been in his uncle Will's arms at a university function over Christmas or I wouldn't have known him. Outside the courthouse, Becca Parsons was standing with Ellen and her family. Ben Sanders's adopted daughter, Alex, stood close beside her stepmother, Tory, who was with Phyllis.

I couldn't see Phyllis well—it was a side shot of her—but just getting confirmation that she's really here made my stomach jump. It does somersaults every time I think about actually seeing her, speaking to her. Sometimes I think I can't possibly wait until next week when school starts. And sometimes I think I won't dare go to school for fear of meeting her. What if I act like a country hick and she can't stand me? What if she somehow recognizes me and is livid that I've come here, disrupting her life? I've sure read enough about birth families to know that's a very common response. Ohhh. One step at a time. And today's step is to occupy the next few hours until bedtime.

I saw John in the still. He was in the background, slightly apart from everyone else. Kind of odd that he'd go all that way to join in the town's support, and then not stand with them. He was wearing a tie. I haven't seen that since the first night I met him.

And there was a woman there, behind John, that I think I recognized—she's noteworthy only because I can't place her! Silly, I know, but I'm kind of relieved about that. I'd begun to worry that I might be getting too obsessed with this crazy need to connect to Phyllis's life. The woman's probably someone's sister.

Mostly what I have to say is—I'm jealous of Tory Sanders and her obvious closeness with Phyllis. I know I shouldn't be. But I am. I hate that about myself.

STANDING AT THE EDGE of the crowd gathered outside the little Italian place in downtown Phoenix that the entire Shelter Valley crew had chosen for dinner after leaving court, John knew a moment that was as near perfect as he'd had in years. They were a family of sorts, all these neighbors and friends. Supporting each other.

A wonderful thing for a man without loved ones. And the safety offered by their number was somehow pleasing, insuring a measure of distance. John could know them all—share his life with them all—without a single one of them getting too close.

"John, congratulations on the new projects!" Sam Montford, Jr., grandson of Shelter Valley's founder, said, holding out his hand for a friendly shake, as they all said their good-byes in the parking lot after dinner. "Will just told me you won the bid."

John nodded. "I—"

"Oh, my God!"

"He's here someplace."

"Everyone look for Billy!"

Sam and John turned together as the alarmed ripple spread around the crowd, whatever John had been about to say completely forgotten.

"What's going on?" Sam's urgent question was directed at Greg Richards, Shelter Valley's sheriff, as he pushed through the crowd, his expression grim.

"Randi told Billy he could climb that little wall to the side of the front door. She turned to answer a question and when she turned back, Billy was gone."

Without a word, or another wasted second, John moved forward through the panicking crowd of friends. What they needed right now was a cool head—someone who wasn't emotionally involved. They needed him.

"He's got to be here!" Randi's terror-filled shriek rose above the collective voices of the people calling out to the little boy as they broke apart to search around.

John's attention shot back and forth across the area. Adrenaline dictated that he move, but he wasn't sure where to go. People were everywhere. Running frantically. He checked behind a wall Phyllis had just looked behind, trying to ignore the fear he'd seen in her eyes.

Billy had to be there. Little boys had a tendency to be curious and to let their curiosity get the better of them.

Phyllis searched behind some bushes and John knelt down in the dirt, inspecting every inch of ground beneath them. It took him several seconds to figure out that the pounding he heard in his ears was his own heartbeat.

"When I was a kid not much older than Billy, I wandered off from my mother in the mall," he said to Phyllis, moving with her to the shrubbery that continued around the building. "I'd seen a midget and thought he was an elf."

She didn't say a word, just nodded jerkily and kept looking, pushing aside the brush, calling Billy's name. John wasn't sure she even felt the ugly scratch that had left a small line of beaded blood on her forearm.

"I managed to get so lost I ended up hiding under a rack of women's dresses. I was sobbing like crazy an hour later when the store manager finally found me."

"Billy!" Phyllis called, sending John a half smile at the same time.

"Billy must have seen his own midget," he said, feeling stupid and scared and hating both emotions.

"Yeah," Phyllis said. She squeezed his hand, an unusual

action from someone who didn't really know him all that well. "Don't worry, John, we'll find him."

He wanted to tell her he wasn't worried.

But what he knew—what he feared Phyllis had recognized in him—was that life was just like this. Its cruelty struck without notice and changed lives irrevocably. The knowledge damn near debilitated him.

HALF AN HOUR LATER, the solemn group stood together in a tight circle, Randi, Zack and Sheriff Richards in the center. It was still light outside, but wouldn't be for long.

"The police are arranging a search," Greg said. "Any of you who can stay to help, raise your hands so I can give them an accurate head count."

Every hand in the circle rose.

"I'll watch the other kids." Bonnie Nielson's voice came from somewhere in the sea of people.

"I'll help her," Becca Parsons replied.

The Sheriff looked at Ellen Moore Hanaran, the reason they'd originally gathered together that day. "Will you stay here, too?" he asked. "We don't want to take any chances with the rest of our troops."

Ellen nodded, while John silently applauded the sheriff. Ellen, still emotionally shaky as a result of her rape the year before, had had a hard day.

"Let's get this show on the road," John mumbled under his breath, impatience tightening his stomach.

"I'm with you," Will Parsons, Billy's uncle and namesake, replied beside him.

Neither man mentioned the possibility that no matter how soon they began their search, it might already be too late for two-and-a-half-year-old Billy. John hoped to God his friends would be spared that unbearable heartache.

CAROLINE WATCHED as another set of headlights turned the corner, coming slowly closer. *Please be him.* She repeated the mantra slowly, again and again, as she had for every other vehicle that had driven down John Strickland's street in the past half hour. No one seemed to notice the woman sitting in the little old pickup parked at the curb. But then, it was dark. They probably couldn't see her, thought the truck was empty.

Would John think that, too?

The car passed, and her heart settled heavily. If he didn't come soon, she wouldn't have the nerve to stay. And then she'd probably be up all night, trying to convince herself that all was well.

Billy had been found. She'd been sitting right there with Mrs. Howard in the kitchen at the boardinghouse when the call came from her friend, Mrs. Williams, who'd heard from another friend that a second call had come from Phoenix and the boy was safe.

John's Cadillac was two houses down before she noticed him. Climbing out of her truck, Caroline figured he must've seen her, because he didn't lower the garage door after pulling inside. Instead, he came out to meet her halfway up the driveway. He'd removed his tie. The first two buttons of his cream-colored dress shirt were undone. He was still wearing the brown tweed sport coat that matched his wrinkled brown slacks.

Not that she was noticing. It was just a long walk up the driveway.

"You heard?" he asked, meeting up with her.

"Yeah." She searched his eyes, not sure what she was looking for, but somehow believing she might find it there.

John, running a hand through his hair, seemed exhausted. "What a night."

"What happened? All I heard was that he's safe."

He shook his head. "No one knows for sure," he said.

"One minute he was there. Then he was gone. An hour later, he was back again. Phoenix police say he must've just wandered off, so that's the official explanation."

"For an *hour*?"

"Yeah."

"And managed, at two years old, to find his way back?"

"They figure he was right there, in the vicinity, all the time."

"Like he crawled under a bush or something?" She supposed it was possible. In his younger years, Jesse had certainly pulled a stunt or two. The infamous haystack episode, for instance. Little boys did things like that.

"I guess. Though we looked under every bush in the area."

She frowned, glad for the cover of night as self-consciousness came over her. She, Caroline Prater, unmarried and pregnant for the second time in her life, dressed in jeans that were faded because they were ten years old and not because they were fashionable, had invaded the personal space of a man who made more money in a year than she'd see in a lifetime.

"But if he was right there, why wouldn't he have answered when everyone was calling him?"

"I don't know."

John stood there, watching her, saying nothing. He didn't seem to be in any hurry for her to leave. Or to go inside.

"I guess I could've phoned," she said, glancing down at her boots. "I just didn't want to leave a message on your machine and I had no way of knowing when you'd be back and I needed to get out of that little room…."

"Caroline." He waited until she looked up at him. "It's okay. You don't know anyone in town yet. And you're going through a lot of changes right now. You're welcome to come over here anytime."

Was he humoring her? Or worse, feeling sorry for her? Because if he was…

"Would you like to come in? I could use a drink and I try my best not to indulge alone."

She didn't know what she should do. But she knew what she *didn't* want to do. Go back home to sit in that lonely little room, with only her computer for company.

"Okay," she said, following him slowly up the driveway. "But just for a minute."

He took her through the neatest garage she'd ever seen and into his kitchen, indicating a seat at the table. She perched on a stool at the breakfast bar instead. It felt less like settling in.

While John poured her a glass of filtered iced water and popped the top on a can of beer, Caroline tried not to stare around her like a kid in a candy shop. She'd never been in a kitchen like this, couldn't imagine cooking in one. He had double ovens, for heaven's sake! And the stove top—there were no burners, just a glass surface. The shiny beige-and-black-speckled counter was a cookie-maker's dream.

"What's this made of?" she asked, enjoying the smooth coolness beneath her fingers.

"Granite."

"It's wonderful."

"Yeah. It's scratch-resistant, so no need for cutting boards, but you have to treat it every year or so."

Treat it? The kitchen counter? Treating the leather on your saddle she could understand, but the kitchen counter? She had no idea what one would treat it with. But she didn't ask.

She'd look it up on the Internet before she went to bed.

"I made the doctor's appointment." It was her excuse for coming over.

"Oh." His beer can indented slightly beneath his grip. "When?"

"Monday at three if that's okay with you. I can change it if—"

"It's fine."

She meant to take a sip of her water. A small sip. And gulped so much she started to choke. After he'd patted her back and waited for her coughing fit to stop, John sat down on the stool beside her, facing her, his knees spread to accommodate hers. But he didn't touch her. Caroline didn't think she could have stayed if he had.

"Relax," he said, his voice soft, more from exhaustion, she thought, than anything else. "I don't bite."

"I know."

"I don't blame you or think badly of you, you know."

She tried to meet his gaze. Managed for a second, but then glanced at the cupboards behind him. "I know."

"How soon will it be before we find out if it's a boy or a girl?"

Warm emotion flooded Caroline. A boy or a girl. Her son. Or daughter. A new baby to cuddle and love and care for. John took another sip of beer.

His baby. Fear and uncertainty replaced the serenity she'd known for a second or two. This wasn't just her baby, to raise as she saw fit. She had to share the cuddling, the loving and decision-making with a virtual stranger. Even down to choosing a name.

She couldn't afford to get sentimental. At least when she wasn't alone.

"Not for a few months yet," she finally answered his question.

She was going to do her damnedest not to get embarrassed, either. Or allow any feelings of intimacy. Their connection was biological. It wasn't emotional. Or legal.

"I had something else to discuss with you," she said, proud of herself for speaking up when she'd feared she'd chicken out.

"What's that?" His tone was warm, easy. His eyes kind.

"About the doctor…"

His head lowered. "I need to be involved, Caroline."

She nodded quickly. "I understand. I'm not about to suggest otherwise, only that…perhaps…there's a better way to do this."

"What do you mean?" His stare was hard. His determination was for his baby's sake; she knew that.

She ran her tongue over her lips, swallowed and took a deep breath. "Well, since your involvement isn't physical…"

He frowned.

"…at this point," she added. "So you could handle your part of the…uh…transaction…over the phone."

He shook his head. "I don't like it." He hadn't taken enough time to give the idea any thought. "I'm that child's father and, as such, I should be present."

"You will be," Caroline said softly, years of living with Randy guiding her words. "I plan to tell her all about you on Monday, explain that you're taking full responsibility and will be actively involved every step of the way. Other than the physical exams, of course." He'd already agreed to that, but she had to make it perfectly clear. "I can have her call you after every visit, tell you whatever you would've heard if you were there, or I can arrange to have you call her. Your choice."

John studied her. He didn't seem convinced. But he wasn't shaking his head, either.

"You won't be able to keep me a secret if you're sitting with me in an obstetrician's office." She almost whispered the words, afraid her voice would reflect how badly the statement hurt her. Not because *he* was rejecting her, but simply because she was being rejected.

"I'm not trying to keep—"

Caroline looked him straight in the eye. "Yes, you are, and

it's okay, John. I understand." She had it all figured out. "This is a small town. You're relatively new here, and yet these people all know you. They've accepted you. You aren't sure how they'll react."

"I'm not afraid of their reactions." His voice was strong, sure. "I am, however, a little sensitive about Lauren's feelings. I broke off our engagement a week before the night I—we…"

Lauren. The physical education teacher from Montford.

"And you're right," he continued, not looking at Caroline. "I could tell her privately, try to explain, but…"

He'd still slept with another woman almost immediately after telling Lauren that he wasn't over his first wife.

"Anyway, in a town this size, people talk. There'd be a lot of speculation about her, people wondering how she was taking things. I'd just like to give her some time to move on before this comes out."

It was as good an excuse as any for putting off the inevitable. As eager as John to avoid the unpleasant aftermath of small-town shock, Caroline was willing to accept his reasoning.

If only she could ignore her fear that the more likely explanation was that he was ashamed of her—the country bumpkin who was carrying his child.

"And you don't think it'll be all over town in an hour if you're sitting in the waiting room of an obstetrician's office?" she asked now, focusing on the issue at hand. "Even if you aren't sitting with me?"

He didn't answer. Stared at the floor.

"I'll talk to the doctor, John," Caroline reiterated. "I can have her call you the second I'm through."

Head still lowered, he peered up at her. "How about you both call me when you're in the office. I'm sure she has a speakerphone. That way you can hear the questions I ask and the answers I receive."

Was it fair to hope the doctor didn't have a speakerphone? "Okay."

"Okay." He sipped his beer. Then again. And smiled at her.

"Have you thought about what you're going to tell them after the baby's born and you have to publicly claim it?" Oh, God, she was tired. She hadn't meant to let that slip.

Or to feel such crushing disappointment when John shook his head. "I'm having trouble getting through each day as it is. I can't think that far ahead." He wouldn't meet her eyes.

He was ashamed of her.

"You aren't ready for their questions," she guessed.

If she was a lawyer or a scientist or even a schoolteacher, would this be so hard for him? She couldn't ask. The answer—even unspoken—would hurt too much.

"I'm not sure I'll ever be ready," he murmured. "Damn, this day was hard." His weary sigh brought her head up.

"Because of Billy." Thinking of someone else always helped.

"Yeah. It happened so fast. One minute he was there with all of us, perfectly safe, and the next…gone, right from under the noses of more than thirty people."

"I, uh, knew a—well…someone who lived right by me whose little boy dug a cave for himself in the haystack in the barn without telling anyone. Apparently he played there fairly regularly until the day he accidentally fell asleep inside and his mother had the entire town on the farm looking for him."

He grinned. "What happened?"

"He woke up. Got the spanking of his life from a father who never quite understood him to begin with, and was forbidden from ever going near the haystack again."

John's eyes on her felt warm, and that warmth soothed her more than it should. "Sounds like you knew them well."

Caroline hoped her laugh didn't sound as nervous as it felt. "Everyone in Grainville knows everyone else well."

She should tell him about Jesse. It was going to come out soon enough anyway. The doctor would need to know this wasn't her first pregnancy.

She should've already told him.

But as she sat there, staring at John's knees, Caroline couldn't find the words. She didn't want John to think any less of her than he already did. One unexpected, unplanned and unmarried pregnancy was bad enough. But two?

It was downright humiliating.

"He's my son."

"Excuse me?"

"The little boy in the haystack was my son."

She heard his beer can touch the counter. "Was?"

The compassion in his voice brought Caroline's eyes up to his. "Is," she corrected. "His name's Jesse."

Eyes narrowed, John cocked his head as he studied her.

"You have a son."

She nodded. Tried to swallow and couldn't.

"Where is he?"

"At school."

"He goes to boarding school?" He couldn't seem to hide his shock at that assumption. And she didn't blame him. Not many boys from dirt-poor Kentucky farm folk ended up in boarding school. Jesse among them.

She shook her head. "He's at Harvard." She couldn't quite contain the proud little smile. "On a full scholarship."

"Harvard?" He frowned. "How old is he?"

"Seventeen."

His brows rose. "He's got his mama's brains."

Caroline waited.

He didn't surprise her. "Seventeen and you're what? Thirty-five?"

Almost. In another few months. Caroline nodded.

"You got pregnant when you were seventeen." He sounded as though he'd solved a puzzle.

"Sixteen, actually," she admitted. "I had him when I was seventeen." And just to save him a step. "An unplanned teen-aged pregnancy."

And this was where true confessions ended. He didn't need to know the rest. That the mother of his unborn child hadn't even graduated from high school. But she'd earned her GED, which was the important thing.

"Did you love the guy?"

Carefully, Caroline took a sip of water. She hadn't expected that question. "Very much."

"Did he stand by you?"

Her heart felt sad as she looked over at a man who would never in a million years understand Randy. "He married me and spent the rest of his life providing for the three of us."

"Randy."

She nodded.

John didn't say any more. Just sat there, his beer on the counter beside his hand, watching her. And then, after long moments while Caroline waited for some verdict, he picked up the can and took a long sip.

CHAPTER SIX

"I HAVE TO BE HONEST with you...."

"Okay." Sitting at the breakfast bar in John's kitchen, her glass of water still barely touched, Caroline braced herself. His silence had given her time to prepare. She needed to know where she stood even if that meant knowing she'd lost his respect.

"That thing with Billy tonight—"

She nodded, waiting to see how it tied in with what she'd confessed about her past.

"It...I'm having problems with the whole baby thing."

"Our baby." A spiral of butterflies attacked her lower belly at the intimate sound of those words. Even after she'd promised herself there'd be no intimacy.

"Yeah." His voice, the look in her eyes, conveyed regret for what he was about to say. Do.

Drawing a slow breath, Caroline told herself she'd be okay. He was having second thoughts about support, but she hadn't planned on his support to begin with. Financially or otherwise. His words weren't going to matter.

Which was just as well, since he didn't give her any. He was leaving her to fill in the blanks.

"Okay," she said. And wondered how best to make her departure.

"When Billy went missing, I saw the terror on his parents' faces. I don't think I can go through that."

Her thoughts skidding to a halt, Caroline sat still.

"It told me something about myself. Something I'm not proud of, but it's true. I didn't break off my engagement with Lauren just because I still care about Meredith, which is what I thought. I broke it off because I somehow knew I can't go through that again—can't go through what I did when I lost her. Today I realized how easily it can happen. And I know that if I care that deeply again, I'm always going to be afraid of what's around the next corner. I can't live every day with that fear."

He finished his beer. Crushed the can in his hand—something she'd already come to associate with his attempts to suppress intense emotion.

He was staring at the crushed can but didn't seem focused on the misshapen piece of aluminum. "It dawned on me tonight that with this baby—a life I contributed to but knew absolutely nothing about—I'm powerless to prevent tragedy from happening. If that had been our son tonight..."

His eyes met hers, and Caroline's carefully guarded heart opened the tiniest crack.

"You know," she began, understanding completely, but not sure what she should say, what she *could* say. "One thing I've learned in my life is that when things happen, you handle them. Because you have no other choice."

His eyes were intent, as though trying to absorb something from her. Gain something.

"If I'd contemplated being unmarried and pregnant at sixteen, or unmarried and pregnant again at thirty-five... If I'd contemplated losing Randy..." Her voice trailed off. Sharing her innermost thoughts and feelings wasn't something Caroline did easily.

"I would never have believed myself capable of handling any of those things," she finally said. "I'm still not sure how

I did. I only know that, at the time, there was no choice but to get up every day, so I did. I got dressed. Made whatever decisions the day required of me and then I went to bed."

John nodded, the glint in his eyes one of comprehension. Or so it seemed to her.

"Just as long as you understand that I'm going to be struggling with it."

She nodded, smiled and before she could change her mind, reached out and squeezed his hand. Life was hard. There were few easy answers. Or even indisputably right answers. She and John had been thrown together under extreme circumstances that promised to be rife with pitfalls and challenges. Pain was inevitable.

But he hadn't turned his back on her and walked away. He apparently hadn't decided, as she had, that finding herself in the single and pregnant mode a second time was inexcusable, and that it served her right to go it alone. Caroline didn't even want to acknowledge how relieved she was about that.

And therein lay the biggest danger of all. The danger of relying on someone else.

She was strong. She could handle whatever came her way. Unless she gave that power away.

"So TELL ME about your son." After the night of Billy's disappearance, John had not expected to speak to Caroline Prater again until Monday afternoon's telephone conference call with her doctor, figuring that the baby didn't need him until then. He'd intended to work, to read, to play a round of golf and have a couple of beers with Will Parsons and some of the other guys. Until he remembered that pregnant women needed exercise.

At least, he was fairly certain they did. It only made sense. So instead of playing golf on Saturday, he was in Phoenix

with Caroline, walking through the Desert Botanical Garden.
He figured, with her penchant for the out-of-doors, she'd like
the place. He'd have preferred something with more buildings himself.

Although she'd refused to come until he'd told her he was
only thinking of the pregnancy, she strolled along beside him,
occasionally reading excerpts from the signs along the trail,
saying not one word about her son. She didn't seem to mind
being there, though.

"It's not personal," he finally heard himself saying. "He's
going to be a half brother to my child, so I figure I should
know something about him." *Lame, Strickland. Really lame.*

"What do you want to know?"

About the fear she must have felt when she discovered she
was pregnant at sixteen. How she'd managed school and baby
feedings. If she'd been able to go to her senior prom.

He and Meredith had gone to senior prom together. It had
been their first date. And the night of their first kiss. He'd tried
for more, gotten his hands slapped and fallen in love.

"What's he like? Other than smart?" Does he have his
mother's thirst for knowledge? Her compassion and open mind?

She sighed, took a path that led to some pavilion—John
missed the name of it. "He's tall like his father, a typical farm
boy with big shoulders and strong arms."

"Already at seventeen?"

"He's been working the farm after school, on weekends,
holidays and summers since he was eight."

John was intrigued. It wasn't a life he knew anything about,
except perhaps from a couple of old television episodes or
movies he might have seen. "Doing what?"

"Anything from milking the cow, cleaning the barn, col-
lecting eggs, helping in the fields—depended on what time
of year it was."

"Did you have beef cattle?"

"A few. We raised primarily crops. Randy worked the land from early boyhood, as well, and he was good at it. He just never made enough to invest in the property or the equipment. Every time there was a little extra money, the tractor would break or the barn roof would spring a leak."

There was no bitterness in her voice. No complaint. Not even any regret that he could detect.

"Did Jesse like the work?" Did she?

Caroline shrugged, glancing back and forth across the trail as different flowering plants came into view. "It was life," she said. "It wasn't a matter of liking it. He just did it." Her expression was placid, telling him nothing, yet John sensed there was much more to know.

"So where does Harvard come in? Does he plan to return to the farm after he graduates?"

She looked over at him assessingly, as though trying to determine if his question crossed the personal boundaries they'd set for themselves. John wished he had her talent for facial camouflage. More, he wished he knew for sure that there was nothing *to* camouflage. He'd been thinking about her a lot. But only, he told himself, because she was carrying his child.

"No, he doesn't plan to return."

They circled the pavilion—a butterfly haven at certain times of the year—and headed down another paved trail through more cacti and bushes and flowering plants.

"How did Randy feel about that?"

Her glance at him was sharp.

"You learn a lot about a teenager by how he relates to his parents," he said, answering her unspoken question. Not that he knew anything about teenagers except what he'd learned from being one.

"Randy refused to discuss college with Jess. He just kept talking like Jesse was going to be working the farm full-time after his high school graduation."

That must've been difficult. For all of them. "But Jesse persevered."

"Yes."

"Mature kid you've got there."

She smiled, slid a rock off the path with the tip of her boot. "Sometimes. Especially since his father died and he's become the self-appointed man of the house. And then other times he'll say something that reminds me of the little boy I used to have to coax to eat his oatmeal."

"Does he know about the baby?" Not that he'd blame her if she hadn't told Jesse. An unexpected pregnancy like this couldn't be an easy thing to explain to a teenager—especially with his own father so recently dead.

"No." Caroline's pace picked up. "He found it hard enough to cope with my move. It's best to break things to him one at a time. It's always been that way with Jesse. Even as a kid. Like the summer I had to tell him that not only wasn't there enough money to go to Nashville on vacation, but there wasn't going to be any vacation at all *and* he'd have to work more hours on the farm until school started. I told him about Nashville and then waited a week before I broke the rest of it."

"How'd he take it?"

"He was angry, stormed out of the house cursing about the unfairness of life. An hour later he was back apologizing and asking for a hug. Both times."

Something tugged at John's stomach as he pictured the woman beside him mothering her son. Something that made their whole situation more complicated.

And he had enough complications.

"You ready to go back?" he asked. They'd only been there half an hour. Hardly worth the eighteen dollars he'd paid for their admission.

"Sure."

No questions asked. Sometimes the woman was so accommodating it annoyed him.

CAROLINE WOKE UP her second Sunday in Shelter Valley and spent half an hour staring at the ceiling, engaged in a mental debate. She'd been going to church every Sunday her entire life. She didn't feel complete just lying in bed without that weekly tune-up. But more than spiritual renewal, church in Grainville had been the social event of the week. Of course, there'd been only one church there—a nondenominational gathering of people struggling to get by in a hard world.

Shelter Valley had three churches, but she knew which one she'd want to attend. David Marks's church. Not only was it nondenominational, it was walking distance from her room. Caroline couldn't bear the thought of pulling up to church in her rusted-out old truck—with people watching her get out. She was going to find it awkward in a big college parking lot, and a church parking lot was so much smaller. Worse, everyone arrived—and left—at the same time. Her presence would definitely be noticed.

Something she'd learned about Arizona—rusted vehicles weren't all that common. Must be because the dry warmth preserved metal here. But whatever the case, it made her truck doubly embarrassing.

Still, one voice in her head argued, she was lucky to have that old truck. Thankful to have it. And she was who she was. A dirt-poor, mostly uneducated Kentucky farm woman who, at not quite thirty-five, had already raised a family. She was also a woman who'd loved to chat with her neighbors and help out whenever she could. A woman who'd looked forward to Sundays, and catching up, all week long.

A woman who wanted to go to church.

But in a town this size, a new parishioner, especially one whose only winter church dress was a hand-sewn brown gingham made from her mother's old living-room curtains, would certainly draw attention. She'd taken on a lot in the past couple of weeks, was still trying to figure out the implications for herself, had no faith that she could come up with the answers she needed. And she felt relatively safe with her anonymity in this town.

She turned over, pulling up the quilt her mother had made her and Randy for Christmas ten years before. Was she ready to risk that sense of safety just to go to church? she asked herself. She hadn't had a full night's sleep since Randy died. Wouldn't it be better to try to doze off?

Was she going to let fear keep her trapped in bed? her other voice demanded. Why was she there if not to live?

What if John Strickland went to David Marks's church? She'd die if he saw her in her old dress and lace-up brown shoes—ones that looked no better than her boots but could manage the snow on cold Kentucky winter days.

Throwing off the covers, Caroline got up, barely noticing the chilly wood floor beneath her bare feet as her flannel gown slid down to her ankles. John Strickland's opinion of her looks mattered not at all and if she was going to start thinking it did, she'd just have to prove to herself that she was wrong. She'd put on her dress and go to church.

And if Phyllis Langford Sheffield attended David Marks's church? Caroline's stomach churned. The thought of seeing Phyllis had been the force compelling her through the worst months of her life. But thoughts and reality were sometimes so different.

Seeing her twin sister was the thing she wanted above all else—except for Jesse's safety and health, of course, and the health of her unborn child. And what if Phyllis turned up her nose at the country bumpkin? Or worse, Caroline made some social faux pas that would haunt her nights with humiliating memories? Wasn't a dream better left a dream if that way it could remain intact?

She looked back at the bed, grabbed the sheet and quilt in one hand, and contemplated diving under the worn cotton and getting a real day of rest. Something she could easily have done in Grainville and saved herself a whole lot of bother and money.

With more force than necessary, Caroline jerked the covers up, yanking them tightly enough to remove the wrinkles, and settled the embroidered pillowcases on top. She was going to David Marks's church. She'd go late.

She'd sit in the back.

And leave early.

And if that was living, her other voice said, then she'd hate to see what dying was.

"MA-MA UP! Ma-ma up!"

"Yeah! Ma-ma up!"

"Uhh…" It was the last Sunday morning before school started, and Phyllis Langford Sheffield groaned, bracing herself to ride out the effects of a couple of two-year-olds clambering onto her bed. She was pretty sure her stomach was divorcing her. Not only that, her tongue was sticking to the roof of her mouth. And her head weighed a ton.

She cracked open one eye to stare into two pairs of dark eyes only inches from her face. "Where's Daddy?"

"Da-da!" Calvin repeated happily and with a notable measure of pride at his accomplishment.

"Da-da!" Clarissa, more often the leader of the two, par-
roted.

The twins—she wasn't sure which one was first—climbed
on her curled-up body and started to bounce up and down.

"Ma-ma up!"

"Ma-ma up!"

She should roll over, find the energy to lift them off her.
The peace that would follow would be glorious to her heav-
ing stomach.

"Giddyup, Ma-ma!" Clarissa's sweet voice would have
brought a smile to her face if her cheeks hadn't hurt so much.

"Where's Daddy?" She was wasting her last vestiges of
strength. There was no way they were going to hear her above
their whoops and giggles. It was also pretty clear—to her at
least—that they had no idea where their father had run off to.

To be fair, he hadn't known she was sick. As production
manager of Montford's theater, Matt had worked late the
night before, overseeing a private rental, a well-known jazz
musician who'd come to Shelter Valley to perform for a sell-
out and very appreciative crowd.

"Daddy's right here," the voice of her dreams said from
somewhere near their bathroom door.

"Oh, thank God," Phyllis mumbled into her pillow.

"What are you two rascals doing to your mother?" he asked.

"Giddyap!" Calvin shouted in his baby voice.

"Did you ask Mommy if she wanted to be a horse this
morning?" Matt's voice was closer, as though he was prop-
ping himself on an elbow beside her.

"Horsey!" Both kids cried with glee. "Horsey!" Their
bouncing gained intensity with each brain-piercing shriek.

"Dead." Phyllis gave everything she had to that one word.

"Mommy, did you tell these two adorable little devils that
you wanted to be a horsey this morning?" Matt asked play-

fully, pushing her hair back from her face. She opened an eye again, just to see the gorgeous smile she knew would be lighting her husband's face.

"Dead," she muttered.

Her eye dropped shut just as Matt's expression fell. "Hon, what's wrong?" Sweeter than his words was the immediate removal of the jumping weights on her body and bed. With another quick peek, she caught a glimpse of her husband with a squirming two-year-old under each arm.

"Flu," she said, her mouth getting tangled in her pillowcase. "Or death."

His frown didn't suggest any appreciation of her sense of humor. Just as well, since she wasn't sure it was going to last. She needed to throw up, pass out or weep.

"Let me get these two in high chairs with dry cereal and a video, and I'll be right back."

They generally didn't let the television babysit their children. But sometimes... *"Blue's Clues,"* Phyllis mumbled. They'd get as much as thirty minutes out of that one.

Matt sat down on the bed, too close to her for comfort. Phyllis groaned. *"Blue's Clues."* Please, God, let him hear her this time. She didn't think...

"They've seen it twice. And *Lion King,* too."

Both eyes flew open. "What?"

"You've been asleep for more than three hours," Matt said, gently moving the bangs from her forehead, leaving his hand there for a few seconds.

"You don't have a fever," he said. Very, very good news. Whatever was killing her probably wasn't contagious—wasn't going to kill her loved ones as well.

"Then it's a migraine."

She'd said a full sentence and tried for another. "I haven't had one in a long time."

The movement of Matt's head as he nodded made her dizzy, so she closed her eyes. "Probably the stress of Billy's disappearance the other night, mixed in with school starting," he said. His fingers felt heavenly as they massaged the back of her neck.

She'd like to be able to agree with him. And, in truth, she was sure he was correct—at least partially. But not totally. There'd only ever been one source of stress in her life that could bring on a migraine of this magnitude.

Her ex-husband.

Since the moment she'd admitted her love for Matt Sheffield, Phyllis had been honest with him. About herself, about everything. After barely surviving her first marriage with psyche intact, she'd vowed never to hide anything from her mate again.

But that was just what she'd done. She hadn't told her husband about Brad's letter.

"Thank goodness, it hit on Sunday," Matt was saying. "You have all day to lie here and rest."

Phyllis's eyes flew open. "I promised Bonnie I'd watch her girls this afternoon." She had to get up. Somehow. Throwing off the covers was an effort that sent pain shooting through her temples to her brain. Tears spilled from her closed eyes when Matt reversed the heroic effort with one swoop of his arm, covering her back up.

"She called an hour ago. I told her you were sick and offered to call Tory. She and Ben are taking them."

Oh. Thank God. And Tory. And Ben. And Matt. And…

Phyllis opened her eyes, forced herself to hold them open and focus on her husband. If he was going to be so kind to her while she suffered, she owed it to him to tell him the cause of her suffering. She owed it to her conscience to come clean. "I had a letter from Brad."

His eyes narrowed, shadowed, and still she forced herself to maintain contact. With halting phrases broken by pauses filled with the deep breathing necessary to retain the meager contents of her stomach, she told Matt about the seemingly worthless investment she'd accepted as part of her share of the assets in her divorce. She explained the judge's willingness to accept the investment's potential value as its worth in the dividing of assets. And after a few slow and even breaths, she told him about the investment's sudden change in value. And Brad's demand that she sign away her rights to it.

"What did you tell him?"

She turned over very carefully, trying to keep her head as still as possible. "I didn't respond."

"Do you think you should?"

Leave it to Matt to ask, not tell. She wanted to nod. "Unless I give him the money, he's going to be livid."

"Then give it to him."

Tears filled her eyes again as she lay there staring up at the man who'd changed her life. He meant what he'd just said.

"I don't *want* to give it to him. He took everything from me," she said, emotion carrying her through the pain. "That investment was a slap in the face, meant to tell me I was worthless, and instead, it tells me I came out of my experience with Brad worth a quarter of a million dollars."

A smile slowly creased Matt's lips as he continued to stroke her tense muscles. "You're worth far more than that, hon."

She wanted to smile back. And rub her face against that caressing hand, like a cat. But if she moved she was going to be sick. "You know what I mean."

"Yeah, I do."

"So?"

"So you keep the money and we'll deal with the bastard's

anger. As long as you can keep yourself okay up here—" he brushed a hand across the top of her head "—there's not much he can do. He doesn't have the power to hurt you anymore."

He was right. Logically she knew that. And as she lay there, feeling like she was at death's door, Phyllis's heart knew it, too. Brad's opinion, anything he might do or say, could only matter if she let it. Matt's love for her, his belief in her, had set her free.

Even feeling this sick, she was the luckiest woman alive.

CHAPTER SEVEN

Sunday, December, 5, 2004

I never planned to meet the man! I went to Frankfort for the dedication, just to be close to someone who knew my sister. I had no idea it would be so easy to get a ticket to the reception, or that I'd actually walk up to a bar to order a drink or that he'd be there at the same time and take pity on me when I had no idea whether I wanted red wine or white because I had no idea what the difference was.

And you know, when I went, I didn't have even a tiny hope that he'd start talking about Shelter Valley, or that he'd be without a dinner companion. I'm still amazed at how easy he was to talk to—how easy it was for me, Caroline Prater, to sit in a fine restaurant and carry on a conversation with a gorgeous man of the world. I just can't believe it!

He really loves Shelter Valley, based on how much he talked about the place and his friends there—without me even asking! He didn't mention Phyllis, so he must not know her well, but he talked about some of Phyllis's friends. I feel as if I know them. At least a little bit.

Anyway, that's not all I can't believe.

I'm so shocked I can't even tell you what I've done....

CAROLINE HAD COME to the clinic prepared to wait. Worn puzzle book in hand, she took a seat in a far corner of the waiting room on the second floor of the Shelter Valley Medical Center—a small strip office complex that consisted of everything from dental and optometry offices to the one specialist in town, the ob-gyn. There were a couple of family practitioners who could double as emergency-room doctors on occasion, a rehabilitation clinic and a weight-loss business. Most other physical needs were handled in Phoenix.

Because Dr. Mason was working her in in between scheduled patients, Caroline had come early and was content to sit there minding her own business for as long as it took. Other than a bit of nervousness over the appointment itself, it felt good to be out of her room and among people. The waiting area was about half-full, but women seemed to be moving in and out fairly quickly, many with smiles on their faces. Which made the young woman who took the empty seat next to Caroline that much more remarkable.

Mostly she was remarkable because—unlike all the other women in the room—she was someone Caroline recognized.

Ellen Moore Hanaran.

Setting the still-closed puzzle book down in her lap, Caroline clasped her hands so that their shaking wouldn't be obvious.

Other than sitting in a pew at the rear of the church, staring at the backs of heads, it was the closest Caroline had ever been to any of the people she "knew" in Shelter Valley. It was the closest she'd been to anyone—besides John—who knew her twin sister.

Ellen glanced over. Smiled. The expression was genuine yet didn't quite hide the uneasiness in the young woman's eyes. Caroline saw something in that brief look.

The girl introduced herself and continued to smile shyly when Caroline did the same.

"Is this your first time here?" Caroline asked.

Ellen glanced down and then back up. She nodded. "I...uh...I've been to the clinic before, just not here. My appointment's actually not for another half hour, I didn't know how much time it would take to fill out the paperwork," Ellen was saying.

The girl seemed so vulnerable, so needy, as though any human comfort, even from a stranger, was preferable to having only her own mind for company. Caroline wanted to ask what Ellen was there for, but didn't.

It was none of her business.

"It's my first time here, too, though it's my second pregnancy," she babbled, hoping she was doing the right thing.

Horrified when tears filled the girl's eyes, Caroline couldn't resist her natural impulse to cover Ellen's hand with her own. "It'll be okay," she said, although she had no idea what was bothering the young woman.

"I hope so," Ellen said softly, drying her eyes before any of the three other women still left in the room noticed her tears. All three, with obviously advanced pregnancies, were in seats close to the door leading to examining rooms.

"Are you afraid of the exam?" Caroline asked, remembering her own first gynecological visit. She'd spent the entire time in the waiting room praying for an avalanche to come and kill her.

It hadn't happened. And it hadn't been long before Caroline was thankful for that. Because those visits had helped her bring a very healthy Jesse into the world.

"A little," Ellen said with a nervous chuckle. "Not really, though. I've been through all that."

Still holding the other girl's hand—mostly because Ellen

hadn't pulled it away—Caroline gave her fingers a gentle squeeze. "So what's upsetting you?"

And then, as if in slow motion, she had a mental rerun of the past several minutes. Saw herself touching a perfect stranger. Prying into an unknown person's business. As if she were a hick in Grainville with nothing better to do than pass the time gossiping about anyone who was doing anything worth gossiping about.

Snatching her hand away, Caroline sat back, her skin burning. "I'm sorry," she said, as professionally as she could manage for a woman who'd never even had a real job, let alone been any kind of professional. "I don't know what came over me, minding your business like that."

"It's okay," Ellen said, giving her a smile as she grabbed Caroline's hand. "I was just thanking God for sending me an angel when I needed one. Don't desert me now."

If Caroline hadn't spent the past thirty years learning how to hide herself from the world, she would've burst into tears of her own at that moment. Instead, she took a deep breath, carefully stored away the memory, and said, "Then I guess, if I'm to do my job well, maybe I should know why you need an angel."

It was Ellen's tighter grasp of her hand, more than the shaky sigh, that spoke to Caroline. "I…have a symptom…. I might have something…." the young woman confessed. "I haven't told anyone."

Caroline's thoughts slowed and her heart opened wide. "Something serious?"

Surely this was just a young woman's ignorance of the relatively normal vagaries of the female cycle. After everything Ellen had been through, any more than that would be just plain cruel.

Her troubled gaze couldn't seem to settle anywhere. "I don't know," she said, the fear in her voice a tangible thing.

She shouldn't be sitting here alone.

"Don't you think you should tell your family?" Her mother would be able to reassure her about whatever she suspected was wrong. She'd have the experience to set Ellen's fears at rest. Or, if things really *were* bad, the love and support the girl would need.

"I've had kind of a rough year…and Aaron, that's my husband, he's been so great and patient and…"

Ellen looked at Caroline, and Caroline had a feeling that it was their combined strength, meeting in that glance, that kept the girl sitting upright in her chair.

She turned her back fully to the room, facing Caroline and the wall behind her. "I…had an experience…and I'm afraid I might have caught something," she whispered, her cheeks flushed.

Guided by the same instinct that had seen her through the raising of a highly intelligent son in a backwoods town, Caroline said, "You're talking about what happened to you last January."

"How'd you know?" Ellen asked. And then, dropping Caroline's hand, she turned away. "I guess you saw the news. I'm going to have to testify in Phoenix sometime later this month or next."

"I know."

"They're still doing jury selection. We all went for the first day, but I'm not going back again until I have to take the stand. It's just too hard."

"And serves no real purpose, anyway," Caroline agreed. Being there that first day, with all her support, was probably a good thing for the girl—took away her fear of having to face the courtroom full of people, of having to face the man who'd violated her so horribly.

But beyond that, she deserved to start a new life. One filled with love and hope and security.

Two of the other women had been called in. The remaining woman was talking on a cell phone. A television talk show droned in the distance.

"Am I never going to escape the stigma of that night?" Ellen's question came softly beside her.

"Of course you are," Caroline hurriedly assured Ellen, sitting back to give her space. "Someday when there's more time, I'll tell you a few things I've learned about life, but for now, I promise you that you'll move on, have a new and different life."

Ellen stared at her. "Did something bad happen to you, too? Were you raped?" She glanced down at Caroline's bare left ring finger. Then at her belly. As if to ask whether the baby she was there to bring into the world was the result of an attack.

"No, it's nothing like that," Caroline immediately assured Ellen. Eventually these people were going to know that John Strickland was the father of her baby, and she could never have anyone thinking that he'd acted in any way except honorably. This was just as much Caroline's doing as his—more so, if the truth be known. Although she hadn't knowingly set out to have dinner with John—and certainly not to sleep with him—she *had* set out to meet him, when he hadn't even known she existed. "It's a long story, too long for here and now, but I promise I'll tell you about it someday."

"Okay," Ellen nodded, still watching her.

"And in the meantime, don't worry so much. I don't know what's making you think you might've caught something from that jerk, but I do know that often what seems like a problem…down there…really isn't anything at all. And even if there *is* something, it can be taken care of."

Ellen nodded but didn't look convinced.

Caroline didn't take time to think, she just let her natural frankness come forth. "You said your husband doesn't know, right?" she asked.

"Right." Ellen's eyes were facing the tile beneath their feet.

"Have you and he been physically active?"

Ellen blushed again. "Yeah."

"Then chances are, you didn't catch anything last January," she said. "I can't promise, of course, but those things are passed back and forth and if you haven't passed *him* anything—and if he hasn't passed *you* anything…" She had to say it.

"Oh, no!" Ellen stared up at her. "He's never…been with anyone else."

"At this stage, it's probably unlikely that you have an STD," Caroline said matter-of-factly.

"But…" Ellen's innocence was heartbreaking as she stared up at Caroline. Caroline couldn't help feeling how difficult this was for the young woman, driven as she was to conduct such an intimate conversation with a complete stranger. And made a silent promise to hold sacrosanct the faith Ellen had placed in her. "If…if Aaron had something, would he be able to tell?" she finally asked.

"Almost always," Caroline told the girl. "It's easier for guys to tell."

The girl continued to stare at her, and Caroline hoped she hadn't mistakenly brought that relief to her eyes. "I'm not a doctor," she added. "I could be completely off…."

Ellen's smile was tremulous. "I know," she said. "I don't think I'm really afraid of something being seriously wrong. I feel I could handle that, you know? I'm just terrified that I was marked by…you know…"

"You felt dirty," Caroline guessed.

"Yeah."

"And ashamed?"

"Yeah."

She took the young woman's hand. "Well, my friend, you're neither. No matter what the doctor finds."

Ellen glanced up, tears in her eyes. "You're being so kind."

Caroline shrugged. "I'm just sitting here."

"No, you aren't." Ellen grinned, looking younger. "Why would you do this for a perfect stranger?"

"I've been in need of a friend a couple of times in my life," she said. "Times when I thought I couldn't go on without one."

Ellen nodded silently.

"I recognized that same look in you."

"Oh."

"And being new to town, I don't know many people yet. It's nice to have a real conversation with someone besides myself."

The third woman was called, and then it was just the two of them in the waiting room. They sat quietly for a couple of minutes and Caroline contemplated opening her puzzle book.

Or finding some way to bring the conversation around to her twin. But it seemed a little…underhanded and creepy, now that she was here, to be trying to get information about someone without her knowledge. Reading public information on the Internet hadn't seemed nearly as invasive in Kentucky as it did to her now.

"So, you said you just moved here," Ellen interrupted Caroline's ongoing mental battle. "Is your husband with you?"

Caroline froze. Somehow the protective bubble that usually surrounded her had slipped away in Ellen's presence. She'd known there'd be questions in a town this size. Being new to Shelter Valley would garner attention in and of itself. But being pregnant and single…

"My husband was killed in a tractor accident last summer."

Ellen's brows drew together, her eyes dark with sympathy. "I'm so sorry. This has got to be awf—" She broke off, her face blank. "Oh."

Obviously there was no way Caroline could be newly pregnant by a husband who'd been dead for more than six months.

Neither could she talk about John to the people who'd become his family. Presenting his child to this town was up to him.

Sitting there, next to the girl she'd befriended, with absolutely no idea of what to say, Caroline felt incredibly stupid. Instead of worrying about her wardrobe and fantasizing about meeting a sister who didn't even know she existed, she should've been planning how *she* was going to present her child to the world. Away from Grainville and all the people who'd known her all her life, she'd begun to feel almost anonymous, and she'd let the feeling lull her into an awkward moment, completely unprepared.

"This was my first holiday season without Randy since I was ten." She had to speak what truth she could. "I...let a moment of loneliness get the better of me."

"So..." Ellen's smile was sincere, sweet, without a hint of judgment. "Does the father know?"

She nodded. Tried for an easy smile, which she feared was more tentative than anything. "He's a good man. I'm ashamed and embarrassed to say that we hardly know each other, but he's insisted on taking full responsibility."

"Don't be embarrassed," Ellen said, tapping Caroline's hand. "Everyone has moments of crazy loneliness. And if they don't, they're just too lucky for words."

Caroline smiled as she studied her new friend. "Well, I don't know about that, but here I am, brand-new to town, and pregnant to boot."

"Don't worry," Ellen said. "Everyone here is really cool. They aren't going to care if you're married or not. I'll introduce you to my mom and Bonnie at the day care and some of the others. Before you know it, you'll have more babysitters and—" she chuckled "—life-sitters, too, than you know what to do with."

Caroline wasn't so sure, but didn't see any point in disillusioning the girl who'd suffered so much. Shelter Valley had come through for her in a big way; her faith in it was well-placed and, Caroline suspected, equally well deserved. From what she could tell, Ellen Moore Hanaran was a gem. Instead, she told the girl that she, too, had grown up in a small town, and spent the next couple of minutes answering Ellen's questions about life in rural Kentucky. The desert-born girl seemed quite taken with the idea of living with so much green.

"It sounds wonderful," Ellen told her. "So what made you leave? Especially now?"

"I'm going to Montford," Caroline said, again choosing her words very carefully, to speak the truth—some of the truth— but not to speak out of turn. As painstakingly as she'd thought through this whole plan, there were some things she hadn't considered well enough. "I got a full scholarship, majoring in English. I've always had this desire to write."

"No kidding!" Ellen grinned. "I'm impressed. Scholarships to Montford are hard to come by. Especially for people from out of state." The girl leaned back in her chair, apparently more relaxed, and Caroline was content to sit and listen. "I'm graduating in May with a degree in Social Work," Ellen said.

She spent the rest of the time until she was called in telling Caroline about the Montford University undergraduate experience. The courses and classrooms, professors and fellow students. The depth of material, long assignments and difficult tests.

Her words made Caroline nervous as hell and still…she couldn't wait.

JOHN PACED his home office for forty-five minutes, trying to come up with a way to solve a roofline problem on his most recent project—an art museum in Idaho. How the hell long did it take for a first pregnancy appointment, anyway? What exactly was there to do?

Glancing out at the little patch of green grass in his backyard desert oasis, he thought about having a grapefruit. Or an orange. His oranges were really good this year.

He really wasn't hungry for a piece of fruit. John checked his watch impatiently and swore. It wasn't even three yet.

His computer signaled a new mail message, calling John. He sat. Deleted the junk e-mail that had just come in, and clicked on his CAD program. He'd get the round, three-story-high solarium and the one-story squared-off oil painting display rooms to complement each other before she called. He just had to focus.

With rapid clicks, John moved walls and doorways, changed the shapes of windows and arches, added a chimney and turret to a roof that was too flat, and took them all away again. He measured dimensions, told his mind to travel along creative paths and thought about having a son named after him. By the time the phone rang at almost four o'clock, he was peeling his third orange.

"Strickland," he said when he picked up after allowing the phone to ring twice so it wouldn't appear that he'd been sitting on it.

Dr. Mason introduced herself. Told him that Caroline was with her. Took a moment to make sure that all three parties could hear each other.

And then she started to talk about John's baby as though the little guy were already alive and real. There were no questions about how he'd come to be in this situation or what he and Caroline planned to do with the baby. No admonitions or warnings about his upcoming obligations or current duties. Instead, the doctor gave a professionally thorough rundown of everything he and Caroline could expect over the next months, complete with lists of appointments that would be little more than just the usual checkups, which occurred once a month, at least for now.

They could expect to hear the heartbeat at the first trimester mark. There'd be an ultrasound in the fourth month, during which they might be able to determine the sex of the child. Based on Caroline's age and good health, she didn't think there'd be any need for amniocentesis, which was fine by him as he didn't even know what that was. Apparently, though, she'd need something called a triple-screen blood test. Fine, but as far as he was concerned, the fewer tests required, the better.

"Do you plan to have the baby naturally?" Dr. Mason's question fell into an awkward silence.

"As opposed to what?" John asked, frustrated with his ignorance. Until now, he'd been deliberately ignorant about the nuances of baby-having; he'd always thought he and Meredith would learn the ropes together.

"There are many options," Dr. Mason said after a brief pause. John wished he could see Caroline's expression, wondering if, even now, it would be as unrevealing as usual. "An epidural is probably the most commonly used. It's an injection in the mother's spine to numb her lower half for the actual birth...."

John stood, walked to the window, ignored the grass and citrus trees growing there, staring instead at the icy coolness of the swimming pool.

Dr. Mason was talking about the pros and cons of epidurals, obviously unaware that John was still focused on the long needle going into Caroline's back.

"Uh…" he interrupted. "Caroline, you've had a baby before. Do you have any preferences?"

"I'd like to go natural."

Then why hadn't she just said so?

"Okay, natural it is," he said.

"Fine." Dr. Mason didn't seem to think it was a bad idea. "We'll need to schedule classes when it gets closer to the time."

Classes. He'd heard of them, of course. But most of what he knew he'd seen on sitcoms. John moved over to the wet bar on the wall opposite the windows. Not to pour a drink; it was too early for that. He just wanted to lean an elbow there and try not to picture himself sitting on the floor next to a prostrate Caroline, the two of them panting….

The doctor talked about diet. Caroline's, not his. And exercise. John grabbed a beer out of the minifridge. Popped the top.

"And obviously, you're to avoid alcohol and tobacco for the duration…"

John dropped the can of beer on the bar and proceeded to a leather armchair by his built-in mahogany bookcase. Sitting down, legs stretched in front of him, he leaned his head against the back of the chair.

"By my calculations, the baby's due August sixth," Dr. Mason said, "which means its going to be a hot summer for you, my dear."

"I'll be fine." Other than answering his question earlier, it was the first time Caroline had spoken.

"You don't have air-conditioning in your room," John said, thinking aloud.

"There's a ceiling fan."

"I'll get you a window unit."

She didn't argue. But probably only because of the doctor sitting in the room with her.

"Since you're going natural, I'd like to have John start coming to your visits." John sat up. Smothered a cough. "We'll make the next appointment for February twenty-first, a Monday, if that works for you both. It's five weeks away but my receptionist says it's my first free appointment. That's your twelfth week and we can be on track for every four weeks after that."

"Is it really necessary for John to be there?" Caroline asked as soon as the doctor had finished.

Silently, he echoed the question. He and Caroline had been through this and she'd talked him out of going.

"He'll be much better equipped to help you if he's familiar with the whole process," the doctor continued. "Besides, by next month we'll be listening to the baby's heartbeat and that's especially important for the father, as it's the only tangible contact he has with the child at this stage."

He was going to have contact with his child. In one month.

John began to sweat.

ON TUESDAY AFTERNOON, after a not-so-good phone call with John—in which he was trying to insist he take her shopping for maternity clothes, in spite of the fact that she still had all the clothes she'd worn with Jesse—Caroline could feel the walls of her room closing in on her. She fled to the streets of Shelter Valley. She didn't want to waste gas driving when she had nowhere she needed to go, but for a woman used to country air and hills as far as she could see, Mrs. Howard's quaint boardinghouse was beginning to feel like a lovely little prison.

She started to feel better, in spite of a nasty dose of the day-before-school jitters, as she walked the quiet streets of her new town. Still not used to all the cacti, rock and flowering bushes in the front yards she was passing, Caroline occupied herself naming as many of the plants as she could, compliments of the Internet and her brief trip to the desert botanical garden with John. He'd been so restless that day, almost as though…

No, she wasn't going to think about him.

She saw a couple of boys in the street, working out with skateboards and a lethal-looking ramp. Thank God, Jesse hadn't been interested in those things. She'd never have survived.

Caroline walked at least a mile before she even thought about how far she'd gone. Never had she experienced such wonderful weather in January. Balmy, high sixties, sunshine. She barely needed the cardigan she'd thrown on over her blouse. The air was clear. Invigorating. Full of life.

She wasn't ready to turn back. She had an hour or more before dinner. Crossing the street, she turned toward town to take the long way home.

A young woman approached on Rollerblades, nodding at her as she flew by.

Caroline was either going to have to ask Mrs. Howard if she could do her own laundry at a lower cost than the older woman charged her boarders or load up the truck and head back to the Laundromat she'd found the week before. Even wearing her jeans twice, she just had one pair left. Unless she wore the two pairs of Jesse's that she'd saved after his departure. They were only a little too big.

A beige luxury car turned onto the street. Caroline's stomach tensed. Then the car passed her—a Lincoln, not a Cadillac like John drove. As her shoulders relaxed, Caroline warned herself to get a grip before she made herself crazy.

"You didn't survive the end of one life to let yourself down in the next," she said out loud, just to be certain she got the message clearly.

She was going to see her sister the next day. Caroline wasn't sure she was ready. Or capable of remaining emotionally stable when her Psychology professor—her twin—walked into the room. What if she sat there and started to cry?

Rounding the corner that led downtown, she slowed her steps, checking to see if she recognized anyone going to and from any of the businesses. And stopped in her tracks. There, on the corner outside the diner, stood an entire group of women she recognized. Becca Parsons was in the middle of the group. And she noticed Ellen's mother, Martha, and the day-care owner, Bonnie Nielson. Caroline wondered what had happened with Ellen at the doctor's, and whether or not her mother knew.

As she moved a little closer, she could see that Randi Parsons Foster was there, too. She and Cassie Montford seemed to be engrossed in their own conversation.

Only Tory and Phyllis appeared to be missing. Were they someplace together? They seemed to be together a lot.

Whether the group was coming or going, she had no idea; she was only aware of the crushing need she felt to join them. And of the fact that she had no right to do so. She was a stranger in town. One who had very little in common with any of these professional women. Her talents lay in milking cows and making ends meet on a rural Kentucky farm.

And yet these women seemed to bring each other everything Caroline had ever longed for. From what she'd read about the "Shelter Valley Heroines"—a name given them by the city's mayor, Becca Parsons, when they'd banded together after Ellen's rape the year before—they gave each other support and a sense of belonging. She wondered what they would do if she walked up and said hello.

In Grainville, she'd have felt no compunction about introducing herself.

Of course, in Grainville, if there'd been a group of women standing by the diner, she would've been one of them.

Caroline couldn't hear what Becca Parsons was saying, but all the other women laughed. Caroline turned around. She'd never spoken to a politician in her life. Besides, Becca was married to the president of Montford University, where Caroline felt like the oldest freshman known to man. Yeah, these women were definitely out of her league.

CHAPTER EIGHT

JAMES MONTFORD STOOD at the floor-to-ceiling windows in his living room Tuesday night, looking down the mountain on which his house sat to view the city before him. Shelter Valley was the only home he'd ever known. Founded by his father, the late Sam Montford, and his mother, Lizzie, the town bore little resemblance to the wide-open and almost savagely undeveloped space he'd played in as a boy. Still, while some of the changes would have his father turning in his grave, many of them had been good.

Glancing down to the spot he knew more by memory than sight these days, James pinpointed a white dot—the statue of his father that had been erected during a special Fourth of July ceremony four summers ago. James's father, Sam Montford, Sr., from a well-to-do Boston family, had fled civilization after the unsolved murder of his infant son and black wife. He'd seen that murder as public protest to his interracial marriage. He'd got on a wagon train west, living with various Indian tribes over the next few years. It was while living with Hopis in Arizona that Sam met James's mother, Lizzie, a Christian missionary come to save the "heathens" at the request of the United States government. Sam, who'd suffered so greatly, was drawn to the peace that was as much a part of Lizzie as the heart beating inside her.

James's eyes grew moist as he remembered his father repeating those words to him so often during his youth. After his parents were married, his father was ready once again to start a family. He wondered if he should return to Boston with the new wife of whom his family would approve, yet every time he thought of going back to that small-minded society, he'd feel as though he was suffocating.

It was a feeling James could relate to more and more these days. Chest heavy with the effort it was taking him to draw breath, he forced himself to stand at the window. He needed the strength this view—these memories—gave him more than he needed to fall into the seat only a few feet behind him.

Carol knew he tired too easily these days, knew the doctor had warned him that his heart was giving out; but she didn't know that he'd started having these spells during which he found it harder and harder to breathe. No one knew. James didn't want them to. He'd been born naturally, grown up naturally and was going to die just as naturally.

Muff, his faithful and obese old cocker spaniel, appeared, plopping down to lean against his ankle. Instead of bending, he moved his foot slightly to rub her side. And continued to stare out at the town that was his heritage.

How's life treating you where you are now, Pop? he asked silently. James wished his father could answer him, to calm his fears just as the old man had so many times when he was a boy.

As far as he'd been able to tell, nothing had scared Sam Montford. When he'd faced the dilemma of where to settle with his new wife, where to raise his family, Sam had gone out into the Arizona desert with a couple of his Hopi friends and came back with a new lease on life. He'd discovered a small abandoned settlement—probably a camp left behind by settlers heading west—and had suddenly known what he was going to do. His share of Montford money was going to be put to good use. And the town before James was a result of that long-ago decision.

James glanced over to the complex of lights and shadows that was Montford University. His father had dreamed of a school of high repute that could rival Harvard, but James didn't think even his father had dared hope for the speed with which the university had gained national prestige. Every year, in growing numbers, the nation's smartest and best came to Shelter Valley to attend Montford.

Just as it took more energy, of which he had less, for James to move these days, just as bones that had once been agile and cooperative were now threatening to quit on him daily, just as his mind crawled in random directions instead of leaping from challenge to challenge, Shelter Valley suffered from having grown older. Land that had been open and free and plentiful was being desecrated in the name of development. An environment that had been unquestionably safe was now tainted by the possibility of evil lurking in its midst. And where once a walk downtown had meant meeting friends, that same journey was often done in the company of strangers.

James stumbled backward a couple of steps to fall into the chair, situated there expressly to provide its occupant with a comfortable resting place while enjoying the view. He figured he'd lived a good life. A blessed life. His son, Sam, at one time irrevocably lost to him, had been back for more than three years and was firmly ensconced in Shelter Valley—and in this home. Cassie, Sam's high school girlfriend, was once again living with him as his wife and there wasn't a soul on earth more precious to him than Brian, his little rascal of a grandson, and Mariah, the adopted daughter Sam had brought home with him. Except perhaps Carol.

God, what a woman he'd been blessed with. Not only was she beautiful, she was loyal and kind and about as interesting as anyone he'd ever known.

Carol wanted another grandchild. James didn't think Cassie was going to be able to give her one. But then, he'd also been sure that she and Sam would never find their way back together again.

Of course, his son and daughter-in-law could always adopt another child. Mariah had been the daughter of Sam's closest friends. But agency adoption was also an option; it had worked out okay for Becca and Will.

Still, Sam had his syndicated comic strip to keep him busy. And his construction business was flourishing so fast his obstinate son would have to find someone to run it for him if he planned to go on contributing to the construction process with his own hands. And Cassie not only had her veterinary practice, but that pet-therapy thing she was doing, which was going great guns. She had some fine friends, too. Strong women, all of them.

Reminded him of Carol. They'd had their ups and downs but they'd made it.

Muff was at his feet, issuing little half barks, wanting to be picked up. James didn't dare bend over just now. If he made it that far without passing out, chances were his arm would lose strength on the way back up and he'd drop her. The weakness was worse tonight. If he had a little more energy, he'd be damned upset about that. With a final huff the dog lay down on his feet and heaved a huge sigh.

His head against the back of the chair, James remembered a day when he could sigh like that.

IT WAS PROBABLY TOO LATE in Boston for Caroline to be calling. Almost eleven o'clock Jesse's time. Caroline sat on her bed, her back propped on pillows against the headboard, and dialed her cell phone anyway. Finger punching each of the buttons individually rather than using the speed-dial button preprogrammed with Jesse's number, she considered what she was going to say.

And wondered if she was being selfish—or wise.

Caroline recognized that she wasn't at her best. With school starting the next day, she would've felt a bit shaky even without the added turmoil of seeing, for the first time, the twin who didn't even know she existed, the only blood relative she had in the world, other than her son.

She pushed the tenth number and read the display just to be sure she'd dialed correctly. Her thumb hung just above the Send button.

Her flannel gown was warm. Caroline didn't need covers just then. Her homey and spotless room was bathed in the glow of light from the lamp on her nightstand. She'd turned it to the lowest setting. If she hadn't been afraid of making Mrs. Howard nervous, she'd have lit a candle, too. Something with chamomile and lavender and sweet marjoram—all natural sedatives.

Caroline's thumb descended. She listened for the ring. If no one answered at the dorm, she didn't know what she was going to do.

Hang up, she supposed.

Seeing those ladies downtown this afternoon had been her undoing. She'd somehow missed seeing the connection between Shelter Valley, a small town like Grainville, and Shelter Valley, the home of Montford University and all of its resident professionals. She'd known she'd have to work hard not to appear backward. What she hadn't expected was to find the people of Shelter Valley such a closed group. The citizens of Grainville welcomed every newcomer with equal curiosity and welcome. She'd been in Shelter Valley almost two weeks, and other than young Ellen Hanaran, she'd yet to see any open arms.

Ten rings. Eleven. Still, Caroline waited. The phone was out in the hall, Jesse had explained when he'd given her the number. And the guys were a lazy bunch. No one wanted to bother getting up to answer it when in all likelihood the call would be for someone else.

Blinking back tears, Caroline tried to ignore the bitter irony of having traveled so far from home, hoping to *find* home, only to feel so homesick.

On the twenty-second ring, a deep voice barked hello— along with a threat that made her darn glad she wasn't Melissa. The tone changed completely when she identified herself.

"Oh, sorry, ma'am. Joe's ex has been calling all night and a few of us are running out of patience. Hold on, I'll get Jesse."

Caroline did as he said—held on. And felt inordinately old. She was a *ma'am* that some cool college kid spoke to in that deliberate way reserved for people you had to respect but couldn't wait to escape. Like the preacher. Or someone else's mother.

Tomorrow she'd be sitting in rooms filled with kids just like that.

And she'd thought she couldn't possibly feel any more isolated.

"Mom?" Jesse's greeting was breathless, as though he'd run to the phone. "Is everything okay? Are you hurt or lost or something?"

You gotta love it. The survival voice inside Caroline, which had deserted her downtown, chose that second to return. *You raise a kid from scratch, solve all his problems, answer ques-*

*tions like "why is the moon white" and then he has a birth-
day or two and suddenly you're incapable of walking across
a room without mishap.*

"I'm fine, Jess." If only her psyche would take heed of the
confident assurance in her voice. "How's school?"

"Good. Really good." He sounded a little doubtful, a little
hesitant, as though his mind wasn't completely focused on
what he was saying, but he spent the next five minutes telling her about the Christmas vacations of a couple of the guys
he'd met. And he talked about his upcoming classes. He'd
purchased his books. And he had a job working a couple of
hours a day bussing tables in a cafeteria.

"Have you seen your sister yet?" he asked.

"No. Tomorrow. I'm in her Psychology class."

"Whoa! That's random, Ma. Your sister's your prof?"

Caroline smiled. If only it could always just be her and
Jess. "Yep."

"So what are you gonna do? Just walk right up and say,
hey, guess what, we're twins?"

"No, Jess." Her head hurt. "I'm not going to tell her."

"Ever?"

"Maybe not."

"Well, what's the point of that? You went all the way there
to meet her."

"That's true," she said, glancing at her computer, a world
where she knew the rules, felt safe.

"What's wrong, Ma?" He was suddenly alert, suddenly
protective.

"Nothing's wrong, Jess, but there is something I wanted
to talk to you about."

"It's not going to be worse than you moving across the
country to some strange town in the middle of the desert, is
it?" His tone suggested that such a thing wasn't possible.

"I don't think so."

Was she being selfish? Or fair? Jesse was going to be a big brother. He had a right to know.

And no need to know until he came home for summer vacation, when he'd have some time to absorb, in peace and privacy, the turns life was taking.

But she needed him to know.

Which was no reason to tell him.

"Ma, you aren't getting married to some cowboy you just met, are you?"

"No!" The answer was sharper than she'd intended. "You couldn't be farther from the truth."

"Thank God."

He might not be so happy about that once he heard the rest of what she had to tell him.

And she *had* to tell him. He was going to be hurt and offended if she waited six months to let him know she was having another child. Understandably so.

"I'm pregnant, Jess." Shadows hung silently on the walls surrounding her, unmoving, as though waiting either to be dispelled or to prevail. The dim light projected more gloom than comfort now. She shivered but didn't pull the covers around her. Instead, as she'd done since she was a child, she twirled a piece of her hair, free from its daily ponytail, around her finger. And stayed quiet.

"Tell me you didn't just say what I thought you said." There was more of his father in that sentence than she'd ever heard before.

"I'm two months' pregnant, Jess. I've already been to the doctor. The baby's due August sixth."

He didn't hang up.

Maybe she shouldn't have told him. He had a lot to cope with, having just lost his father, moving away from home for the first time, starting college so young. God, it was so hard to know what to do, what was right.

"Jess?" Caroline said softly after what seemed like several minutes had passed. "Say something."

"I've got nothing to say."

She wished the light was off—leaving her in darkness. It might be easier.

"Are you angry?"

"No. It's your life."

"Disappointed?"

"No."

"Are you lying to me? *Are* you upset?"

"Ma? Let it go, will ya?" Randy was the one who'd taken the brunt of that impatient tone in the past. Never her. "I don't know what I am, okay? I can't believe this is happening."

"It doesn't change the way I feel about you. You know that, don't you? Nothing will ever change that."

"I wasn't even thinking about that," he said. "I know I'm a teenager, but I do have thoughts that aren't about me."

Caroline stopped fighting the tears that sprang to her eyes, letting them slide slowly down her cheeks. "I know that, Jess. But it would've been a perfectly understandable and natural reaction."

"I'm too busy trying to figure out how we can make this all work to think about feelings," he said. "Someone's gonna have to make enough money to support us all."

Had she not been engaged in a conversation, Caroline would have broken out in sobs at that. She might've messed up many things in her life, but Jesse sure made her look good.

"Those aren't your concerns, Jess," she told him, hoping there was enough authority in her voice to convince him. "I've got everything figured out, and we'll be just fine."

"I'd like to finish this year, at least, and if the kid isn't coming until summer, that shouldn't be a problem…."

She sat up straighter, clutching the phone so hard she activated the volume control. "You will finish all four years there, young man. I won't hear anything different."

"You said you weren't getting married."

"I'm not."

"Then who's going to take care of you and the kid if I don't? You might think you're a superwoman, Ma, but not even you can raise a baby and run that farm all by yourself."

There'd certainly been times she'd felt as though she was doing exactly that. If she had a little more emotional energy, she might have argued with him.

"I'm not going to be running the farm," she said, though she realized he wouldn't want to hear that, either. "I knew about the baby before I came to Shelter Valley, Jess, and I came anyway. I'm here on a full scholarship. You're there on a full scholarship. With the money from your father's life insurance, as long as we're careful, we can both finish school."

His harsh sigh gave her an indication of the words he wanted to say and didn't.

"Do you want to know who the father is?"

"Not really."

That hurt. It shouldn't. But it did.

"I only slept with him once, Jess. And he's the only one—"

"I said I didn't want to hear it."

"The holidays were just so hard without your father, and I—"

"Ma, please." The word was ground out from the back of his throat.

"Are you ashamed of me, Jess?" It was what she'd feared most.

"No."

"I wouldn't blame you if you were. I know it's going to be embarrassing for you and I'm sorry. I never would've chosen to have this happen."

"I know, Ma."

"And maybe it'll be a little easier for you with me here instead of in Grainville."

"Maybe. Have you told Gram and Papa?"

Her parents. She was doing her best not to think about them. Other than worrying that her mother was all right, feeling guilty for deserting her. "No, and I'm going to ask you not to do so, either," she said, her chest tight. "I talk to Gram every week, but she has enough on her plate and she'll make herself sick fretting about this from now until August."

"I'm not telling anyone," Jesse said, his tone making clear that it was the last thing he'd do. "But I think you ought to give her more than a week's notice," he added. "She's your mother. And it's her grandkid."

He was right, of course.

"I will, Jesse. Once I'm further along and know for sure that I'm going full term, I'll tell her."

"You mean there's still a chance that you'll lose it?" He seemed almost relieved.

"There's always that chance, Jesse, but it's not likely. The doctor said everything looks great and I'm healthy—"

"Oh."

She had to get off the phone before she started to cry in earnest. Jesse wouldn't know how to handle that.

"I love you, Jesse, more than life."

"Yeah."

"You don't love me anymore?"

He sighed again, sounding more tired now than anything else. "Of course I do. And I know you, Ma. I'm sure you haven't done anything to make me ashamed of you. And I'm not. I just don't know what I do think. You're gonna have to give me some time on this one."

"Okay, Jesse." Her hand was so sweaty the phone was slipping. "Take all the time you need. And if you want to talk about it, you call, okay?"

"Yeah."

"Bye, Jess."

"Bye, Ma. Take care of yourself…."

Reaching over to turn off the light, Caroline slid down until her head was on the pillow and, lying there on top of the covers, the phone still in her hand, she cried herself to sleep.

"I HEARD LANGFORD MAKES freshman English look like a party, man."

"Yeah, this class is gonna suck. I tried to get out of it, but everything else I needed was either full or too early in the morning." The knowing chuckle that followed grated on Caroline's nerves.

She moved down a step into the lecture hall.

"…and that's when he kissed me…"

Another step.

"…did you see the reading assignments? She had the syllabus posted online."

Damn, Caroline hadn't even known such a thing was possible. She could've been using all her empty hours getting a head start on assignments. Another step. There must be about fifteen or twenty of them.

"We're getting a full keg, man. You should come…."

"I heard her tests are mostly from her lectures…."

"My roommate says she's cool, as far as profs go…."

"No kidding! I heard them in concert…."

Another step. And another. She passed a young man in black leather pants, a black leather jacket with painful-looking silver studs around the bottom edge and black lace-up leather boots. He had more earrings in one ear than were in the whole jewelry case in the drugstore back home. He was slouched in a seat sound asleep.

"Is anyone sitting here?" she asked a blonde wearing jeans, a white Arizona sweatshirt, tennis shoes and a ponytail.

"No."

Not particularly friendly. But not rude, either.

Caroline slid into the seat midway down the lecture hall in Psych 101 just after the lunch hour on Wednesday, trying not to let the conversations around her, the nervous energy in the air, affect her. She was going to sit here, listen, takes notes and leave. Just like she'd done at her English class that morning and like she planned to do in every classroom she entered over the next four years.

She was here to get an education. A college degree. She was here to further her life, catch up with the tail end of her destiny.

And…

"Good afternoon, everyone!"

She was here to see her twin sister for the first time in her life.

"Welcome!" The voice came again.

Pressure built at the back of Caroline's eyes. She tried to take a deep breath, but her throat was too tight to let the air pass. She put down her pen before she dropped it.

The lecture hall was eerily silent except for the clatter of pumps coming down from the door at the top of the room. People around her turned toward the sound. Caroline squeezed her eyes shut.

"Did everyone have a good holiday?" The voice—strong, soothing, compelling, confident—washed over her, carrying chills in its wake. It was *her* voice. Or could have been if she'd ever felt that confident about anything in her life.

She was burning up in her jeans and gingham blouse and blue cardigan sweater. And, in spite of the seventy-degree temperature outside, she was freezing.

She was also afraid that she might have her first serious bout of morning sickness.

"Okay, we've got quite a large group here."

Caroline opened her eyes as the voice, amplified by a microphone now, sounded from the front of the room. And stared at the woman she recognized from the photo in her wallet and yet, didn't recognize at all. Phyllis wasn't just a collection of grainy lines on a worn piece of paper. Her head wasn't turned slightly, exposing only one side fully, her mouth wasn't pursed as though she'd been caught in speech. She wasn't one-dimensional at all.

She was real.

And beautiful.

And Caroline didn't know what to do.

CHAPTER NINE

"TELL ME ABOUT YOUR FAMILY." Hands in his pockets, John walked beside Caroline to the entrance of the Arizona Sonoran Desert Museum near Tucson on Saturday morning.

She was hugging her sweater around her, as though warding off a bone-chilling cold instead of the sixty-degree sunshine.

"Only because they'll be related to the baby," he added when she didn't immediately reply. He'd learned one thing about Caroline Prater in the two weeks since she'd arrived in Shelter Valley. The more uncomfortable she was, the quieter she became. He wished he could tell her that she wasn't a kid in a family that didn't understand her anymore. She could speak up for herself without fear of standing out or being deserted.

John paid as they reached the entrance and ushered her inside.

"You really didn't need to do this," she said. "I don't have to visit all the state's outdoor museums."

"It's good exercise."

"And outside Shelter Valley."

There was no point in arguing the obvious. She was right. He didn't want to be seen with her in town. He'd already explained all that. He had Lauren to think of.

And his own answers to find and come to terms with before he could share them with his friends.

"Welcome to the museum." A young man in a park ranger uniform, carrying a hairy tarantula about the size of a small orange on his arm, approached them.

John wondered at the guy's choice of welcoming committee.

"Does he have a name?" Caroline asked, moving in for a closer look.

"Tammy."

"It's a she." She reached a finger out to entice movement from the lethal-looking spider.

"She's here to serve as an ambassador for her wild relations," the ranger said. He told them where they could find more spiders and scorpions within the confines of the outdoor zoo and museum, encompassing more than one hundred acres of natural desert. "Enjoy your visit."

Eyes taking in everything around them, Caroline moved forward, John following. "I had no idea this place was so big," he said, pleasantly surprised. He'd really just intended to keep her company while she got some exercise for their baby, and planned to be home in time for an afternoon round of golf. He was heading out of town the next day to drop in at his Chicago office and then go for a site visit or two. He'd wanted to do his part before he left.

"They have over forty thousand plants, more than fourteen thousand fossil and mineral specimens, seventeen hundred animals and six thousand catalogued books to read about it all."

John glanced down at her, enjoying the color in her cheeks, the light in her eyes. "I only told you about this place a couple of hours ago," he said. "How do you know so much?"

"I went on the Internet while I was waiting for you."

Over the next hour, they saw everything from rattlesnakes

to mountain lions, an impressive tortoise collection, more fish than he'd seen in any aquarium back east and a botanical garden that was every bit as impressive as the one they'd visited in Phoenix the week before.

"How's school going?" he asked as they veered toward the fish and amphibians. The toe of her boot caught on a crack in the blacktop and she stumbled. With an arm around her waist, John steadied her.

She pulled quickly away from him. "Fine." She was looking at a map she'd picked up at the entrance. For all the attention she was paying him, he might as well not have been there.

Which was fine. This was about exercise for her. Nothing more.

"Do you have a favorite class?" He followed as she moved toward an enclosure, happy to tag along.

"Psychology."

"You're interested in psychoanalyzing people?"

"I like the teacher."

Caroline didn't seem the type to prefer one class over the rest just because of a teacher. He wondered what she wasn't telling him. Or if, perhaps, she was telling him in Caroline-speak to mind his own business.

He was stepping dangerously close to boundaries that he needed to keep intact. "Who is it? Maybe I know him."

"Her. Phyllis Langford, and it's not like she knows *me*. I'm a little dot in a very big classroom. She doesn't even do roll call."

And he'd bet his life's savings that Caroline Prater didn't ever speak out in class. Any class.

"She's good friends with Becca, Will's wife," he said. "Nice woman."

She shrugged.

Yep, he was pretty much being held at arm's length. For a second, John considered challenging her on that. Until he remembered that he was the first one to establish that distance.

In any event, she'd entered the lizard enclosure and started asking questions of the ranger there, and that was that.

A ROADRUNNER STREAKED BY the path and John stopped abruptly. He reached for her arm, to get her attention, and pulled back in the nick of time. Her reaction to him when she'd stumbled earlier had been very clear—and he agreed with her. If he and Caroline were to get through this, they had to enforce a hands-off rule.

"Did you see that?" he asked, pointing in the direction the desert bird had run.

"Yeah, but I can't believe it! Other than the drab color, he looked exactly like the character in the old cartoon I used to watch. He was really running that fast!"

The cartoon she was referring to had played a prominent part in his Saturday mornings as a kid. There was satisfaction in knowing she'd liked it, too.

"I've been in Arizona on and off for more than four years and I've never seen one."

She turned, grinning. "Then you're either blind or completely unobservant, John, because I've been here two weeks and *I've* seen one."

He might have responded to her teasing if, in that moment, her face hadn't been so strikingly beautiful.

"YOU STILL HAVEN'T TOLD ME about your family," he said later, heading with her toward the bighorn sheep.

"I told you before, I'm adopted," she said after an obvious hesitation. "Their bloodlines aren't going to have any effect on the baby." Her voice wasn't sharp, but it wasn't as calm as he was used to, either.

"But their relationship with him will."

She sighed, pausing to watch the sheep—and to read about them. And then it was on to the otters.

"My parents still live on the small farm in Grainville where I grew up." She was leaning over, smiling at a beaver swimming toward them in the stream. "Their parents are dead. I have one uncle on my father's side whom I barely know. My mother had an older sister who died of kidney failure a couple of years ago."

She entered a circular enclosure housing some colorful parrots.

She didn't ask about his family. "My parents are divorced," he told her after she'd read about the parrots and moved on to macaws. "My mother remarried several years ago and lives in Paris. I haven't seen my father in years. I have one sister, younger, who's married to a Parisian and lives down the street from my mother. She has a couple of kids. There're a few aunts and uncles I haven't seen in years. No history of disease."

The jaguarundi and ocelot were both endangered species. They'd circled around to the magnificent cats. John wondered if there was someplace he could send money to help save the lives of these lithe beasts. He decided to look into it.

"My father's an alcoholic."

He did a double take, not sure Caroline had even spoken. She was watching a bobcat sniff the air. "You grew up with a drunk?" The thought angered him. She deserved better than that.

"He was dry for years." She reached back to tuck a strand of hair back into the ponytail he'd never seen her without.

Except the first night he'd met her, when that long auburn hair was tangled around his hands...

"Was he violent when he drank?"

"Sometimes."

"Did he ever hit you?"

"Once."

He wanted to ask if that was when the man had quit drinking. But he'd already crossed the personal line. He only needed to know things that would affect the baby.

"And now?"

"He's drinking again."

Back in Grainville. Which she'd left to have her baby.

There seemed no end to the depths he saw in this woman. Javelinas, lizards, the walk-in aviary—they did it all. He'd assumed that pregnant women got tired easily, but Caroline sure didn't seem to.

"Do you drink a lot?" Her question came out of the blue as they stood in front of a woodpecker.

"Define *a lot*."

"I saw you with a beer the other night. To me, more than one or two is a lot."

"I've had occasion to have more than one or two, but generally, no, I don't drink a lot." He supposed it was a fair question, considering what she'd told him earlier about her father.

"Randy was drinking when he was killed. He was drunk, actually."

"I'm sorry," he said. "About Randy."

She nodded. "The accident wasn't his fault—if it had been, his life insurance probably wouldn't have paid. It was a tractor-engine default. But he lay out there for a couple of hours before he died. I hope the alcohol made those hours more bearable."

She was a strong woman.

John had to get her back to Shelter Valley before he started liking her—too much.

Monday, December 6, 2004

I can't stop thinking about what I did. Or thinking about him. What's wrong with me? I've only been a widow for six months! And only EVER did it with Randy. I never even liked it all that much. Before. It's like I'm a different woman. I don't even recognize me. Or the way he made me feel.

Maybe it was that sparkling wine he had me order at the bar.

I want so desperately to believe that. To blame the wine. But I only had one glass. I'm not even sure I finished it!

It's partly that I've never been to Frankfort at Christmastime. And there were decorations lining the streets and the building being dedicated was strung with the most beautiful lights. I heard a little boy ask his mother if they were going to see Santa Claus after the ceremony. I've never felt as alone as I did at that moment, knowing I was going home to Grainville and Daddy's problem and no Jesse to go to the Christmas pageant with or cut down a tree with or hide presents from. He's not coming home until the day before Christmas! It'll all be done by then.

I just wanted to feel like I belonged, even if it was only for an evening. All I could think about was grasping a brief escape from the dark and lonely future that stretches before me. I'm afraid of what I've done. I'm afraid of what I'm going to become. I'm afraid I'm going insane….

THE PROBLEM WITH JEANS was that they didn't have a lot of give for an expanding stomach. Especially when the stomach they'd been purchased to cover had been flat and firm. Still, she wasn't big enough yet to fit into the elasticized denim pants that had seen her through most of her pregnancy with Jesse. Caroline sucked in a deep breath every morning and squeezed until she could fit the metal clasp into the stiff denim hole and, inch by inch, coax the zipper to close. A process that worked relatively well—and saved Caroline the expense of purchasing new maternity slacks.

At least, it worked relatively well—until the last Wednesday in January. Right after lunch, Caroline took her seat in Psychology 101, and the light meal she'd forced herself to eat for the baby's sake began to make its presence known. Phyllis—no, Dr. Langford, she reminded herself—wasn't even there yet and Caroline was so nauseous she was afraid to stand up.

She couldn't miss this class. She just couldn't. It was only the fourth time in her entire life that she'd get to watch and listen to her sister. An amazing and completely intimidating woman.

With some very deep breaths and a lot of willpower, Caroline managed to stay in her seat and not embarrass herself. Then Phyllis came in from the door at the top of the room, walked down the steps to the podium and began to speak.

Caroline's awareness of any morning sickness vanished. She'd done all the reading for the class. She always did. But every word Dr. Langford uttered was fascinating. At least to her two-minutes-younger fraternal twin.

"Today we're going to talk about John B. Watson," Phyllis said after a couple of minutes of friendly dialogue with her students. Dialogue to which Caroline loved to listen. Her sister not only had intelligence, but she had an engaging wit and warmth, too. She wondered why, with her obvious compassion and people skills, Phyllis wasn't in private practice.

"He wasn't covered in the assigned text, but is certainly pertinent to today's discussion. Does anyone know who he is?"

The founder of the behaviorist movement. Caroline's heart sped up. She'd been reading voraciously about the man and his beliefs since discovering him from the syllabus of suggested readings. Montford's library had become, next to her computer, her best friend.

"No one?" Phyllis said, the clicking of her heels on the tile floor resounding around the cavernous hall. "Come on, someone at least take a guess."

"Someone to do with Sherlock Holmes?" suggested a young man who wore his confidence with ease.

Phyllis grinned, slid one hand into the pocket of her short, tailored navy suit jacket. "Good try, Sean, but no." The hem of her skirt moved against her knees as she walked to the other side of the room. "Anyone else?"

Phyllis's gaze traveled around, and Caroline looked down, careful to be unobtrusive from her place in the middle of the hall, surrounded by more than a hundred other faces. It wasn't as if Phyllis was ever going to notice her—or know her. She just didn't trust herself not to say something foolish.

"Anyone ever hear of the behaviorists?" she asked next.

They believed people became what they were programmed to become. That human beings were the products of their environments. Their theories sounded logical to Caroline, but she couldn't entirely believe them. And yet, look at her. She was a country bumpkin because of the environment in which she'd grown up.

With a series of questions meant to provoke thoughtful replies from her students, Phyllis taught the class a lot of what Caroline had read over the weekend.

"Later in the year we're going to have a nurture versus nature debate," Phyllis was saying toward the end of class. "Are we products of our environment or of genetics? Or both?"

The mass of cells that was slowly becoming Baby Prater took that moment to wage war against its own environment, and Caroline stared at the floor, trying to relax.

"You'll all be assigned different research projects that'll be presented to the class. You will wage the debate that has been keeping scientists and psychologists active for centuries."

In the front of the room, a dark-haired girl with olive skin raised her hand. "Will we get to choose our areas of research?"

"To some extent," Phyllis nodded, gathering papers and books and pens and putting them back into the satchel she always carried. "We'll be focusing on various twin studies—"

Shoving her notebook into her homemade bag, Caroline put her head between her knees. And stayed that way until most of the class, including the teacher, had cleared out.

Then she stumbled to the bathroom and threw up for the first time in years.

JOHN CALLED THAT NIGHT. Caroline recognized his cell-phone number on the LED screen of her cell phone. She didn't pick up—precisely because she wanted to. He'd been in Atlanta since Sunday and hadn't known for sure when he'd be home. She watched the phone where it lay on her desk beside her, counting the rings until voice mail picked up and took a message.

Was he back in town? Or calling to say he wasn't coming back? Or just calling to make certain he wasn't shirking any unknown responsibilities?

The ringing stopped. Caroline stared at the half-written five-hundred-word descriptive essay on the computer screen. And almost came up with a topic sentence for the new paragraph she was starting. She was writing about a pebble. One paragraph for each of the five senses. What did a pebble smell like?

The phone rang again. Without moving anything but her eye muscles, she glanced at the little lit-up screen.

It was John again. Guilt—because she'd already ignored him once—had her picking up the phone.

"Hello?"

"Caroline? I was worried when you didn't answer. Are you okay?"

She was having a little trouble breathing at the moment, but it would pass. "Fine."

"Where are you?"

"My room." She didn't ask where he was—it wasn't her business. She knew his number if she had problems with the baby.

"Doing homework?"

She hated being so predictable. And boring. "Yes." He was probably on his way to some fancy cocktail party to schmooze with politicians and wealthy people.

"Are you always so talkative?" His voice was soft, teasing, and her stomach melted.

A reaction that was nothing to worry about. John was the only person she could talk to about the baby, and that was the only reason his attention meant anything to her.

"Sometimes less."

"Getting smart with me, are you?"

Boring as she was, she could make him chuckle. "Maybe."

"I like that."

She liked that he liked it. Until she remembered who she was. Who *he* was. And what they weren't.

"Are you in town?"

"I'm supposed to be, but no." His sigh was deep. "I'm stuck in an airport hotel in Minneapolis, grounded due to weather."

Minneapolis. Two hours later than Arizona's eight o'clock. Caroline looked away from the blinking cursor that reminded her she had something else she should be doing. "I'm sorry."

"Why should you be sorry? You don't control the weather."

"I'm sorry for you."

"And I'm just tired and frustrated enough to accept your pity."

She smiled. "Long week?"

"The longest and it's only Wednesday." He went on to describe the power struggle that had held up final approval of his designs for a new art museum. Approval he hadn't yet attained.

And then he told her how he'd won the bid in the first place. About members of the investors' group in Atlanta who'd been family to Meredith—family torn apart by a divorce that had taken place since Meredith's death.

The conversation had nothing to do with the baby that had brought them together—the only reason they were conversing at all. But Caroline couldn't be rude to him. She stood, turned off all but one light and propped herself up on pillows at the head of her bed.

"I'm sorry, I'm taking up your study time," he said eventually, his voice low, husky…and curiously lacking in repentance. "Do you want to hang up?"

"No." Apparently she couldn't lie to him. "I mean, unless you want to." God, she sounded like an idiot. "What I mean to say," she tried again, "is that I'm ahead with my homework and can spare the time if you have something we need to talk about."

There, was that impersonal enough? Because even though she hadn't been able to stop herself from talking to him, to stop the pleasure that flooded through her when she saw his number on her screen, she wasn't kidding about wanting nothing from him. There was too much at stake.

He was silent for so long she started to worry that she'd offended him.

"Have you ever thought about marrying again, Caroline?"

Caroline's chest tightened around her lungs. Her stomach tightened, too, squeezing so hard it hurt. Surely he wasn't suggesting…

She didn't want to hang up—especially with him sitting all alone in a strange town late at night—but…

"I look around me at all the people I've known who either are married or have been married and I tell you, I find very few who are examples of success. The people I've been dealing with this week sure aren't. Each side's primary goal was to see that the other side didn't get what it wanted. Each side knew the other's vulnerabilities and had no compunction about using that knowledge."

Ah, it was just general conversation. That she might be able to handle. She inhaled deeply.

"I've seen some happy marriages," she said. "Seems there's at least one fiftieth anniversary celebration in Grainville every year. Of course, there were also painful divorces. Sometimes it's inevitable, you know?" Damn, it felt good to express herself, to really take part in the conversation. "But a lot of times it just depends on how hard the people are willing to work. Happiness doesn't seem to come easy."

"Were you and Randy happy?"

"Yes." To a point. She hadn't been unhappy. And for most of their years together, neither had Randy.

"So you think, if the circumstances were right, you'd consider doing it again sometime?"

She thought about that. Really thought about it. "I don't think so," she said, feeling free to speak honestly because her answer meant nothing at all to him. Unlike Jesse, or her parents, or the women she knew in Grainville who couldn't imagine her being happy without a husband.

"I've spent most of my life feeling like I couldn't be who I was because of my responsibilities to others…and the expectations they had of me. Now I have the freedom to be true to myself."

It was the second time since she'd known him that she'd talked about things she hadn't previously discussed with anyone but Jesse. John was safe. He had no expectations of her, other than that she include him in his child's life. She couldn't disappoint him or be hurt by any lack of understanding on his part.

"Don't you think you might get lonely?"

She didn't have to think it. She felt it. Every day. "Yeah. But the question is, would it be lonelier living apart from yourself or living apart from other people?"

He didn't say anything and she tried to replay her words from his perspective.

"I guess I sound pretty selfish, huh?" she muttered.

"Not at all. In fact—" his voice was muffled, as though he was moving around "—I was just figuring that maybe you'd hit on something."

Jesse used to think she had a lot of insight. But then, he was a kid. Her kid. He also used to think she had the power to make the sun rise when he was having a bad night or to make thunderstorms go away so he could play ball.

"Maybe the answer is to find someone with whom you can be yourself," he went on.

"Maybe." Caroline freed her hair from the ponytail,

thought about undressing and getting ready for bed. She didn't want to consider the possibility he'd just raised. She couldn't. She was afraid to hope. Afraid to open the door to more disappointment. She wasn't sure she had the emotional capacity to sustain her if despair came knocking again.

And she sure as hell didn't want to think about having someone like John Strickland knocking at her door. Someone who was intelligent, who challenged her, someone who didn't bore her to tears, someone who understood and seemed to appreciate her ideas, someone who was sexy as hell, someone whose voice—even on the phone—could raise those peculiar little knots of tension… Therein lay the biggest danger, the largest risk of foolhardy behavior. And that was a damn *huge* risk, considering that she was a woman experiencing the second unplanned pregnancy of her life.

And, to complicate things further, she was pregnant by that very same man.

The intelligent, interesting, sexy John Strickland himself.

CHAPTER TEN

"I'M TAKING A TRIP down to Tucson on Saturday afternoon to drop off some plans," John was saying. She had no idea what she'd missed in between that and her last "maybe." "It might be a good time for you to come along and get some maternity clothes."

Her nightgown was on the end of her bed, waiting for her, but even though she recognized that she was being ridiculous, she couldn't take off her top, her bra, while he was on the phone.

"I told you, I'm not having you buy me clothes."

"Have *you* bought any yet?"

"No." She was going to leave the button undone on her jeans. And wear blouses and sweaters to cover it.

"I've been thinking about what you said, about the clothes being yours and personal. The truth is, if it weren't for the baby, your clothes would continue to fit. It's not really you we'd be clothing, but the baby who's sharing your body. So I should pay for half of that." He sounded pleased with this logical conclusion.

"I have maternity clothes." Of sorts. She'd opened the box that afternoon after being sick at school. The bout of retching in a public bathroom surrounded by made-up and fashionably clad young women wasn't an experience she was eager to repeat.

"And they're what, seventeen years old?"

Almost eighteen. Which had been evident in the dead elastic she'd discovered when she'd pulled on a couple of pairs of jeans. They'd made a crunching sound and had not sprung back to a less stretched state.

"Maternity clothes don't date as rapidly as other fashions." As though any of her clothes had anything to do with fashion.

"You were pregnant in Kentucky, not Arizona," John said. The rustling had stopped on his end of the line. She wondered if he'd climbed into bed. Or if he'd already been there and what she'd been hearing was the movement of his sheets and bedspread. "You heard what the doctor said about the heat."

"I'm a Kentucky farm girl, John. I'll make do."

"I'm not insisting on buying *everything*," he said. "Although it goes against my better judgment, I'll let you pay half."

He just didn't get it. "I can't afford to buy maternity clothes."

Silence fell and the knot in Caroline's stomach started to dissipate. Maybe he was falling asleep. It was after midnight there, and he'd had an exhausting couple of days. If she waited just a few more minutes until he'd drifted off completely, she could quietly click off and—

"I have a compromise for you."

"What?" She wouldn't have taken the bait but he'd surprised her.

"There's an outlet mall on the way to Tucson. Pretty much all the merchandise there is half off. We'll buy only what we find there and I'll pay for it all. It's the perfect solution. I'll be spending the same amount and you can afford the rest."

Caroline chuckled out loud. He'd sounded so little-boy proud of his ingenuity she couldn't help herself.

"I wouldn't have figured you for a man who knew his

shopping malls," she said, trying to come up with a reason to refuse his generous offer. A feat made harder by the fact that she desperately needed the clothes. At home on the farm, she could get away with looking like a hillbilly, but at Montford…

"I broke my putter a few months back," he said. "It was an older version, but I was pretty partial to it. There's a golf outlet there that still had some in stock."

She'd never met a man so enamored of chasing a little white ball around a plot of grass. But she figured it was better than drinking.

Not that his habits in either area had anything to do with her. As long he didn't get drunk around her baby.

"I have a tee time with Will and Matt Sheffield on Saturday morning," John said. "How about I pick you up around two?"

Caroline was too tired to fight him anymore.

ONLY IN ARIZONA could a group of friends party around the pool on Valentine's Day. In his swim trunks and white muscle shirt, John threw darts with Will, played a rousing tournament of water volleyball with Matt and Ben and David Marks, scoring three wins in a row against Zack, Sam, Will and the sheriff of Shelter Valley in the Richards's solar-heated pool. Which was saying something, as Zack was the largest, most athletic one of the bunch.

And all around them, beautiful women lounged in varying degrees of undress and filmy cover-ups—wives of the men who'd become his good friends. He knew most of the women well, having been included in their group for every holiday and most other social occasions over the past two years.

"I'm going for another glass of wine. Can I get you anything?" Jennifer Mason stood from her seat beside John, her long tanned legs straight out of just about every fashion magazine known to women. None of which he'd read.

Jennifer, the only unmarried woman in the bunch, was a friend of Beth Richards, visiting for a couple of weeks between photo shoots. She was a model. Divorced. And John's date.

"Please," he said, smiling at her. "Another beer would be great, thanks." She grinned and he watched her backside as she moved graciously through the crowd, chatting unselfconsciously as she went. She had to be, hands-down, the most physically beautiful woman he'd ever met.

He was kind of sorry that he didn't feel anything about that.

"I'm worried about my old man." Sam Montford, builder extraordinaire, spoke from across the room. "He's not himself lately." John had been trying to talk Sam into teaming up with him in a business partnership. He hadn't been successful yet, but he suspected eventually he would be.

"We're annexed almost all the way out to Wal-Mart." Becca Parsons was sitting a little closer to John, speaking to Ben Sanders, who was graduating from Montford with a degree in business. Ben, the curly-headed Montford heir, was already running the office side of things for his cousin Sam. "If we grow much more, we're going to lose the small-town feel we all value so much."

"Billy went to the potty all by himself today," Randi Foster, Montford's athletic director, said to Ben's wife, Tory.

"No kidding!" Tory smiled. "That's early. Chrissie was almost three."

John quickly looked away when he realized how avidly he'd tuned in to that particular conversation.

Jennifer returned, and the conversation rolled on around him. Sitting there, in a circle with his closest friends, John told himself it was the best Valentine's he'd had in years. And he figured that, with this beer, he just might believe it.

It had to happen with this beer. Two was his new limit.

"I'm surprised Ellen and Aaron preferred watching our whole pack of kids over going to dinner in Phoenix," Beth Richards said. She was sitting with Martha and David Marks, who'd offered the newlyweds an all-expenses-paid dinner to a restaurant of their choice.

"Shelly's helping them," David said, referring to Martha's second-oldest daughter, a seventeen-year-old who was in the process of pulling her life back together after making some unfortunate choices during her junior year of high school.

"Ellen isn't eager to leave town just now," Martha added, giving a toss to hair that was already short and sassy-looking.

John thought back to the few dates he'd had with Martha when he'd first come to town. Older by three or four years, she'd never looked her age to him. He'd suspected a time or two that if circumstances had been different for either of them, they might have ended up together.

Instead, the new preacher got lucky.

"Besides, our kids are great!" Bonnie Nielson, keeper of the town's children, piped up. "Ellen, Aaron and Shelley are probably having fun."

"This is the first time Tory's left the baby with anyone," said Keith, her husband and a colleague of Martha's and Matt's.

I'm going to be like that. The thought came out of nowhere. Yet it rang true. No matter how hard he was taking this baby thing, how resistant he was to the whole idea, once that kid was born, he was going to watch it like a hawk.

Poor kid.

Paper plates full of food were passed around, with plastic tableware rolled up in napkins. Balancing his plate, John grabbed Jennifer's wineglass and held it while she settled her food in her lap.

"Phyl's been having some trouble with her ex," Matt Sheffield told Greg Richards as their host finally left the grill and joined their circle. It had grown quiet as they'd all begun eating the delicious ribs and potatoes and corn, prepared on Greg's built-in outdoor grill.

Greg took a seat next to his wife. John wondered if anyone else had noticed the way the back of the sheriff's hand brushed Beth's shoulder as he passed. Or the way his leg was pressing against hers where they sat.

"Anything I need to be aware of?" Greg was asking Matt.

"No," Phyllis said, shaking her head with total confidence. She was one of Caroline's teachers. He wondered what the professor thought of her.

"Maybe," Matt said. With his considerable bulk and black hair and eyes, he looked almost as intimidating as the sheriff. "The guy's definitely unstable. And apparently he's just declared bankruptcy."

"What's he want from Phyllis?"

"A quarter of a million dollars."

All eating stopped. Everyone stared at Phyllis, and then six conversations broke out at once.

"I'm sorry about this," John said quietly to Jennifer. "Must be hard not knowing any of the people we're talking about."

"Actually I'm enjoying myself." Her smile was generous. And genuine. "I spend so much time on the road, it's great to be a part of small-town family life—even if only vicariously."

His attention strayed to the cleavage showing from her brightly flowered tankini top. A man could lose himself in cleavage like that. If he gave enough of a damn to try.

"Be careful," he teased. "That's how I used to feel when I visited Will, and look where I ended up."

"I could do a lot worse than living in Shelter Valley…."

So she might be around in the future. Something to think about.

Dessert appeared. Blue-and-pink cupcakes. Unusual fare.

"We have an announcement to make," Greg said, as the plate was passed around. With a lingering look at his wife, he took her hand and glanced around the circle. "Beth and I are going to have a baby."

John's congratulations were genuine, if perhaps lost among the whoops and hollers of their friends. Jennifer was smiling as though she'd known all along, but still got up to hug Beth, whom she'd known since college. Greg and Beth had both come through a lot and had continued to press forward, having faith that happiness was possible.

Just like someone else he knew.

As baby advice started to rain down, John quickly finished his beer. Said his goodbyes, avoiding the disappointment in Jennifer's eyes, and left.

The leather seat in his Cadillac was comfortable, familiar. The car seemed to be the only thing that hadn't spun out of control in John's world. He just needed some sleep. He'd feel better in the morning. Experience had taught him that.

So John didn't understand why his car was parked outside Caroline Prater's boardinghouse. Or why he was looking at the light in the window of her room, wondering if she was up there studying on this night made for lovers. Other than messages he'd left on her cell phone, at times specifically chosen to insure she'd be in class and not answering her phone, he hadn't spoken to her since he'd called from Minneapolis almost three weeks before.

He'd invited her to shop for clothes, told her what time he'd be by to get her and then failed to show up. Because, just hours before he was due to pick her up that Saturday, he'd thought about Caroline in a way he'd only ever thought of

Meredith. He'd frozen. Known he had to avoid her at all costs.

Throwing the car into park at the curb, John sat back in his now-dry trunks and tank top, staring up at that window. There were so many reasons he didn't need to speak to her. So many reasons he shouldn't.

Any kind of relationship was just too dangerous. They were already facing far too much built-in intimacy for either of them to be comfortable introducing any more.

He'd been a jerk.

And he was angry with her, too.

CAROLINE WAS IN HER ROOM, preparing for a section exam in algebra Valentine's night, when a knock sounded on her door. Jumping, surprised at the interruption, she rose slowly. She'd been in the house over a month and had hardly seen the other two tenants, smiling at them while passing in the hall. They'd both chosen the room-only option and either had something on a hot plate in their rooms or ate out, so she never saw them for meals. Since neither of their cars had been in the parking area today, Caroline had assumed they were out.

And Mrs. Howard rarely climbed the stairs, except when she did her weekly cleaning.

It was Mrs. Howard. Caroline had a visitor. And Mrs. Howard didn't allow visitors in the rooms. But for Caroline, and because the visitor was a friend of Will and Becca Parsons, she'd make an exception. For one hour.

Caroline wanted to beg her not to do that.

She didn't want to see him. Had assumed she wouldn't have to until their doctor's appointment the following week.

But her upbringing wouldn't let her leave him standing there, rejected. Smoothing a hand over the new forest-green, stretch denim pants she was wearing, she nodded her head.

JOHN CLIMBED THE STAIRS SLOWLY. He shouldn't have come. And he damn sure should've gone home and changed first.

But if he had, he wouldn't be here.

She was waiting for him in the doorway, not looking any heavier at all, though he supposed her shirt hid whatever changes there might have been.

He hadn't felt so guilty since he'd stolen an apple off his neighbor's tree in first grade and had to go confess to his sins. Without an apple to return.

"John, it's nice of you to stop by. Come on in." Her welcome grated on him. He'd been rude beyond measure and deserved sarcasm at the very least.

A quick search for a seat as he heard the door close behind him revealed only the bed and the chair by the desk. He took the chair—although it appeared from the notes and books, the calculator and pencils to one side of the computer, that she'd been occupying it. The rest of the room was pristine.

"You made it back," she said, standing awkwardly at the end of the bed before perching on one corner.

His last message, left on her cell phone the previous Wednesday, had told her he was flying in from Kansas the day before. He nodded. Waited—giving her plenty of time to berate him. He'd take whatever she handed him. He deserved it.

And then he'd ask for her forgiveness. He couldn't promise he'd never stand her up again. He didn't trust himself to keep his word. He could only promise that he'd never stand up his kid.

She shifted her feet against the floor. Glanced at the desk and then at him, her eyes shying away from his exposed shoulders.

"Sorry about the attire," he said, shrugging, a selfish part of him wondering if she liked what she was trying so hard not to see. "I just came from a cookout." And then he felt compelled to add, "I left early," as though that somehow made the fact that he'd been out partying on Valentine's Day while she sat there alone, pregnant with his kid and studying, seem less cold and heartless.

Not that he was in any way responsible for her social life.

"Don't worry about it," she said, with a smile that was almost natural. "I'm used to guys coming into my kitchen straight from the manure. Chlorine smells a lot nicer."

He cleared his throat, tapped a hand against his leg, noticed that she was wearing new clothes. And noticed the little piece of lace sticking out from beneath her pillow.

So she was one of those women who stored their pajamas under their pillows. And she wore lace to bed.

He wondered what the lace was attached to. And didn't think it would matter. If he had her in his bed, he was fairly certain she wouldn't be wearing whatever it was for long.

Not that he'd have her there. Ever.

Or, at least never again.

"Did you get enough to eat?"

His gaze returned to her. He liked the lighter green shirt she was wearing in contrast to the slacks. It matched her eyes.

"Yeah, sure," he said, getting a little impatient with the waiting. He deserved to be raked over the coals. He'd told her he'd take her shopping, had practically coerced her into agreeing and then he'd neither showed up nor called to tell her he wasn't coming. He'd been a total jerk. It was completely unlike any action he'd ever taken in his life.

She had every right to give him a piece of her mind.

He wished she'd get on with it so he could try to apologize. "Some friends of mine got together, barbecued ribs," he murmured. She probably didn't want to hear about it.

"Some of the same people who went to that court case in Phoenix?"

He nodded. And waited again.

Until it became painfully obvious that she wasn't going to do anything but sit there, making restless little movements that were driving him nuts.

"I see you got the clothes." Maybe a little baiting would help.

She glanced toward the window. "Yes. Thank you."

If John hadn't been so frustrated, he might have smiled at her insincere but perfectly polite response.

He sighed, leaned forward, elbows on his knees, hands clasped. "Look, Caroline, I'm sorry. I should've called."

"You have called. Several times."

"I stood you up."

"You don't owe me anything."

"I owe you—anyone I give my word to—the respect of doing what I say I'm going to do."

She didn't speak, just sat there looking at him with that placidly blank face, her thoughts closed to him.

"I told you I'd be here at three to take you shopping and I wasn't." Maybe if he reminded her of his shoddy treatment, he could get a response out of her. A little anger wouldn't be amiss.

"And I told you that you had no obligation to buy me clothes."

She had, yes, and he'd been obstinate about the whole thing, insisting she put aside time for him to take her right after his golf game.

And then he'd shot four under par, mainly due to a hole in one that had everyone cheering and patting him on the back, and his first thought had been that he could tell Caroline on the way to Tucson. Until that moment, whenever anything good had happened to him, Meredith was the only person he'd wanted to tell.

He'd showered at the clubhouse and sped off to Tucson—alone. Two days later, he'd gone to a mall in Phoenix and, with the help of a saleswoman, had purchased enough clothes to get Carolyn comfortably through her pregnancy. He'd had them delivered to her.

"You're wearing the clothes I bought, though," he said now.

She shrugged, looked pointedly at the work spread out on her desk. "Seemed wasteful not to. All the tags had been taken off, making it virtually impossible to return them. Especially since I had no idea what store they'd come from."

He'd done that on purpose.

"I know."

"Well." She stood. "Thanks for stopping by…."

"Dammit!" John stood, his voice purposely soft in deference to the other people who might be in the house, but also because he'd learned a long time ago to control his anger. "What's the matter with you?"

"With *me*?" She glanced up at him. "Nothing. I'm fine. I was afraid I was going to suffer from morning sickness, but except for a brief bout or two, I've been fine."

He stepped closer, cocked his head enough to catch her wandering gaze. "That's not what I'm talking about and you know it. I treated you like shit. How can you expect the world to give you what you deserve if you don't demand it for yourself?"

She didn't say a word. Just stared at him.

"You think you can go through life being nice and expect people to be nice back?" His tone was full of frustration—with her, with himself, with the whole damned world. "The Golden Rule is great, but it doesn't always work." He couldn't

An Important Message
from the Editors

Dear Reader,

If you'd enjoy reading romance novels with larger print that's easier on your eyes, let us send you TWO FREE HARLEQUIN SUPERROMANCE® NOVELS in our NEW LARGER-PRINT EDITION. These books are complete and unabridged, but the type is set about 25% bigger to make it easier to read. Look inside for an actual-size sample.

By the way, you'll also get a surprise gift with your two free books!

Pam Powers

Peel off Seal and Place Inside...

FREE BOOKS
LARGER-PRINT EDITION

84

THE RIGHT WOMAN

she'd thought she was fine. It took Daniel's words and Brooke's question to make her realize she was far from a full recovery.

She'd made a start with her sister's help and she intended to go forward now. Sarah felt as if she'd been living in a darkened room and someone had suddenly opened a door, letting in the fresh air and sunshine. She could feel its warmth slowly seeping into the coldest part of her. The feeling was liberating. She realized it was only a small step and she had a long way to go, but she was ready to face life again with Serena and her family behind her.

All too soon, they were saying goodbye and Sarah experienced a moment of sadness for all the years she and Serena had missed. But they had each other now, and that's what

She held

Printed in the U.S.A.
Publisher acknowledges the copyright holder of the excerpt from this individual work as follows:
THE RIGHT WOMAN Copyright © 2004 by Linda Warren. All rights reserved.
® and TM are trademarks owned and used by the trademark owner and/or its licensee.

The Harlequin Reader Service™ — Here's How It Works:

Accepting your 2 free Harlequin Superromance® books and gift places you under no obligation to buy anything. You may keep the books and gift and return the shipping statement marked "cancel." If you do not cancel, about a month later we'll send you 6 additional Harlequin Superromance larger-print books and bill you just $4.94 each in the U.S., or $5.49 each in Canada, plus 25¢ shipping & handling per book and applicable taxes if any.* That's the complete price and — compared to cover prices of $5.75 each in the U.S. and $6.75 each in Canada — it's quite a bargain! You may cancel at any time, but if you choose to continue, every month we'll send you 6 more books, which you may either purchase at the discount price or return to us and cancel your subscription.

*Terms and prices subject to change without notice. Sales tax applicable in N.Y. Canadian residents will be charged applicable provincial taxes and GST.

If offer card is missing write to: Harlequin Reader Service, 3010 Walden Ave., P.O. Box 1867, Buffalo, NY 14240-1867

BUSINESS REPLY MAIL
FIRST-CLASS MAIL   PERMIT NO. 717-003   BUFFALO, NY

POSTAGE WILL BE PAID BY ADDRESSEE

HARLEQUIN READER SERVICE
3010 WALDEN AVE
PO BOX 1867
BUFFALO NY 14240-9952

NO POSTAGE
NECESSARY
IF MAILED
IN THE
UNITED STATES

seem to stop. "If you let people walk all over you, they will. You have to be willing to ask for what you're entitled to."

As his delivery continued to grow in intensity, Caroline continued to stand there and take it, spurring him on further. He was acting like a total ass.

"Look at this," he finally said. "*I'm* the one who misbehaved and I'm standing here calling you down, as though *you* did something wrong, and still you don't defend yourself."

She didn't flinch. Hardly moved, except for the even intake and exhaling of breath. John shut up. He stood there trying to stare her down, but it was a contest in which she refused to engage.

"Are you through?" she asked after a full sixty seconds had passed.

"Yes." At least he hoped he was. With her, he could never tell. She raised all kinds of emotions that were unfamiliar to him.

"Then it's probably best if you go. Mrs. Howard only gave us an hour."

He was being dismissed. So be it.

"It's only been half an hour."

She wrapped her arms around her waist. "I have studying to do."

"I thought you always read ahead." He'd lived his whole life as a nice guy, and this country woman from Kentucky was turning him into a first-class jerk.

"I have a section test in algebra."

Of course, that had nothing to do with the baby, which was all they were supposed to be discussing. She was right to get rid of him.

"How are you doing?"

"Fine."

"Getting good grades?"

"We've only had one test in Math, Biology and Psychology, and a couple of papers in my two English classes, but yes."

"How good?" It didn't matter to him. What did matter was the little glint he'd just seen in her eyes. Anger? Or pride in herself?

He didn't know. But wanted to.

She didn't answer. Her way of telling him to mind his own business. He'd crossed a "not baby" boundary.

"I'm interested," he said. "After all, there's a lot you're going to be teaching my child," he offered in return.

"All As."

Chin jutting out, John nodded. "Impressive." He wasn't the least bit surprised.

She moved to the door, reached for the handle.

"You know, in spite of what Dr. Mason said, you don't have to come to the appointment next week. Someone might see you there and get the wrong idea."

"Or the right one," he shot back. "I'll take my chances."

With one hand out, John leaned forward, covering her hand on the knob. "For what it's worth, I'm sorry," he said, his eyes directly connected with hers.

She nodded. All the acceptance he was going to get.

He released her hand and stepped back so she could open the door. He was halfway down the stairs when he heard her softly utter, "Thanks for the clothes."

It sounded as if she meant it that time.

CHAPTER ELEVEN

THE FRIDAY AFTER Valentine's, Carolyn sat in Psychology class, wondering if she'd made a mistake in coming to Shelter Valley. Phyllis was so many leagues ahead of her, there was no way she could ever tell anyone they were related.

John had called every night that week, and while she wasn't forthcoming, she was beginning to expect to hear from him—which was dangerous. And stupid.

She'd run into Ellen Hanaran a couple of times on campus. Had grabbed a quick snack with her at the campus food court once, and been thrilled to hear that the young woman didn't appear to be suffering any lasting physical effects from the rape, despite her fears. "A yeast infection," she'd whispered to Caroline.

Still, those few conversations with a woman more than ten years younger than her were the closest she'd come to developing any friendships in this town.

Dressed in black slacks and a green silk tailored blouse, Dr. Langford faced the lecture hall still crowded with students, even after the final drop date. "Who can tell me what psychophysics is?"

The study of how physical stimuli are translated into psychological experience.

"Kayla?"

Phyllis's compassionate smile almost brought tears to Caroline's eyes—and a kind of detached pride to her heart.

"Something to do with how we process what we see and hear?"

"Something," Phyllis said, moving her mic wire as she walked toward one end of the room. "Anyone else?"

She wore her hair much shorter than Caroline's, but it was the same color. Did Phyllis like the muted shade of red as much as she had growing up?

"It has to do with how our experiences affect our perceptions," a young man called out from behind Caroline.

Phyllis nodded.

"Like the rose in the book," another girl said. "Some people saw it as a rose and one guy thought it was a red shape with a green line because he'd never seen a rose before."

"Right." Phyllis lifted her right hand to the cord that came together at her neck, and Caroline had another glimpse of the ring her sister always seemed to wear on her right hand. From this distance, all she could make out was a plain gold band, thinner than the one on the wedding finger of her left hand. Was it the opal her mother had given her? "It's the study of how physical stimuli are translated into psychological experience." She continued with her lecture, talking about absolute thresholds, the JND—just noticeable difference—and psychophysical scaling. Caroline had found these topics fascinating a week ago when she'd first read about them.

Now all she could do was stare harder at that ring, trying to convince herself it was the one she'd read about in the letter.

She had to get over this obsession. It didn't matter if Phyllis was wearing the ring or not. Even if she was, it wasn't about Caroline. Or about them. Phyllis didn't know Caroline existed. The ring, if she'd kept it, would simply be a keepsake from their parents.

She'd had parents Phyllis knew. Parents she'd never meet. She looked away, and forced her thoughts to move on. She wondered if she'd ever be able to wrap her arms around her sister and give her the hug she so desperately longed to give—and receive.

"Subliminal perception, scientifically speaking, is the registering of external stimuli without conscious awareness."

As Phyllis Langford expounded on this newest topic, citing several examples including a woman who wound up in bed with a man she barely knew because her unconscious self had picked up on signals he'd been sending, Caroline paled. Had her twin somehow read her mind?

That was impossible, Caroline quickly assured herself.

And prayed to God John wasn't still sending out messages that her body answered without first checking with her. She was having enough trouble dealing with the challenges she *knew* she faced; she'd rather not have to worry about hidden problems, too.

Class ended. Finally. For the first time since school had begun, Caroline was eager to get away from Psychology 101. And it would appear that her sister shared her eagerness. Where normally Dr. Langford stood at the podium, available to take questions from her students, today she had her mic off and was rushing with the rest of them toward the double doors at the top of the room.

When Caroline turned around, she saw why. Tory Sanders was standing there, and judging by the look on her face, whatever she'd come to share with Phyllis was important. Caroline's heart caught when she saw an answering urgency on Phyllis's face. Clearly these two were close. As close as any sisters could be.

She watched as, heads together, the two women walked out into the sunshine. And hated the jealousy that flooded through her. She'd never been a small or petty person. And she had no desire to become less than she already was.

Maybe she'd made a mistake in moving to Shelter Valley.

"THEY CALLED THIS MORNING!" Tory's excitement was palpable and Phyllis grinned right along with her friend as the two women chose a shaded bench in a gazebo. "I've been approved to adopt Alex!"

"Oh, sweetie, that's wonderful!" Phyllis hadn't been in any doubt that Tory would eventually be a legal mother to her husband's adopted eleven-year-old daughter. Tory, on the other hand, who'd both nurtured and been nurtured by the little girl since Alex came to live with Ben as an abused seven-year-old, was a little slower in the trust department.

They talked about court dates. Phyllis agreed to be there no matter what. And then there'd have to be a party—a birthday party, Tory said.

"Alex is special enough to have two birthdays a year," she continued, grinning and fidgeting as she sat beside Phyllis. In that moment there was no sign of the tentative and fragile young woman who'd first come into Phyllis's life pretending to be her dead older sister, Christine—Phyllis's best friend—four and a half years before.

Tory was a living example that people could heal. That life could go on…

"Brad called." Phyllis hadn't meant to blurt out the words. Hadn't been planning to tell Tory at all once she saw the state her friend was in. They'd worked too long and too hard, waited through excruciating months of torment for these moments of unadulterated happiness.

But she didn't have anyone else to tell. Tory was the only one who'd understand her irrational fear of her ex-husband— and her refusal to give in to him.

"And?" Tory's brow furrowed as she studied Phyllis.

"He's threatening to make me miserable until I let him have what he wants."

The tender touch of a hand against the side of her knee

gave Phyllis more strength than Tory would ever know. "What can he do to you?" the younger woman asked quietly.

Shrugging, Phyllis didn't immediately reply. She'd been asking herself the same question since the unexpected telephone call in her office the previous day.

"Show pictures of me when I was fat," she said, trying to make light of a situation that probably held no danger at all.

"And you can walk right behind them skinny and beautiful," Tory said, her rare militant side showing its face.

Phyllis tried to smile. Didn't quite make it. "Brad's an unknown quantity," she said, watching as students walked, some hand in hand, some alone, others in loud groups, throughout the campus. God, she loved it here. Loved the peace and warmth and sunshine. The green and browns of the desert. Loved the blue sky and the stucco and, most of all, she loved the people in Shelter Valley.

"He's spoiled and weak. He's always the victim. And he believes that whatever he wants is his due. A person like that, who finds himself alone, broke, virtually powerless—who knows?"

"You know enough to watch out."

"Yeah," Phyllis agreed, pressing her knee against Tory's hand, taking comfort from the small contact that represented the entire network of friends and loved ones they'd both found in this town.

"So, really, what can he do?"

"Find some way to ruin my reputation."

"Not gonna happen."

Phyllis hoped not. Just when life was everything she'd always wanted it to be, she couldn't bear the thought of seeing it come crashing down.

"Who's that woman?"

Alerted more by Tory's protective tone than her words,

Phyllis glanced over to a tree in the distance, where a lone woman was standing, facing them.

"Oh, nobody to worry about," Phyllis said, relieved when she recognized the thirty-something female dressed as usual in plain pants and a nondescript top. She was leaning against an old paloverde. "Just one of my students."

"She seems awfully interested in us."

Phyllis glanced again, in case she was missing something, then shook her head. It was definitely the same woman. If the clothes didn't give her away, that ponytail sure did. Not many women her age had hair that long. Or if they did, they tended to style it. "No, she's in my Psych 101 class—the one I just finished. She's so quiet and unassuming I never even noticed her until the first exams came in. Other than the fact that she doesn't participate in class discussion, she's holding a perfect score."

"In your class?"

"Yeah." Phyllis smiled. "It's a first."

"Have you ever seen her before?"

"Nope. Her name's Caroline Prater. I don't know of any Praters around here."

"Me, neither," Tory said, still watching the woman. "And I still don't like how she's looking at us. What makes you so sure she's not someone posing as a student to…to…"

"To do what, Tor?" Phyllis asked, nudging her friend. "Rob the lecture hall? Not everyone comes to town under false pretenses," she reminded the younger woman. On the run from an abusive husband, Tory had posed as her older sister, an English professor, for her first six months in Shelter Valley—teaching classes at Montford when, in reality, she didn't even have a college degree.

She almost had one now, though. Even with giving birth to Phyllis Christine and raising Alex, Tory only had two more semesters to go before she graduated.

"Well, what makes you so sure she isn't someone Brad hired?" Tory asked. Phyllis wondered if, even in fifty years' time, Tory would still have difficulty trusting. And hoped not.

"She's a registered student," Phyllis answered slowly, watching as Caroline turned and moved slowly down the walk all alone. She'd never seen Caroline Prater with anyone else, not even talking to fellow students before and after class. "I have no idea why she's watching us, and I don't particularly like it, either, but I just don't get the feeling that she's harmful." She frowned. Caroline aced every test and yet never once had the woman spoken up in class when Phyllis asked questions. "It's kind of like when you first came to town. I'd never met you before in your life, you were impersonating my best friend, lying to an entire community, teaching under false pretenses, but I *knew* you weren't a threat."

Tory glanced down for a moment and then raised eyes filled with tears. "Okay, you're the best judge of character I've ever met—Brad being the exception that proves the rule. Whoever that woman is, she must be okay. But you have to admit, she looks kind of weird."

"Maybe she lived on some secluded mountaintop somewhere," Phyllis offered, giving Tory's hand a reassuring squeeze. "You worry too much, you know? And you and I have a birthday party to plan…."

THERE OUGHT TO BE A RULE against men who were strangers being fathers.

Caroline turned her head to the side, staring at the white cement blocks that made up the wall a couple of feet away as Dr. Mason lifted her blouse, exposing Caroline's bloated stomach to the cool air of the examining room—and to John Strickland's intense regard.

He hadn't been in the waiting room when she'd arrived for her appointment, but he'd run in just as her name was called. She'd been hoping he was going to make a habit of standing her up.

No such luck.

"You say the baby has a recognizable shape?" he asked, his body just inches from hers.

If she moved her eyes at all, she'd see the brown leather belt hooked through tan dress pants at his waist. As it was, her peripheral vision was focused on the different shades of brown and tan in the tip of his tie.

"Not only does your baby have shape," Dr. Mason was saying, pressing her fingers lightly into Caroline's abdomen, "but some of his or her internal organs are already in place."

Her baby also had a facial profile as of this week, not that Caroline felt like contributing that piece of information to the conversation. And intestines. And by next week, there'd probably be ribs and maybe even a thumb in the mouth.

"Next time you come, the baby should be about four inches long and weigh a couple of pounds. We'll do an ultrasound then and take a look."

"Can I be there for that?" John asked.

"Of course."

"And we'll actually be able to see the baby?"

"It'll be murky to you at first," Dr. Mason said patiently. "A mass of black-and-white shadows that move, but you'll soon recognize what you're looking at."

Caroline remembered the one and only ultrasound she'd had with Jesse. She'd been almost eight months along and, right then, had fallen so deeply in love with her baby that she'd somehow believed she'd never know another unhappy moment as long as she lived.

"How's the morning sickness been?" Dr. Mason asked,

forcing Caroline to focus exactly where she didn't want to—the present. She glanced up at the doctor, feeling like a specimen under a microscope with faces peering down at her.

"Good," she said. "Pretty much nonexistent." She wouldn't look at him at all. That might help.

Dr. Mason pulled a special obstetric stethoscope out of her pocket, handing one set of the attached earpieces to Caroline. "What do you say we have our first communication from this little one?" Dr. Mason slid the other set of earpieces onto her head.

With shaking hands Caroline put the earpieces in place. Tried to relax as she felt the cool head of the doctor's instrument slide along her belly. And waited.

Please, God, let him be there. Let him be strong and healthy.

The doctor moved the stethoscope again, her brows pulled together—in concentration or in worry? Caroline couldn't tell. And then moved again.

So far, Caroline had heard exactly nothing.

She felt one more move on her stomach and she was looking for John. She'd expected him to be staring at her belly—or at the doctor. But his gaze was locked on her face, his eyes warm and reassuring. Did he have some sense that everything was all right? Or was he just completely ignorant of the fact that it shouldn't take this long to hear signs of life?

She wanted to ask him. To hear him tell her anything at all in that deep, confident voice of his. But she didn't want to make a single sound and perhaps have the doctor miss the critical thump they were seeking.

Placing the cold instrument up beneath Caroline's ribs, Dr. Mason seemed to stop breathing. And then smiled.

"Here it is," she said, just as Caroline picked up the signal the doctor had already noticed. It was just as she'd remembered with Jesse. A beat so rapid she'd been scared to death, at sixteen, that her baby was about to have a heart attack. Now she welcomed the sound with unexpected and very happy tears.

Embarrassed, she blinked, pulled off the earpieces and handed them to John.

Still watching her, a curiously intimate glint in his eyes, he put the stethoscope to his ears and listened.

And paled.

He didn't say anything for several seconds and Caroline could only guess what might be running through his mind. Based on his stark expression, she figured it couldn't be good.

John didn't want this child. Since little Billy's disappearance, he didn't want any child—any person—in his life that he might love and lose again.

He'd told her he was struggling. Perhaps she'd underestimated how much.

Maybe he'd be standing her up again, soon.

The idea shouldn't be frightening. Shouldn't really matter to her at all.

But it did.

"It's so fast." His voice cracked as he spoke.

"It's perfect," Dr. Mason said, smiling at both of them, seemingly unaware of John's reaction. "You two have a living, growing baby on the way...."

"WE HAVE TO TALK about where you're going to live."

John had followed Caroline out to the parking lot after the doctor's appointment. She just wanted to be alone.

"I have a room." Stepping off the curb, she continued across the blacktop toward her truck, parked in the back corner of the lot.

"I mean after the baby's born."

"I have lots of time to figure that out."

His Cadillac was in the second row. He passed it.

"We need furniture."

"I have Jesse's stuff back home."

With a hand on her elbow he brought her to a stop. "You're leaving?"

He didn't look any happier than he had in the examining room.

"No," she told him, although she wasn't as sure about staying as she'd been even a couple of weeks ago. "Jesse will drive it out to me this summer."

Her son had agreed to do that during their last conversation, almost two weeks before, adamant about not wanting his mother to travel so far in her condition.

"You told him about the baby?" They started walking again.

"A month ago." Breathing in the soft, fresh air, needing its cool, sixty-degree bite, Caroline slowed her steps. How could she be feeling so inadequate, so trapped, when the skies overhead were so perfectly blue?

John slipped his hands into the pockets of his slacks, adjusting his stride to hers. "How'd he take it?"

So far, other than saying he'd bring out the furniture, he hadn't given her any indication of his feelings. It was the only other time she'd talked to him. She'd called several times, but her son was avoiding her. "Okay."

"He's not angry?"

"No." Just distant—refusing to acknowledge that her life was changing so drastically. Refusing to share in the changes. In their one conversation, Jesse had spoken as if she was the same old mom she'd always been.

Maybe John was right about Jesse being angry.

They'd reached her truck. John opened the unlocked door

for her and after she sat, lifted a foot to the running board, with an arm resting on top of the door, effectively blocking any escape she might have made.

"What did you tell him about me?"

"Nothing."

"Nothing?" He bent, staring in at her.

She shook her head. "He didn't really ask."

She could tell she'd surprised him. He stood there, apparently at a loss for words. Or deciding not to say whatever words had occurred to him.

"You tell your son you're pregnant and he doesn't want to know who the father is?" he finally said.

"He asked if I was getting married."

"And?"

"I told him I wasn't."

He nodded, his dark hair shadowing his brow.

Caroline swallowed, shoved her bag off her lap to the console beside her. "I told him it was just a one-night thing. Because I was lonely."

"How'd he take that?"

"It made him uncomfortable," she said. "You know, seventeen-year-old boys don't like to think of their mothers as sexual beings." She slid her key into the ignition.

He nodded, his expression relaxed for a moment. "I remember."

Caroline meant to start the truck, put it in gear, give him a huge hint that she was planning to move his footstool. Instead, she couldn't look away from the reminiscent grin on his face.

"The night of my high-school graduation, I came home unexpectedly to get some albums I'd said I'd bring to a party one of my buddies was throwing and interrupted my parents hard at it on the living-room floor."

She'd have died a thousand deaths. But then, her parents

would never in a million years have been "hard at it" on the living room floor. That kind of thing, if it happened at all, took place only in the bedroom with the door closed. And no one ever spoke about it.

"What did you do?" Curiosity got the better of her manners.

"Went back out and pretended I'd never come home." He shook his head. "I couldn't look at my mother for weeks after that."

"What about your father?"

"That was different. He's a guy."

She supposed that made sense in a strange way. "So you went to the party without the music?"

"Yeah. There was supposed to be a keg of beer there and I planned to drink as much of it as I could manage to swallow."

The sun was starting to lower and she had to squint to see him. "Did you do that a lot when you were younger?"

"What, plan to get drunk?"

"Get drunk."

"A few times in college, but I went through that stage rather quickly. The night before never seemed worth the morning after. How about you?"

"I've never been drunk in my life," she told him. Not only did her father's example give her a firm reason to avoid the stuff, she just plain hadn't had the chance. "I was pregnant at sixteen, and every minute after that, I've been a parent with no time for that kind of partying."

"What about *your* high-school graduation?" he asked. "Didn't you at least get to go out that night?"

Something about John Strickland made her relax in ways she never relaxed around other people. Maybe because she had nothing to lose, she could reveal more of herself with him.

The experience was both freeing and far too dangerous.

Because she could easily tell him far too much.

"I didn't graduate from high school."

She had to hand it to him—he didn't let his jaw drop, but she knew she'd surprised him. "When I got pregnant with Jesse, my parents and Randy's decided there was no reason for me to finish school, since I was going to be a wife and mother. We already had enough against us, starting a family at such a young age, they said. They were afraid the added pressure of me going to school, trying to do it all, would be too much."

"And you didn't think to disagree with them?"

She shrugged. "What would be the point? Not one of them, Randy included, would've understood."

"So you got your GED." It was a statement, not a question.

She nodded. "I was almost twenty-six, but yes, I got my GED."

"How'd Randy react to that?"

Not well. Glancing out the front windshield, Caroline wondered if she could ever explain to him how it was with her and Randy. And how much Caroline had loved him in spite of their differing goals.

"He was okay with it at first."

"At first?"

She took a breath. "He started to feel a little threatened when he found out about the book."

"What book?"

"The one I'd decided I was going to write."

"Going to? You didn't do it?"

She'd said too much. Just as she'd feared she would.

"I started to. Several times." And then, always, the burning fire that had propelled her to the keyboard would be doused by Randy's misgivings, by his emotional distance, followed by her own admonishments to herself about her foolishness. She didn't even have a high-school diploma. How the hell could she consider herself capable of finishing a book?

"What happened?"

"I don't know," she said, looking away. Because she did know. "Life happened, I guess."

"Or maybe it just wasn't time yet," John told her. "Maybe there's a book or two in your future."

Maybe. Her interest in writing was why she'd chosen to major in English. But Caroline had grown leery of looking any further ahead than the next day. The future was fraught with unanswered questions and more fear than she'd ever faced in her life. She'd pretty much abandoned her journal-writing—uncomfortable with what she might discover about herself.

If she did write a book sometime, she'd stick to fiction.

CHAPTER TWELVE

"HI, IT'S ME." John stood at the window of his Chicago hotel room the second Thursday in March, looking out over Lake Michigan, wondering if Caroline had ever seen a view like this.

Or stayed in a room like this.

"Hi." That was his Caroline, effusive as always.

His Caroline. With a sweating hand John held the cell phone to his ear and slid his other hand in his pocket, pretending a calm he didn't feel.

"How was school today?"

"I didn't go."

His chest tightened. "Why not?" If something had happened to the baby…

There'd been no message from her on his cell phone.

"Ellen Hanaran had to testify in court today and she asked me to be there."

A boat was leaving the harbor, its lights on to combat the falling dusk. John's head hurt.

"I didn't know you knew Ellen."

Things were spinning so far out of control, John wasn't sure if his axis was vertical anymore. Maybe he should've stopped for dinner before rushing up to his room. He hadn't eaten anything since breakfast.

And wasn't hungry now.

It didn't matter who she knew or didn't know. Her personal

life didn't matter. *Caroline Prater's personal life doesn't matter.* And if he kept repeating that to himself over and over, at least once every five minutes for the next week, he might start to believe it.

"So we're supposed to report to each other on every acquaintance in our lives?" she said.

"No." She was right; he was being ridiculous.

The boat was a speck of light in the distance—a small dot compared to all the city lights coming on in front of him.

"You never say much about the other two boarders. Do you see them often?"

"No," she said. "We pass in the hall sometimes, but we keep different schedules and neither of them has meals with Mrs. Howard."

He should order room service. Probably would if he had any appetite. Maybe later.

"You've been in town, what, a couple of months, and you hardly know anyone," John said, trying not to feel guilty about how much time she spent alone in that little room of hers.

Not that he had any reason to feel responsible for any of her choices.

"My studies are the most important thing right now," she said. "I didn't finish high school, John. The last class I attended was almost eighteen years ago. Going to lectures and taking notes, figuring out what'll be on a test, classroom technology—that's all new to me. Besides, I spend my days with kids my son's age. I don't have a lot in common with them."

Good. He felt better.

"And I'm pregnant," she continued, her voice softer, more vulnerable. "Until we decide how we're going to present this to the world, or until I'm showing so much I can no longer hide the truth, it's kind of necessary for me to keep my distance."

The guilt was back. In force.

"You can present whatever you want to present. It's your body."

"And your baby. What if people ask about the baby's father? Like, is he still alive? Will he be helping me? What do you want me to tell them?"

Nothing. He had no idea. That he was the father. No…nothing. "I don't know."

"That's what I thought." There was no recrimination in her voice. "We've got a little more time. Maybe it'll become clearer to you."

And in the meantime, his indecision, his issues and struggles, were holding her hostage.

"I'm not all that eager for people to know, either, to be honest." Could the woman read his mind? "It's hard enough being new to town, new to school, without having everyone know right off that I'm also pregnant—with no husband in sight."

"Does Ellen know?"

"Yes, although not who the father is. And for now, she's keeping quiet about the baby."

Ellen would. She might be young, but she'd be a good friend to Caroline.

"How did things go for her in court today?"

She sighed, and John wondered where she was. Sitting at her desk? Propped up against pillows on her bed? It was almost five in Shelter Valley; she'd be having dinner soon.

"Good, I guess, although how you define something like that as good, I don't know. The best thing was there was no press. She cried once, but she got through it. Only the prosecution's questioned her so far. She'll have to go back for the defense."

And that would be much harder. They weren't on her side.

"Thank God she has Aaron."

"And a loving family," Caroline added. "And an entire town that adores her."

Support that John hadn't had when he lost Meredith. Once he'd married her, he hadn't thought he needed anyone else.

And then something else occurred to him.

"If you went to court, you met some of my friends today."

He would've liked to be there, and yet he wasn't sure why. It wasn't as if he could be open about his association with Caroline Prater. He had Lauren to think about.

Or so he told himself.

"Not really," she said. "Most of them couldn't be there. I saw Martha and David, of course. Ellen introduced me to them. But I didn't hang around."

"What did you think of Martha?"

"I liked her. She doesn't put on any airs. Or pull any punches. If I were in a battle, I'd want her on my side."

John nodded. "You're a good judge of character."

"Probably comes from being silent for so many years," Caroline said with a dry chuckle. "Keeping my eyes open and my mouth shut." It was an uncharacteristic response, but he figured it was the kind of acerbic observation she made often—silently.

He liked it.

Which brought back the day he'd just had, the fear he'd experienced, the reason he'd picked up the phone and called her when he'd told himself he wasn't going to.

Night had fallen, wiping out any sight of the water or the ships passing by. Wiping out most evidence of people and life down on the streets. His universe had become this elegantly appointed room looking out over a world of darkness and lights.

"I visited Meredith's grave today."

"She's buried in Chicago?"

Green lights rimmed a skyscraper in the distance. John stared at it, planning to sit down soon. Take off his tie and his shoes. Maybe have a drink.

Just one.

"Yeah."

"Is that where you two lived or where she was from?"

"Both."

"So you're home."

Technically, maybe.

"I grew up here," he said, "but I don't have family here anymore. I have a small office and the people I work with, but Shelter Valley is home, now."

The tightening in his stomach eased, as though saying the words validated something inside him.

"So how'd it go?"

"How'd what go?" But he knew. And as he'd discovered, he wasn't ready to talk about it. He shouldn't have called.

"The visit with Meredith."

Unexpected tears stung his eyes. He *had* visited his wife, not her grave, not the headstone and the few feet of land beneath which her remains lay. But he hadn't needed to go to a cemetery to do that. It was all in his head, anyway.

"I told her about you."

She was silent. If he was going to tell her, he should've waited to do it in person, when he could see her face. Although Caroline's expression didn't give away any more than her silence did.

And suddenly, he was sitting in the armchair in a room lit only by one dim lamp, talking. About Meredith. His life with her. And without her. About how he used to talk to her all the time, and hardly talked to her at all anymore. About how he knew he was really just talking to himself, thinking things through. About how much he missed her.

"I told her about the baby."

"And did you tell her how guilty you feel that she's not the one carrying it?"

"I don—"

"John, it's okay." If it was possible to send compassion through a phone line, she'd just done it. "Really."

"That's not the only thing I feel guilty about," he muttered.

"What else?" Her voice had a soft quality to it that he hadn't heard before—but he suspected that her son, Jesse, would recognize it.

"You," he said. "I feel guilty because of us."

"There is no us."

"Not in a romantic sense," he agreed. "But there's still an us. Because there's a *you*."

"What does that mean?" Her tone had grown thin.

"I don't know." Yet maybe he did. Where he used to talk to Meredith, he now looked to Caroline; where he used to trust Meredith's judgment, he now trusted Caroline's. It wasn't something he could talk about, wasn't something he felt comfortable with.

"I meant it when I said I don't ever want to get married again," she told him, her voice growing stronger with conviction.

John stared up at the shadowy ceiling. "I understand," he assured her. "I feel the same way."

He wanted to break the silence that fell then. Searched for the right words, some statement that would let them back out of this door he'd just opened.

"I'm pretty stretched to my limit right now, John." Her voice startled him. It came slowly, with obvious difficulty. "I can't handle any more complications."

"Me, neither."

"So let's leave it at that, shall we?"

He hadn't heard anything so good in a long time.

Unless he considered the sound of that little heart beating so rapidly in his ears a couple of weeks before.

THE THIRD TUESDAY in March, while walking to her English class, Caroline was pretty sure she felt the baby move. It was too early—she was only fifteen weeks—but she was pretty sure, anyway.

And for the first time, she really started to think about the little life inside her as more than a responsibility.

Who are you, my baby? With one hand on her belly as she walked, her bag slung over her shoulder, she spoke silently to her child. *What shall I call you?*

Would it be a boy or a girl? Another boy would be perfect—her years with Jesse had been the best of her life. She had boy clothes and had saved a lot of boy toys. She knew all about raising boys.

The strange butterflies in her stomach continued and Caroline smiled, until a young guy dressed all in black leather with purple hair and silver chains adorning his body passed by and gave her a strange look.

She'd love to have a little girl, too. Someone she could dress in pretty clothes. Someone who wouldn't have to be ashamed of her mother's tears or embarrassed by her joy.

She could name her Sara. She'd always loved that name. Her one and only doll had been named Sara.

And if it was a boy, Jacob. It was solid-sounding. Successful.

She felt another little flurry of movement inside of her. And remembered that this baby had a father.

Who might want to name him John.

ON THE THIRD TUESDAY of every month, the "Shelter Valley Heroines"—whoever was available—met for lunch at Montford, sometimes in the faculty lounge, often outside at a picnic table. On this particular Tuesday, they met in Martha Moore's office. Martha's students had a big film production coming up and she'd missed more work than she'd have liked due to Ellen's trial. She wanted to be available to her crew if they needed her.

Phyllis offered to pick up salads for everyone on her way over.

Beth, head of the Music Department at Montford, was dressed as usual in professionally casual clothes, her straight blond hair loose and falling around her shoulders. She was already there when Phyllis arrived. As was Tory.

"How's the mama?" Phyllis asked, smiling as she approached.

Tory jumped up to help her with the plastic containers full of salads, handing the tuna to Martha, the Caesar to Beth, egg for herself and a garden salad for Phyllis. It was a small group today. Becca was at a one-day conference in Phoenix, Randi was supervising an intramural tennis match, and Cassie had emergency surgery at the veterinary clinic.

"Fine at the moment." Beth smiled. "But you better get that to me fast while I'm enjoying my fifteen minutes of appetite."

"Morning sickness got you bad, huh?" Martha asked, her brow creased with sympathy.

Beth nodded, but was wearing a huge grin all the same.

Phyllis felt an uncharacteristic moment of envy. She had her hands full with the twins—had two more children than she'd ever thought she'd have. There was no reason for her to want more.

"I was that way with Shelley," Martha said. "And as it turned out, of the four, she was my easiest baby. Hardly ever cried, slept through the night almost right away."

"How's she doing?" Beth asked softly.

"Okay." Martha, sitting with them at the round table in a deserted corner of the studio, took a bite of tuna, chewing slowly. "Good, really. She's completely cleaned up her act and she's getting all As."

"How'd the doctor's visit go?" Phyllis asked. They'd all encouraged Martha to get Shelley checked out after her association with a less-than-reputable crowd the year before.

"Fine," Martha said, her eyes more peaceful than Phyllis had ever seen them. "All clean."

"Thank God," Tory whispered as she scooped up some egg salad.

Beth nodded. She put down her plastic salad fork after only a couple of bites. "And the trial?"

"Prosecution rests at the end of the week," Martha said, fork suspended as her focus turned inward. "She'll probably be called in Monday or Tuesday so the defense can question her."

Phyllis laid a hand over Martha's on the table. "It'll be okay," she said. "She's ready. She'll do fine."

Martha's eyes filled with tears, which caused all three of the other women present to exchange glances. Martha was their staunch heroine. "I'm not going to let them make it look as if what happened was her fault," she said. "She already struggles with enough guilt."

"I know." Phyllis said. Although Ellen had a therapist in Phoenix, Phyllis had talked to her enough to be well aware that the girl was struggling. Not that she would've needed to talk to Ellen to know *that*. A young woman didn't go through a rape and not struggle with it.

"Ellen's on her way to recovery," Phyllis said. "She's had that trial looming over her for months and once it's over…"

Martha's smile was slow in coming, but genuine. "She's made a new friend," she reported to her friends.

Phyllis's heart lightened even more. "There you go, then,"

she said. "That's a sure sign that she's back with us. She's reaching out—maybe ready to trust again."

Martha nodded, frowning, but not with disapproval. "I think she really does trust her," she said softly, glancing over Phyllis's shoulder to the cavernous room behind them. Turning, Phyllis saw that Martha's crew was gathered around a sound board in a little glassed-in room across from them.

"She asked her to attend the trial last week," Martha continued.

"Did she go?" Tory asked, eyes wide with apprehension. Someday Tory was automatically going to expect the best out of people, out of life. Phyllis was determined to see that happen.

"Yeah," Martha said.

Beth picked up her fork, speared some greens and held them a couple of inches from her mouth. "So you've met her?" she asked.

"Yeah."

"And?" Phyllis wondered at the hesitation in her friend's demeanor. Surely Ellen, who was so careful, wouldn't choose her friends unwisely.

"She's older."

"How much older?"

"I don't know. Our age."

Phyllis grinned. "That could be anywhere from mid-twenties to late forties!"

"Your age, then," Martha said with a chuckle. "Maybe a year or two younger. And she usually dresses in a way that's, I don't know, out of it."

"Out of it how?"

"Oh, polyester stretch pants that my grandmother might wear and an old button-down calico shirt that looked like someone's kitchen curtains. And she had on cowboy boots."

Phyllis felt the look Tory was giving her. "Her name wouldn't happen to be Caroline, would it?" Phyllis asked.

Martha turned toward her. "Yes, why?"

"She was watching Phyllis and me one day when we were sitting on campus talking," Tory said. "It was the day I found out about Alex."

"She's one of my students," Phyllis quickly added. "I don't know a lot about her, other than that she appears to have a new wardrobe. I'll see what I can find out."

"Is she a good student?" Beth asked, chewing slowly. At the rate she was going, she'd be through with her salad by dinnertime.

And still, Phyllis was envious.

"In my class, she is."

"I'm sure she's okay," Martha said. "It's just kind of... weird."

"Did Ellen say where they met?"

"No," Martha said, frowning again, and then her expression cleared. "But since she's a student here, I'd guess they met on campus. It would make sense. Ellen doesn't feel she has a lot in common with the kids her own age."

They all nodded, gave a moment to their salads, and then moved on. To Tory, and the imminent court date that would make her Alex's official mom.

HAVING SPLURGED on a tuna sandwich for lunch, to celebrate Sara/Jacob's movement that morning, Caroline was feeling almost peaceful as she enjoyed the balmy March weather on her way to Psychology class Tuesday afternoon. She could have eaten the peanut-butter crackers and banana she picked up at the bargain-priced grocery outlet in Phoenix over the weekend. She now had an entire case of crackers in her closet at Mrs. Howard's. They were high in protein. She had fruit cups, too.

But just for today she'd spoiled herself.

And Sara/Jacob.

The sun was shining, and the eighty-degree heat felt glorious on her skin, as though she was being gently held, caressed. Contentment bubbled up inside her. Coming to Shelter Valley *had* been the right decision.

Sara/Jacob would have a safe, secure place to grow up. Caroline had a friend now and would eventually make more. As soon as she got settled, figured out how she was going to explain her baby, got her first set of grades...

Jesse would eventually come around, too.

She was holding her own in school. And John lived nearby. She could be happy here.

Drawing herself up, Caroline glanced around, as though someone in the vicinity could have read her thoughts. Her happiness had nothing to do with John. Shelter Valley was a good choice where he was concerned only because her baby deserved to know its father.

A couple of girls brushed past her on the walk. They were both wearing low-cut jeans and tops that didn't quite cover their bellies. One of them was swearing.

It could work, living with Sara/Jacob in Shelter Valley. Cutting across the lawn, past one of many latticework gazebos, toward the Psychology building, Caroline wove one of her stories....

She's dropping Sara/Jacob off at Little Spirits Day Care. Bonnie Nielson is there, dressed in a colorful sundress and flat sandals. She asks Caroline about a social at church. All the women who associate with Phyllis are involved. Caroline is organizing the food. Becca Parsons is helping her.

Caroline had to wait for a cyclist with a backpack to pass and then crossed to the opposite side.

She flipped ahead to the social itself. *Everyone is there.*

The kids are all playing together. Sara/Jacob is about one and toddling around, being watched over by some of the older kids in town. John is speaking with a group of men across the room. He laughs and hearing his voice, she looks up from behind a table where she's arranging some gourmet something that she's made.

With the Psychology building in sight, Caroline decided she'd have to figure out what the gourmet delicacy was later. She wasn't familiar with gourmet cooking, had never cooked anything gourmet in her life and she didn't want that small fact to interrupt her.

Back at the social… *John glances over at her and smiles just as Phyllis walks up behind her and gives her a quick squeeze with one arm around her shoulders.*

Adjusting the hand-sewn bag holding her books, weighing down her shoulder, Caroline figured life was good.

She just needed to be patient. She sometimes said hello to people when she walked across campus. The rest would come.

Approaching the steps of the old building that housed the Psychology lecture hall, Caroline grinned as she saw someone she recognized standing by a tree not far from the building. It was a young woman, in her mid-to-late twenties. As Caroline climbed the stairs, she watched the woman, first to try and place her, and secondly to see why she was just standing there.

She was sitting in the lecture hall, waiting for class to begin, when the first answer came to her. It was the woman she'd seen in the picture taken at court, the first day of Ellen's trial. She'd stood behind John. Someone's sister, Caroline thought. The one person she couldn't name.

Maybe tonight after she finished her reading she could look up some of the old articles. And if all else failed, she could always ask John. He called every night now, at nine o'clock sharp, whether he was in town or not.

The conversations usually lasted only a minute or two— generic renditions of the same theme. Yes, she was fine. Nothing new happening.

But occasionally, like that night he'd called from Chicago, there was more.

CHAPTER THIRTEEN

"CAROLINE, CAN YOU STAY for a second?"

Caroline froze, all the good things in her day evaporating to leave her feeling limp and insecure as she heard Phyllis Langford's voice address her just before the professor removed her mic after class.

Unable to call loudly enough to be heard from her middle row, Caroline nodded jerkily. She turned to head slowly down the wide steps toward the podium in the front of the room. She was so hot she might pass out. Or be sick.

Surely everyone was looking at her, wondering what she'd done wrong. Truth be told, she was wondering the same thing. In her entire life, she'd never been asked to stay after class before. The closest she'd come was the day Randy'd been caught chewing gum in fourth grade and had to stay late to write *I will not chew gum in class* one hundred times on the board. She'd only been in second grade then, but she'd waited to walk home with him.

Other students milled around, asking questions about a missed quiz, an assignment due date, outside reading over the upcoming spring break, which was to begin the following Monday.

The day of her ultrasound appointment.

She should call her mother. It had been almost a week.

Wishing she dared draw attention to herself with a reassuring hand on Sara/Jacob, Caroline thought of her baby, wanting him or her to have a mother who could speak confidently with her doctorate-degree twin sister and handle herself with aplomb. Or at least not do something horrible like throw up.

Trying to ignore the roaring in her ears by concentrating on bits and pieces of the conversations taking place around her, Caroline worried about the scarred tips of her boots. Maybe she should just go ahead and splurge on a pair of thongs from Wal-Mart. Everyone seemed to be wearing them. And she'd seen them for less than five dollars.

She'd worn her blue-and-red flowered shirt today. It'd always been one of her favorites. She hoped that after the next few minutes, it still would be.

"I'm sorry that took so long."

With a hand wrapped around her ponytail, worrying it, Caroline dropped the hair when she realized that her professor—her sister—was speaking to her.

"Uh, n-no problem," she said, hating the stammer in her voice. Hating a lot about herself at that moment, including the fact that she was being so critical.

Phyllis picked up the satchel she'd loaded while talking to her other students and slung it over one shoulder. "Walk with me?"

"Sure." Praying that she wouldn't stumble or have her knees give out on her, Caroline followed Phyllis up the steps, hating the loud *thunk* her boots made against the stairs.

"Where are you from, Caroline?" Phyllis asked, glancing sideways at her as they moved together down the hall.

"Kentucky."

Phyllis nodded, and Caroline swallowed. She was so close. And they had the same eyes. Did Phyllis notice? Not that she'd be looking.

Caroline was looking.

"What brings you to Montford?"

Phyllis reached out with her right hand, pushing open the door. And Caroline stumbled, the toe of her boot catching on the floor.

Phyllis was wearing the ring. It wasn't identical to the one around Caroline's neck—the stone was different. But it was very similar.

"Uh, scholarship," she said, her face flaming.

"I'm not surprised." Phyllis smiled and Caroline's stomach melted.

"You're not?" Her throat was so dry she was afraid she might choke.

"My tests are difficult. I've hardly ever given perfect test scores before."

A little smile started to flower inside Caroline. She wouldn't allow it to emerge, but she enjoyed the moment just the same.

She had no idea where they were walking, hoped it wasn't far, and yet hoped they could keep walking together forever.

There were hundreds of students around them. An in-line skater passed. Caroline was oblivious to them all.

"What's your major?"

"English."

Phyllis turned toward the walk that led to the Performing Arts center—where her husband, Matt, worked as the director.

"Did you manage to find an apartment nearby?"

"A room, yes." How strange to be having such an ordinary conversation with the only other person in the world who shared her genes.

"I don't see a wedding ring. Does that mean you aren't married?"

She felt like a little kid, warming to her teacher's attention. And wondered if Phyllis was this attentive to all her students. Judging by the size of the class, she doubted it.

Of course, Phyllis kept office hours. A lot of the kids visited with her then. Caroline had heard various mentions of it.

"I'm a widow."

"Oh." Phyllis glanced over, her familiar green eyes filled with a sympathy Caroline had seen in her own eyes many times over the years. "You're so young. I'm sorry."

She couldn't react to that. Couldn't tread emotional ground with this woman. Not and survive with her life intact.

"You don't say much in class," Phyllis said.

"It's been a while since I was in school."

"I just wanted to make sure there wasn't a problem," she said. "You can hear me okay? No one's giving you a hard time?"

Caroline fell in love with her sister all over again. Whoever heard of a teacher caring so diligently about her students? "Everything's fine."

Phyllis nodded, her shorter auburn hair bouncing on the shoulders of her light gray suit. "Well, if you're sure…"

Because she looked as though she had more to say, Caroline waited. And wondered if Phyllis noticed that their hair color was identical.

The same hair and eyes. Same height. Different mouth and chin.

They were turning thirty-five in a couple of months.

"Okay, then." Phyllis's demeanor changed, became more businesslike. "That being the case, I'm warning you that I'm going to be calling on you."

Caroline nodded, not at all put out. If Phyllis wanted something from her, that was just fine.

"You can't get a perfect mark in this course without class participation."

"Okay."

They'd reached the door of the Performing Arts Center. "I'll see you Thursday."

When she'd be calling on Caroline in class. Feeling as though she and her sister had formed some kind of bond, Caroline nodded. Then she turned and walked calmly, slowly, out to her truck.

Where she promptly unlocked the door, fell inside and started to sob.

FULL OF AN ENERGY he could hardly comprehend, John walked Caroline to her truck after their appointment at the clinic the following Monday.

"A girl," he said, for at least the fourth time.

"Sara."

"Who?"

"Sara. I want to name her Sara." Caroline paused, glancing up at him. "If that's okay with you."

"Sure." He hadn't thought much about names. "I like Sara." He also liked the fact that Caroline had spoken up about her preference.

He was going to have to call his mother. And his sister. Maybe even his dad. The old man, if he could track him down, might want to know that he was going to have another granddaughter.

He'd have to tell his friends.

"The baby's grown a lot since last month." He'd been hard put to hide his shock when the technician had lifted Caroline's smock, exposing the smooth expanse of her belly. She'd looked pregnant.

"They have a tendency to do that."

John glanced down at her. Grinned. Then instantly sobered. "I couldn't tell under those shirts."

Her reply was a self-conscious shrug and John hated that he'd made her uncomfortable. If he didn't have so much at stake—though he wasn't sure what or why—he'd offer to preserve her privacy and opt out of all further doctor's visits.

Or if he didn't feel so compelled to be there. She might need him.

Even if she did, she'd never ask.

"Are you going to call Jesse and tell him?"

"Yeah."

He passed his car, walking toward the back of the lot where her old truck was parked. Did the woman have an aversion to people parking near her?

"You don't sound too enthusiastic about that."

"He's been avoiding me."

"Still?"

"I've talked to him once in the past month."

"Do you want me to call him?" John had no idea why he'd said that. Of course she didn't want the father of her illegitimate child calling her son.

"No, thank you." She had the grace not to tell him how stupid the suggestion had been.

"I'm sorry."

They'd reached her truck. She pulled out her keys, unlocked the door. "It's okay," she said. "He'll come around."

"Sounds like you've been through this before."

"Not really." She climbed in, looking up at him. "I just know my son."

For a second there, John was jealous of a seventeen-year-old kid. And of his mother. And the relationship they shared.

And then it dawned on him that his chance was coming. She put the ultrasound video they'd been given on the seat beside her.

Something else occurred to him.

"You don't have a television."

"I know."

He should close her door, walk away. Head over to Will's or Matt's. The Valley Diner. Anywhere that was far from Caroline Prater.

"You didn't get to see much of the show earlier." She'd been lying flat on her back, having to stay still and turn her head at the same time.

"I saw everything I needed to see. Ten fingers and toes. A healthy heartbeat."

"But you didn't see her put her hand in her mouth."

Her smile was a little nostalgic. "Maybe I'll ask if Mrs. Howard has a VCR."

"Have you told her about the baby?" Last he knew, she hadn't told anyone. Except Ellen Hanaran.

Caroline shook her head. And he realized she had no real intention of enlisting her landlord's help in video-viewing.

"Listen." He tapped a hand on the top of her truck. "Why don't you follow me home? We can throw on some spaghetti and you can watch the video as many times as you like."

He expected an immediate no.

"I've got a large screen TV." He pushed his advantage, not kidding himself for a second about the reason for her interest. It had nothing to do with him. And everything to do with that little life growing inside her.

"I remember," she said, and he blinked. He'd forgotten that she'd been in his living room. It was that first day she'd come to town.

The day he'd found out he was going to be a father.

And today, he'd seen his daughter for the first time.

"I'd like to make a copy of the tape," he told her.

"Okay."

"Really?" That had been much easier than he'd expected.

She nodded. "But only if you let me cook. I've been dying to get in front of that stove."

Feeling inordinately happy for the moment, John stood back, ready to close her door. "Then it's all yours."

"YOU CHANGED THINGS."

They were standing just inside his front door several minutes later, and John watched as Caroline glanced around the large family/living room combination. "What's missing?"

Her observation shouldn't have surprised him. The woman missed nothing.

"I packed away most of the things that were there simply as reminders of Meredith."

The main event of a weekend spent drinking too much and then regretting it. But he'd completed a difficult job.

"How do you feel about that?"

Not quite an "about the baby only" question—not that they hadn't veered before.

"Better."

She nodded. "I felt better after packing up some boxes...." Her voice trailed off and a faraway look came into her eyes. He wondered if she still thought about her husband first thing in the morning.

He didn't think about Meredith when he woke up anymore. Wasn't sure when he'd stopped. Or if he was losing the capacity to love so completely. He'd been praying for numbness for a long time.

"You want me to make dinner first?" Caroline moved slowly toward the kitchen.

"Sure."

As proficient as though she'd frequently been in his kitchen, Caroline quickly found everything she needed and set to work.

And as he chopped vegetables for her, John wondered why he didn't feel numb. Why he felt alive.

DINNER WAS DELICIOUS. Nothing fancy, just full of flavor. Or maybe it was having someone to share it with—even if that someone was completely off-limits.

He offered to take care of the dishes later, but Caroline insisted on cleaning up the kitchen before following him into the other room. While he turned on his entertainment system and loaded the VCR, she settled into the middle of his brown leather couch. When he turned, she was leaning forward, elbows on her knees, anticipation lighting her expression.

He deliberately chose the chair next to the couch. It was angled for a good view, but far enough away to keep his distance.

A distance that was suddenly becoming important.

And more necessary, too, although he wasn't sure how he knew that.

He pushed the button on the remote, and forgot everything but the grayish movements on the screen in front of them.

"Oh, look!" Caroline cried a couple of minutes later. "She *did* put her hand in her mouth! I can see it!"

The animation in her face was new to him. And oddly beautiful. Something that stuck with him as they watched the video three more times, noticing new things each time. When they finally turned off the television, John had begun to think their daughter was the most astonishing human being ever to be conceived.

Caroline stood.

He wasn't ready for her to go. The mood was too soft, too amiable, for an instant return to the emptiness that usually accompanied his evenings at home.

"Would you mind staying just a little bit longer?" Hands folded and resting on the chair between his spread knees, John glanced up at her. "I think we should talk about what we're going to tell people."

He wasn't ready. But it had to be done. And the mood was going to dissipate anyway.

She sat down again. Squeezed her hands together. And then reached for the chain he'd occasionally noticed around her neck. She wore it beneath her collar, whatever was hanging from it beneath her shirt.

He'd wondered more than once if it was Randy's wedding ring that lay there between her breasts.

He knew she hadn't had it on that night in Kentucky. His lips had been all over her neck, her chest. And below.

She'd tasted like the country. Fresh and flowery. And she'd opened to him as eagerly, as innocently, as any woman he'd ever known.

"What did you want to say?"

Her head wasn't lowered, but neither was she looking at him. With her attention seemingly locked on the now-dark television set, she sat like a criminal waiting for sentencing. Alert. Present. And dreading the outcome.

"I don't know," he told her honestly, leaning forward with his elbows on his knees, turning to look at her. "I was hoping we could come up with this one together."

He needed some direction.

She shrugged, her shoulders slim in the blue-checked blouse she was wearing. He wanted to get up, pull the band out of her ponytail, letting that glorious hair fall free around her shoulders as it'd been on the night that started all of this.

Why was he thinking about that night so much?

Because he was trying to figure out a way to explain what had happened? That had to be it. Please, God.

"I always try to tell the truth," she finally said, giving him an apologetic smile. "Saves a lot of time and creative energy."

He'd agree with that. "What version?"

She glanced away, looked back and then away again. But not before John had caught an unusual glimpse of emotion in her normally pleasant but unrevealing expression.

"As abridged a one as possible."

"Agreed." He waited.

He wasn't being much help here. And there didn't seem to be anything he could do about that.

Her knuckles were white where she was clasping her hands together in her lap. "You're her father."

He nodded.

"That's my version."

Nothing there he could argue with.

"Where did we meet?"

"In Kentucky."

He could see where the truth came in handy.

"When?"

Eyes clouded, she glanced over at him. "During the holidays?" Her voice was a little higher than normal.

And suddenly John felt like a total jerk. Here he was worried about answering to his friends, people who knew and respected him. People he knew would support him, regardless. He got up from the chair and sat beside her. Reaching out, he smoothed a stray strand of hair behind her ear. The almost imperceptible movement of her jaw against his hand spoke volumes to him.

"I'll stand beside you every step of the way, Caroline," he assured her, even while he wondered how he was going to find the strength to do that. Not because he was in any way ashamed of her, or embarrassed by her, but because he was so completely averse to ever being attached again.

And the minute this came out, people were going to think…

"We'll tell them it was a whirlwind courtship," he said with conviction.

"They'll think we're a couple." The horror in her voice almost had him doubting the clarity he'd arrived at.

"Yes."

"But we aren't."

"I know."

She was frowning, but the lost look was gone from her eyes. "We don't want to be."

"I know."

"That's not the truth, then, is it?"

He took a deep breath. Thought for a minute. "Would you prefer to tell them we had wild sex all night long the first time we met and then never intended to see each other again?"

She blushed. And John wanted to kiss her.

He stood instead. Went to get a beer. Took several deep swallows. He'd planned to remain standing until they got through this and he could usher her to the door. But when she tilted her head to peer up at him, he sat down beside her.

"We *are* a couple in a sense," he told her. "We're partners in a very intimate process here. And we'll continue to be partners for the rest of our lives."

"But we don't live together."

"That can be remedied."

"No!" Caroline shook her head, leaning away from him while staring straight at him.

"I didn't mean like that," he quickly said, though he wasn't sure how much truth the statement held.

The day, the video, the weekend, the memories of that night in December were all ganging up on him, attacking him with nonsensical possibilities and half-crazed emotions.

"No."

She wasn't going to budge.

"I have plenty of room here. You'd have your own room. For that matter, you could have your own side of the house."

"No."

"Okay, so we're together, but not getting married yet."

"We aren't ever getting married."

"Anything's possible." He didn't mean that, was just trying point out the truth in his story.

"John? I can't marry you." Caroline had never sounded so certain of anything. For a woman who hardly ever seemed to stand up for herself, that statement was particularly effective.

Which relieved him. Greatly. He thought.

"I know," he said softly, his heart—what he had left of it—going out to her as she sat there, pregnant with his baby. Alone. Defenseless.

"We're too different. I've made that mistake before, marrying a man who wasn't like me. It's damaging. No matter how much I loved Randy, it was never enough to make up for the differences between us. The last time this happened to me, I got married and I'm not sure it was the best thing for any of us. I might have repeated part of the mistake, but I'm not going to repeat the rest of it. I can't."

With a hand around her jaw, John moved a little closer to her, turned her to face him. "It's okay," he continued, the words coming from someplace inside he was hardly aware of. "I'm not suggesting we be anything other than what we are. I'm only trying to give us a safe place in which to exist while we bring our daughter into the world."

Her eyes glistened, and he thought she might cry, but she didn't.

"You know what it's like in a small town, Caroline," he said, rubbing a thumb along her temple. He'd forgotten how soft her skin was. And how silky without the makeup he was used to finding on women's skin. "If it looks as if we aren't headed on a happy course, everyone in Shelter Valley will be wanting to give us advice. And because you're new to town, you'll unfortunately be the one who'll be blamed for making the untraditional choices."

He'd been engaged not too long ago. His friends all assumed he wanted to get married again. They were sure it was what he needed.

"We can be a couple until after the baby's born, and then break up. How would that be?"

She gazed up at him for so long, John had no idea what to expect.

CHAPTER FOURTEEN

"Okay."

Caroline knew she was going to regret the decision she'd just made. Possibly more than any other decision she'd ever made.

John's plan made complete sense. Try as she might, she couldn't find any loopholes. Or a better way. And still, she knew she was walking straight into a pit of flames....

"Don't look like that." His voice was thick.

His thumb was hypnotizing in its soft heat against her temple. "Like what?"

"Like you just found out you have a terminal disease."

It was how she felt. But that made no sense at all. He'd said they'd break up as soon as Sara was born. Five more months. It was no time at all.

"I'm scared." It was the most honest thing she'd ever said, exposing a part of herself that had been hidden from the time she was seven years old.

"I know," he said, his tongue briefly licking his lower lip. "I am, too."

Though neither of them spoke, she continued to stare at him, almost as though she could read something in his eyes that he couldn't say. And that she couldn't translate into words.

His head came closer and she let herself sink into that look, taking an odd comfort in the feelings he was arousing.

Caroline gave comfort. She didn't often take it. Didn't know *how* to take it.

And when John's lips touched hers, she just kept taking. His touch was soft, warm, tender—a simple caress against her closed mouth. Until she opened it—and started giving.

"STOP." CAROLINE HAD no idea how much time had passed or even realized that she'd said the word, except that she'd felt its rawness scrape her throat. "We can't…"

She couldn't. Not again. She'd lost herself in this man's arms once. She couldn't do it again. She just couldn't. At some point she had to learn from her mistakes.

If she didn't start now, it might be too late.

And she had—would have—a daughter who'd be needing a mother soon.

"I'm sorry." His forehead rested against hers. He was breathing as heavily as she was.

"Don't apologize."

Slowly they pulled apart. Caroline wanted to stand, to leave. Her legs needed a second or two.

"Why did you do that?" Asking wasn't polite. Or even particularly nice. But she had to know. Had to understand. The agonizing and second-guessing that would result if she didn't would be too excruciating.

"I don't know."

A blank wall. She hated those. She nodded, still shaky, and picked up the videotape he'd brought over earlier. Then she managed to stand.

"It's probably a good thing it happened, though," he said, surprising the heck out of her. How could he think that had been good? For either of them?

Deliriously sexy, maybe. Dangerous, of course. Neither of which ranked as a good thing in her book.

"For the next five months we're going to be a couple to my friends," John explained, standing, too. "They're going to expect to see some affection between us."

"Or start giving us that advice we're hoping to avoid." She was beginning to understand the ramifications of what they'd taken on.

For a very short time, she'd be appearing in John's circle—conversing, socializing, pretending. In Phyllis's circle. Her sister was going to know that she was pregnant with an illegitimate baby. Not that it wasn't bound to happen anyway, since she'd be showing before the semester was through. But now, with John standing beside her, the pregnancy didn't feel quite as shameful. They all liked and respected him. He was one of them.

One thing was for certain. She'd have to spend some of her carefully guarded funds to buy some new clothes to supplement what John had bought her. "I'll go shopping for more fashionable clothes over the weekend," she told him.

"I'll take you."

She shook her head. They'd been that route before. "This is something I need to do for myself, John." Partially so she could do it at some bargain-basement place. She'd look on the Internet for one of those shops that sold seconds. Surely she could find some outfits with flaws that wouldn't be too obvious.

And partially because she'd never even dared to think about spending money on a fashionable outfit. She wanted to savor the experience without having to worry about looking like a wide-eyed bumpkin when she saw herself in the mirror.

He walked her to the door. Opened it. "There's a barbecue on Saturday at Will and Becca's. It'd be a good time for us to break our news."

She stepped out into the night, thankful for the cool air on her skin. She couldn't breathe. "Will Phyllis Langford Sheffield be there?"

"She's supposed to be."

"She's one of my teachers." Caroline stumbled on the words. "Won't that be awkward?"

"No," he said. "Tory Sanders will be there, too, and she's also a student at Montford."

She'd forgotten about Tory. Maybe if she concentrated on how envious she was of Tory's relationship with Phyllis, she wouldn't die of panic before the weekend.

"Okay," she said. Sara deserved this.

And if she could keep telling herself that, Sara's mother just might survive.

JOHN WAS STANDING on the eighth tee of the Shelter Valley country club with Matt Sheffield, Will Parsons, Greg Richards and Sam Montford on Saturday morning when Sam's cell phone rang.

"Damn," he muttered, reaching for the small leather pouch attached to the waistband of his jeans. "I forgot to turn the damned thing off."

"Ever think about leaving it at home?" Greg taunted good-naturedly.

"Ever think about Beth in trouble and not being able to reach you?" Sam shot back.

It was obviously a situation that struck to the core of both men. John remembered a time when he'd been that attached to Meredith. In the end, his being there had made no difference at all.

"It's Cassie." Sam's voice brought John back to the present. The younger man was looking at the outside LED screen of his phone.

"Hey there, sexy, what's up?" he greeted his wife of many years but lover of only a few. John had heard only the basics of how Sam and Cassie had lost a baby and eight years of marriage.

And that, having been given a second chance with his estranged wife, he was one of the luckiest guys around.

The pinched look that came over his tanned face didn't suggest a lucky man. "When?" Sam paused, obviously receiving an answer that didn't make him feel any better. "Is Mom with him?"

He nodded then, and John wondered if Sam realized his wife had no idea that he'd just agreed with whatever she'd said.

"I'm on my way."

Without even saying goodbye to the woman he adored, Sam snapped his phone shut.

"My father collapsed," he said, heading off across the golf course without the cart he'd driven up in or the wood iron he'd just dropped.

"Sam!" Will Parsons ran for the cart. "Hold on, I'll drive you."

Grabbing Sam's club, John jumped into the back of the cart with him, leaving Greg and Matt to follow in the second cart.

"Has anyone called Ben?" John asked, filled with a familiar urgency that required action where no action would help. Ben was Sam's cousin and would want to be there.

"No," Sam said. "Cassie's a mess." Sam's knee was bouncing up and down, his hand pounding without rhythm against his thigh. "Once again, she was there shouldering my burden," he muttered.

"Whoa, man, don't do that to yourself," Will said, but John understood the anger that was consuming Sam. It happened to a man who loved someone fiercely and was powerless to do anything when that loved one's life seemed to be slipping away.

The lack of control was debilitating.

"I'll stop by and get Ben," he offered. Not because he and Ben were particularly close, although they certainly knew each other. But because he preferred to have something to do rather than go home and wait for a string of phone calls to finally reach him and tell him what was happening.

James Montford was an institution in Shelter Valley—the direct descendent of the town's founder, the first Sam Montford. A life-size monument of James's father, the elder Samuel Montford, held a place of honor in the square downtown. James, like his father before him, exemplified everything Shelter Valley had come to mean to its people. He was an example of life as it should be lived, with integrity, love, faith and joy.

Even to John, a slightly jaded man who hadn't been in town all that long, the elder Montford represented a kind of security—proof of what life could be. Though he'd only met the man a few times, John thought of James anytime he was in serious jeopardy of losing all faith. He'd recently considered going to talk to Sam's dad as he tried to find sense in a world where nothing made sense to him. As he tried to understand feelings he couldn't understand—like the fear that consumed him whenever he thought about the little girl who'd soon be joining him in this world. He didn't even know Sara yet, but he knew he'd never survive if anything happened to her.

And he knew he had very little control over what might happen to her. Hell, she could die in her crib at night.

That thought scared the hell out of him.

By the time John had tracked Ben down at Sam Montford's construction office and driven him and his wife and their two children—who were with him at work that Saturday—to the Montford estate, James Montford had passed away quietly in his bed.

He'd never regained consciousness.

John gave his regrets and quietly left. But not before he'd heard the animal-like wail of grief that erupted from Carol Montford when the doctor removed his stethoscope from her husband's chest and shook his head.

John recognized that wail. He'd heard it once before, from deep within his own chest when Meredith, bleeding in his arms in the back of a New York City ambulance, took her last breath.

They'd had to pry his arms away from her body, wet and sticky with blood but still warm when they'd arrived at the hospital. They'd taken him inside, stitched up a cut he hadn't even realized he had, just beneath his hairline on the left side of his head. Treated a series of other scrapes and bruises and burns. But they hadn't been able to do anything about the broken state of his heart. Nor could they give him anything to warm the coldness that had permeated every cell of his being.

As soon as he'd made arrangements to have Meredith's body sent to Chicago, he'd left the hospital and taken a cab back to the hotel room he'd shared with his wife the night before. An investigation of the accident was in progress, but no one had expected any charges to be filed, and there'd been nothing more for him to do. John had quietly packed their bags, careful to put her makeup in her cosmetic bag, just as he'd seen her do so many times before. He'd loaded their dirty clothes into a laundry bag, moved their clean clothes to one end of their suitcase, zipped everything in and left for the airport.

The fact that he didn't have a flight out—or anywhere in particular to go—didn't seem to matter to him. He was alive, but he might as well have been dead. As dead as Meredith…

He couldn't do it again. He couldn't face love knowing

that, even in a life as perfect as the Montfords', this was how it ended. How it would always end. For everyone.

He *couldn't* care. It was the only way he could survive.

"JESSE? IT'S MA."

"Yeah, Ma, I know it's you."

Standing in the parking lot of a Phoenix strip mall, trying to justify going inside the bargain fashion store and spending money that wasn't necessary for physical survival, Caroline clutched her cell phone to her ear. "Do you have a minute to talk?"

It was Saturday. He didn't have class to rush off to.

"I'm just leaving to play basketball. You're okay, aren't you?" He always asked. Still. "Yes, I'm fine."

"Did you tell your sister yet? The professor?"

"No."

"Okay then, I'll talk to you later, Ma."

The heaviness in her heart was hard to bear.

"Jesse?"

"Yeah?" A car drove by, the teenage girl in the passenger seat giving Caroline an odd look.

"It's a girl."

"A girl?" His voice cracked in a way she hadn't heard since he was fourteen.

"You're going to have a sister. I'm naming her Sara."

"A girl," he repeated in an odd tone.

"Yeah. Her father's name is John. He's an architect, Jess. He lives here in Shelter Valley."

"So that's why you went there." He said it with only a hint of accusation.

"In part, yes, but that wasn't my main reason." It was seventy-nine degrees and the sun was hot on her head. It radiated up from the blacktop.

"Are you going to marry him?" He didn't seem to be reacting to the idea one way or the other.

"No, Jesse. I did that once before, got married because I felt I had to. I'm not going to do it again."

"I thought you loved Dad." A little more accusation, but it wasn't full of heat and anger.

"I did. As much as I've ever loved anyone, except maybe you. But I didn't marry him because I loved him. I married him because I felt I didn't have a choice. And I lived the next eighteen years that way, too. I can't do that anymore."

"Whatever."

"Jesse? How important was it to you to have the choice to go to Harvard?"

"Very." He sighed. "And you don't need to say any more, Ma. I'm a jerk, huh?"

"No." She smiled as tears sprang to her eyes. "Just a kid."

"It's weird, you know, having a ma who's been knocked up?"

Caroline cringed, glanced at the store, wondering what the hell she was doing. "I know."

"It just takes some getting used to."

"I understand."

"A sister's cool, though."

She walked toward the building. "I love you, Jess."

"Yeah, me, too, Ma. Take care of yourself."

"I will."

And that was that. He was gone. Off to play basketball and to try to forget that he had a mother who was "knocked up."

As she contemplated the night ahead, Caroline wandered around the racks of maternity clothes, alternating between deciding whether to actually buy the clothes in her size and feeling sick to her stomach.

She was finally going to be a part of the club—the closed

circle of strong and admirable women who were her sister's closest friends.

Who was she kidding? She wouldn't be *in* that circle. She'd be sitting outside it, in the role of John's pregnant girlfriend, watching them all. John could marry her and she'd still be on the outside. Caroline wasn't an educated woman who understood the ways of the world. She was a self-taught Kentucky farm girl who probably wouldn't recognize a thing that was served tonight and wouldn't know how to eat it if she did.

Pulling out a pair of jeans that were cut off above the ankle, she wondered how much a pair of sandals would cost. She sure as heck couldn't wear her boots with these.

Nor would she know when to laugh at the party, when to speak up or be silent. What were the proper topics to discuss? In Grainville you said whatever you thought, unless you were Caroline and then you mostly said nothing.

Would they think she was stupid if she just sat there? Or would they all get quiet if she talked about the weather like they did in Grainville?

Phyllis knew she wasn't stupid. Caroline was one of the few students she'd ever had with perfect marks.

But how perfect was she to appear tonight? Pregnant and unmarried.

How perfect would she appear to any of them if they knew her secret? Would Phyllis be so kind to her if she knew that Caroline was not only her blood relation but her twin? She'd kept the news to herself out of respect for Phyllis, but had that been the right thing to do?

"Can I help you?"

Startled, Caroline glanced up at the girl with a nose piercing and bright red lipstick smiling at her. The clerk had a belly button ring, too, visible between the tight black pants she was wearing and the T-shirt that ended shortly below her ribs.

"No, thanks, I'm just looking."

"'Kay, well, we've got some great maternity swimsuits right over there," she said. "They're on sale. Some really cute tankinis, too."

Tankini? Caroline had no idea what that was. And wasn't sure she wanted to know. She'd thought all pregnant women wore big billowing clothes to hide their expanding waists. Apparently fashionably pregnant woman showed them off.

In any case, she hadn't owned a swimsuit since she was about fifteen.

A white stretch top matched the jeans—had the same floral stitching along the collar that the jeans had along the hem—but if she wore that, her belly would show like a big balloon.

Many of the maternity shirts were that way.

Still, Caroline added it to her growing pile.

A lot of birth families didn't want decisions from the past to disrupt their current lives—to haunt them—hurt them. What right did she have to force Phyllis to see her parents in a different light? To tell her that the person she saw herself as, the adored only daughter of a loving older couple, wasn't really who she was? What right did she have to hurt her?

What right did she have to link Phyllis to a country bumpkin in front of her peers and friends? She could be devastated. She could be embarrassed.

Caroline didn't want to be responsible for any of that.

She pulled out a pair of bright yellow pants with a colorful print of purses and shoes. It had a matching shirt. She put them back. Moved to the next rack—summer dresses.

She'd never owned more than one or two dresses at a time in her life. Other than Sunday church and funerals, there just hadn't been a need for them in Grainville.

The first dress she pulled out, lightweight navy-and-white

silk, calf-length with a subtle pleat just under the bustline to accommodate a growing stomach, took her breath away.

Not only did she not want to embarrass Phyllis, she also wasn't sure she had the emotional resources she'd require if Phyllis out and out rejected her. She wasn't at her strongest.

Insecurity should be her middle name.

A hard thing to handle for someone who was used to being calm and capable, contained, a pillar of strength during crises.

Her cell phone beeped a voice message. The phone hadn't even rung, which wasn't all that unusual inside stores.

Maybe Jesse had canceled his basketball game and wanted to talk. To tell her he understood. That he loved her. That they were who they'd always been—on the same side, the two of them against a world that didn't understand them.

John had called. The party that evening had been canceled. Caroline wanted to drop the clothes she was holding and run home to her room, her computer, the only thing she felt sure about.

He said he needed to see her. He had to talk to her. He wanted her to call.

CHAPTER FIFTEEN

CAROLINE BOUGHT THE DRESS. And several pairs of slacks
with matching tops. And a pair of white sandals she found in
her size at seventy-five percent off. On her way into Shelter
Valley from the freeway, she called John.

If they weren't going to meet his friends, she didn't have
to see him. Whatever he had to say could be said over the
phone.

"James Montford died."

Oh. God. She hadn't known. Had no idea.

"I can't believe it." She missed her turn.

"Neither can I."

Caroline slowed, pulled to the curb until she could think
straight. "I'm so sorry."

"Yeah, me, too."

Death was inevitable. A part of life. So why did some lives
seem immune? Exempt?

"How did it happen?"

"They aren't sure. He collapsed this morning and within
an hour he was gone. They're thinking either heart attack or
stroke."

"His poor family."

"I was with Sam when the call came."

"He's an only child, isn't he?"

"Yeah. He's got a cousin in town, though."

John's voice was almost deadpan. Not just weary-sounding. It was beyond that.

"Did you know James?"

"Yes, but not well."

"I didn't know him at all, but you can't live in this town without feeling his presence, can you?"

He was quiet for a few seconds. "That's a good way of putting it."

A car passed her to pull into a driveway a couple of houses down.

"Well, if there's anything I can do…"

"Can you come by?"

She hesitated, hating to deny him anything when he was obviously so down. "Okay…" She drew out the word. "Why?"

"I think we need to talk."

That sounded ominous.

"And I want to stay here in case any of them try to find me. If they're out and about, they're just as apt to stop by as call."

Caroline wondered if maybe he needed to be surrounded by the security of being in his own space. It was a feeling she could understand—more now than ever.

It was something she'd unknowingly robbed herself of when she'd left Grainville.

"I'll be there in a couple of minutes."

JOHN WAS READY when Caroline arrived. He was just going to tell her, outright, that she could count on him for money and that was all. The baby wasn't even born yet and he was having panic attacks about losing her. He couldn't live like that.

He'd only heard it once or twice, but he recognized her tentative knock. Threw open the door.

And stared.

"You look…"

She didn't push past him when he stood rudely in her path, gawking at her, although the confidence her clothes implied suggested she might do exactly that.

"Wow."

Glancing down, Caroline otherwise stood completely still.

"You're wearing sandals."

She nodded. "Even I knew the pants would never work with my boots."

"I like them."

She raised her eyes, sweetly hesitant. "The pants or the sandals?"

"Both. And your hair. I've never seen it down—well, almost never."

Caroline blushed and he wished he could take back the words. Take back his entire reaction. They were only clothes, after all.

"I'm sorry," he said, stepping back. "Come on in."

"I feel a little stupid," she told him, walking through to his kitchen to sit on a stool at the breakfast bar. "But after trying on all these clothes, I couldn't make myself put the jeans and boots back on."

She looked fabulous.

"I hope you bought enough to do away with the jeans completely."

"I got four outfits. I'll be fine until after the baby's born. And," she added, "everything was on sale."

"Good."

He poured her a juice. Grabbed himself a beer. He stood on the opposite side of the counter, facing her. Opened his mouth to tell her what he had to say, searching for a way to do so that would emphasize his sincere intent to follow through on his responsibilities.

"I didn't even know James, but I feel like Randy just died all over again," Caroline said, staring blankly ahead.

John looked at her. Took a sip of beer. He'd thought something was wrong with him, this obsession he had with Meredith's death. His inability to get over it. Get beyond it and start anew.

"I had an older woman at church tell me, shortly after the funeral, that there's a part of me that will always feel this way, but that, in time, it becomes less like a stab in the heart and more like another level of living. She told me I'd find a strength and an ability to endure that I didn't know I had, making life deeper, fuller."

Fullness of life was not at all what he was feeling. She pulled her glass of juice closer, held it on the counter with both hands.

"I'm not there yet," she said.

"Me, neither." He was afraid he never would be.

She took a sip of juice. He gulped some beer.

"Would you like some dinner? We could put a couple of steaks on the grill."

"Okay."

SITTING OUTSIDE on his patio at the round table with its matching padded metal chairs, John slowly cut his steak. It tasted good. As did the baked potato and salad. The breeze was slightly cool but not cold. Track lighting broke through the darkness of the night that had fallen, illuminating the table, the dinner, Caroline.

These were good things. All things he could handle, making life worth living.

"Were you alone when you found out Randy was dead?"

They'd touched on other topics, but somehow kept coming back to the day's events. And the memories evoked by them.

Will had called to tell him that funeral services were planned for the following Tuesday. Public schools and the university would be closed.

"Jesse was there," Caroline said, breaking off a piece of roll and dabbing it in the butter on the table. He'd never seen anyone eat a roll that way.

She didn't eat it, either, just dabbed and held on to it.

"When Randy didn't come in for dinner, we both went out looking for him. We'd split up but happened to run into each other just before we found him. The tractor had thrown him several yards."

"Was he still alive?"

She shook her head. "Neither of us knew that, though. As soon as I saw him, I knew it was bad. I sent Jesse back to call for help. I ran over to him...."

She dropped the bread, wiped her hands on her napkin and then clutched it, wadded between her fingers.

"I was crying so hard I couldn't tell if he was breathing or not. And I was petrified to touch him. I didn't want to make him any worse than he was."

John's chest constricted around the piece of steak he'd swallowed.

"As it turned out, he'd been dead for over an hour. Doc said he'd been unconscious the whole time, but I've wondered if he said that for my benefit so I wouldn't think of him out there all alone, suffering."

"You think of it anyway."

She glanced up, looking surprised. "Yeah. How'd you know?"

"I do the same with Meredith," he admitted. It was something he'd never told anyone. "Not so much lately, but I used to wake up at night and grieve over how she spent her last minutes. She wasn't alone. I was with her. But did she know I wasn't doing anything to save her? That I couldn't?"

He shook his head. Picked up the second bottle of beer he'd been nursing for more than an hour. Drained it.

"What we do to ourselves—it's silly, isn't it?" Caroline said, a sad smile curving her lips. "Things feel entirely different than you expected when you actually go through them. Like driving for the first time. It's nothing like you expected. Or…sex."

"Yeah." He wasn't sure where she was going with this, but wasn't comfortable with the sex discussion. He had a rule against thinking about sex and Caroline together.

"So, none of us can have any idea what it feels like when you're on the verge of death. For months before I had Jesse, I imagined what the birth was going to feel like. I'd wake up in a panic, certain I couldn't do it. But when I actually went into labor, it wasn't anything like I'd expected."

"You aren't going to try to convince me it didn't hurt, are you?"

"No." She gave him a wry grin, then turned back to the fork she'd been toying with. "The pain was there, it was me that was different. I was so filled with—I don't know, adrenaline or something—so eager to finally hold my baby, that I wasn't afraid of the pain. I just accepted it."

"Do you worry about it now?" His stomach muscles gave a twinge as he thought about the impending birth, thought about being there, watching his own daughter come into the world.

He wanted that.

He just didn't want to live the rest of his life after that moment, knowing his daughter could be taken from him at any time.

"Not really," she said. "To be honest, I have so many other things pressing on me that a few hours of physical pain doesn't concern me too much."

"So we sit here and worry about what it must've been like for Randy and Meredith, but we're probably off the mark because we have no experience to work from."

"Exactly." She picked up her fork. "Looking at their suffering from the perspective of someone who's not in pain, not in shock, someone who's lucid and rational, isn't all that logical. Which is why it's silly that we do it anyway."

She made sense.

"And that doesn't even take into account what else they might know at that point that we have no concept of."

Intrigued now, as well as interested, John sat back. "Like what?"

"Like some kind of spiritual knowingness. You hear about near-death experiences where people see white lights. How do we know there isn't some kind of force that comes and fills you with euphoria as you leave this life? How do we know that isn't exactly what Randy and Meredith were feeling? That, given the choice between euphoria and this imperfect life, they chose euphoria?"

Meredith might have made the choice to leave him? That was something he'd never even considered.

CAROLINE RINSED the plates and silverware. And while John was in the middle of loading the dishwasher, Ben Sanders called to ask if he'd be one of the pallbearers. David Marks was going to be officiating and there'd be loudspeakers outside the church for all those who couldn't fit inside.

"I told him I'd do it," he told Caroline as he hung up the phone. "Sam and Ben want to be able to sit with Carol."

"It's an honor," Caroline said, glancing at him over her shoulder. "They must think very highly of you."

He didn't look at it like that. He was just glad to have a job to do.

"YOU'VE GOT THE BEST of both worlds here, don't you?" They were in the family room where Caroline had dropped her purse on the way in.

"How do you mean?" he asked, hands in the pockets of his chinos. The night stretched ahead.

"You're completely free and yet surrounded by friends at the same time. Friends who are practically family."

He nodded. "I guess. I'm lucky, wouldn't you say?"

"I'm not sure."

John's head fell back. He stared at her, frowning. "Why?"

She grabbed her purse, turned away.

"Caroline?"

"You don't really want me to answer that," she said, walking to the door.

He grabbed her by the shoulder, gently pulling her around. "Yes, I do. You have good insights, Caroline. I'd like to hear what you think."

"This town, the feeling of being part of a family, has allowed you to hide. You have a sense of belonging without ever really opening your heart." She didn't look at him as she spoke.

He looked at her, though. At the bent head, the docile demeanor, and was consumed by a fear he couldn't explain. This woman was such a conundrum, he couldn't understand her, couldn't grasp why she'd burst into his life.

He didn't know what to do with the feelings she made him face, about the past and the future. And didn't know what to do with *her*.

He wanted her to go. And he wanted her to never leave him alone, trapped in his private prison, again.

And he couldn't let her stay, couldn't risk giving her what she'd take whether she meant to or not.

The door opened. Closed behind her. Waiting until he heard her truck start, John turned off the front lights and let her go.

PSYCHOLOGY CLASS on the Thursday after James Montford's funeral was a subdued affair. While Caroline had attended the funeral with the majority of the town's population, including a large number of Montford students who weren't full-time residents of Shelter Valley, she'd stayed on the periphery and had not taken part in any of the other functions. A funeral was not the place for her to meet John's friends.

She wasn't convinced that any place—or time—would be right for that.

Wearing her capri jeans with the flowery stitched hem and matching top that made her look pudgy, not pregnant, Caroline sat in class, trying not to be upset that she hadn't heard from John all week.

"Sorry," a young woman said. Coming in ten minutes late, she stumbled over Caroline's sandaled foot as she brushed past her.

"We've been discussing intelligence factors and the topic cannot be complete without taking a look at the nurture-versus-nature debate," Phyllis was saying.

Heart rate picking up as Phyllis's words registered, Caroline glanced down at the blank page of her notebook. She hadn't done a good job taking notes today. She'd start now.

"Caroline, tell us what you think."

In the week or so since she'd spoken to her sister face-to-face, Caroline had begun to hope that Phyllis would forget to call on her.

Perhaps Phyllis had just been waiting for a topic, a question, Caroline couldn't possibly have an answer for. "The nurture-versus-nature debate has been going on since before Psychology became a science," she said, staring at the black-board and hoping the entire class wasn't wondering why such an old lady was going to school with them. Not that she was really the oldest student there. She just felt as though she was.

Montford had many students in its adult continuing-education program.

"You're right about that," Dr. Langford said. Her expression was serious as she continued to watch Caroline. "But I wanted to know what you *think*."

I think I'd give half my life to have nature win. "Anyone who says that environment is not a factor in a person's psychological and emotional makeup is mistaken."

"So—to put it crudely—you think that someone can be born with the ability to be smart and then end up stupid?"

Phyllis had walked over to the side of the room, but was still facing Caroline. "I think that people could be made to believe they are." She swallowed, willing her chest to lighten enough to allow her to breathe. "And if reality is what we believe it is, then the reality is, if we believe we're stupid, we are."

The professor moved up a step. "But what if reality changes?" Phyllis was enjoying this.

Somehow that knowledge gave Caroline courage. "You mean if someone who's always considered himself stupid suddenly finds himself in a position to learn?"

"Yes."

"He still won't learn."

There were rumbles in the class. "Why not?"

"Because he doesn't believe he can."

Phyllis nodded, resting a hip against one of the vacant seats. "So you'd say that testing someone's intelligence isn't enough," she said. "You'd also have to test his or her belief system."

"Yes."

"Interesting." Phyllis stood, then moved back to the front of the class. "I agree with you, by the way."

Heat surged into Caroline's face. With a sweaty hand, she

picked up her pen and began to scribble on the page in front of her. Phyllis went on to talk about an incident Caroline had never heard of, illustrating exactly what she'd said. A young girl who'd frequently been told she was stupid had been unable to learn to read and write. It was only after she'd been adopted by a couple who were convinced she *could* learn that her belief system changed and she became literate. She told the class the woman's name and everyone gasped. She was well-known throughout the world of science for her many forward-thinking theories.

"So what about twin studies?" someone asked.

Caroline paled, praying that her teacher wouldn't call on her a second time. She was too close to this one. Couldn't be impartial. Didn't know what she thought. As many times as she'd read through the material, and the extra material she'd found on the Internet and in the Montford library, she still didn't have a sense of clarity about the various findings, still didn't know if environment or heredity played a bigger part.

She wanted so badly to believe that it was heredity but feared it was environment. And that, if she didn't turn her tail and run home soon, her environmental influences were going to embarrass her, expose her for the stupid country bumpkin she really was. Even if she happened to be a bumpkin who read constantly, voraciously. Because without much formal education, she had no framework for what she learned, no way of judging it.

Her only hope for a different outcome was Jesse. That was one intelligent boy. And he'd come from her.

Whether Phyllis planned to call on her or not, Caroline didn't find out. Her teacher didn't have a chance to call on anyone. The door down on the floor behind the podium flew open. Matt Sheffield quickly surveyed the room, spotted his wife and loped toward her. He said something and, in the next instant, Phyllis was pulling off her microphone, yelling that class was dismissed. Leaving her briefcase and books behind, she followed her husband out.

There was a flurry of papers and pens as students packed up around her. Caroline stood, all the blood draining from her face. Something was terribly, terribly wrong. Her sister was in trouble.

And she didn't know how to find out what kind of trouble. Or how to help.

CHAPTER SIXTEEN

Phyllis's two-and-a-half-year-old son, Calvin, was missing. The twins had been with their father in town. He'd bent down to tie Clarissa's shoe and when he'd stood up again, Calvin was gone. Less than half an hour after the interrupted Psychology class had been dismissed, an announcement had been made on the local radio station. It was now spreading by word of mouth around the campus.

Caroline, standing with several other members of the class, was one of the first to hear. The Sheriff's Department was asking for volunteers to form a search party. So far, more than three hundred people had gathered.

"Come with me."

Caroline jumped as the voice spoke just behind her left ear. It was John. And he was dragging her through the crowd of people to the front, where Phyllis was surrounded by the rest of the Shelter Valley Heroines and their husbands. She looked for Ellen, didn't see her, and figured she must be watching some of the younger kids.

Clarissa, she soon heard, was at home with Beth Richards.

"We're going to split up into groups," Greg Richards was speaking into a bullhorn, which he lowered to say, "Matt, take three people with you. Phyllis, you take another three. The two of you know Calvin's habits and are most apt to figure out where he might go. You're also most likely to recognize any sign of his presence—a piece of clothing, a wadded-up wrapper of some kind of candy he likes."

Looking at her twin, Caroline could *feel* the panic riding up Phyllis's spine.

Greg lifted the horn. "For now—" he gazed out over the growing crowd "—I'm inclined to think Calvin's just wandered off. But time is of the essence. A two-year-old alone after dark, even in Shelter Valley, isn't something we want to face."

Heads nodded as murmurs rippled through the crowd. "Let's break up into groups of two," the sheriff continued. "Everyone start with your own neighborhood and any play areas you might know about. Go to the grocery store, comb Wal-Mart. If there are ten of you looking in the same place, fine. Someone has to see what someone else might miss."

Greg had a few more quick instructions and gave out a couple of emergency phone numbers that would be taking any information. An office had been designated to receive reports of each search.

Taking Caroline's hand, John walked over to the Sheffields.

Raising a shaky hand to her temple, Phyllis was frantically searching the faces in front of her.

"Tory, Becca…" she said at the same time that Matt called out to John and Will. "And…" Phyllis's eyes caught Caroline, standing there with John. "You. Please come with me."

"But I—"

"Please, you're smart. I need your help." Phyllis's voice was sharp with fear.

With a nod toward John, Caroline quickly introduced herself as one of Phyllis's students to Tory and Becca, following just behind the other three women as they set off for the ice-cream shop in town—the last place Calvin had been seen. They were going from there to the day care.

Matt and his group were going to the park across the street and would work their way home.

"HE ISN'T HERE." Phyllis blurted, looking around the ice-cream parlor. She'd checked every closet in the shop and every stall in the both bathrooms, even examined places a child, no matter how small, could not possibly hide.

With an arm around her back, Tory led Phyllis outside and up the street toward the day care.

"We'll find him, hon," Becca said. "Even if he was here, he'd have left by now. You know Calvin, always figuring he knows just what to do."

"I can't believe he left Clarissa," Tory muttered.

Caroline wondered where a small boy would go if he suddenly found himself free....

"My son hid in a haystack," she said, thinking aloud. "He was just playing. We wouldn't even have known he was gone except he fell asleep there and we discovered he was missing. I thought he was with his dad.... He woke up when we found him and wondered what all the fuss was about."

"See?" Tory said. "It's going to be something like that."

Caroline hoped she was right.

"He's bound to be scared by now," Tory said an hour later. With dusk falling, the women left Little Spirits Day Care and headed back toward the ice-cream shop, watching every movement on all sides of them. They encountered various other groups of searchers, but no one had news.

"He'll be hungry, too," Phyllis said. Becca, walking beside Caroline, said nothing. Her eyes were intently focused, seeming to be everywhere at once.

"The first time my stepfather hit me, I ran away from home," Tory said. "I don't remember how old I was, but I remember I got scared whenever it started to get dark. I hid in the closest corner I could find."

Caroline started studying every single crevice and corner they passed. So Tory Sanders had been abused. No wonder Phyllis was so protective of her friend.

MATT AND HIS GROUP were waiting at the ice-cream shop. Caroline stood back, unable to keep the tears at bay as she watched her sister fall apart in her husband's arms. Matt cried, too, his head bent, but quickly straightened.

"Okay, Phyl, he needs us now." The words were filled with love and a curious kind of strength. It wrapped around the small crowd gathered there, touching even Caroline.

"I just talked to Greg. He suggested a few of you wait here. Often when a child wanders off, he'll eventually make his way back to where he started from."

"I'll stay," Phyllis said immediately. Matt nodded. "Becca, if you and Will could handle the phone lines, that would be great. There's been a lot of questions from the press and you're the two best suited to handle that job."

They nodded.

"How're you doing?" Caroline hadn't heard John walk up.

"Okay." Better with him around. He knew her. Somehow, that made a difference to the emotions that were threatening to overwhelm her.

"I'm going with Matt and Ben to search the desert areas around town."

Caroline's heart sank. "They aren't still thinking he just wandered off," she concluded softly.

"They aren't sure, and no one wants to take any chances."

Oh, God. This couldn't be happening. Not here. Not in Shelter Valley. Suddenly Caroline was reminded of something Ellen had said one day, something about thinking the exact thought when she'd heard the hotel-room door shut behind her and felt her attacker's hands on her breasts.

"Someone needs to tell Phyllis." Her sister wasn't the type to hide things from; Caroline's senses told her that much.

"Matt's telling her."

As John spoke, Caroline looked over and saw her twin fall against her husband a second time. And then watched her nod. Stand. Straighten her shoulders.

It was what Caroline would have done if Jesse had been in trouble. There'd be time for falling apart later.

For now, Phyllis's son needed her.

Nothing else mattered.

FOR A WHILE they looked around the ice-cream shop again, and then, convinced there was no other way in, and that the little boy hadn't fallen asleep in some corner, the three women sat down outside the building, leaning against the wall.

The green-silk pantsuit that had been so crisp during class hours before was snagged from the cement. And stained. Phyllis seemed oblivious to the condition of what had to be a very expensive garment.

Caroline wouldn't have cared, either. While they'd been walking back from the day care, Caroline had heard more about Tory's past, the abusive childhood that had led to an even more abusive marriage. The more she heard, the more her heart went out to the other woman.

"So how'd you two come to meet?" she asked now, attempting to keep Phyllis's mind at least partially occupied with something other than panic.

"My older sister, Christine, and Phyllis were best friends," Tory said, sitting between them.

Blinking, Phyllis appeared to be mentally joining them at just that moment.

"You and Tory's sister were friends?" Caroline had known that Tory had a sister from an article she'd read, but Phyllis had never been mentioned in connection with her.

"In Boston. Before I came here. We lived in the same complex, taught at the same university. She was an English professor."

Caroline knew what had happened to Christine and didn't want to broach that subject. Especially not then. She searched for something else to say.

"Christine was killed," Tory said. Her voice was thick, but she was otherwise composed. "My ex ran us off the road. He was after me."

What was meant to be a happy topic—Tory and Phyllis finding each other—had become just the opposite. Caroline had never wished more fervently that she'd kept her mouth shut.

"I'm so sorry." She needed to say more but couldn't find any words.

Sorrow consumed her. For Tory. For Phyllis and little Calvin. For John and his Meredith. For Jesse, who'd lost a father too young. For herself... She was sorry that life held so much pain.

"IT'S GOT TO BE BRAD." Phyllis hadn't spoken in more than twenty minutes. She'd paced the block. She'd been in and out of the ice-cream shop that had agreed to stay open in case Calvin hadn't been found by closing time. But she hadn't spoken. When she did, her voice rang with conviction.

"Brad's her ex," Tory told Caroline. All three women were standing on the street corner, watching for movement. The other businesses on Main Street were all closed, their owners either out looking for the missing boy or home with their own children.

Peering up at Phyllis, Tory asked softly, "Do you really think so? He's deranged, Phyllis, but he's never done anything against the law."

"Why would your ex-husband kidnap your son?" Caroline asked. At least they were doing something besides going quietly crazy. Even if it was only talking about what they were all thinking.

Without moving her gaze from the street, Phyllis told Caroline about an investment of her ex-husband's and how, during their divorce, his broker had made the stock seem far more valuable than it was, awarding it to Phyllis in exchange for liquid assets. And his subsequent harassment of her when the loss suddenly turned into a gain and she was sitting on a nice sum of money that still bore his name.

In listening to Phyllis's explanation, Caroline learned a lot more about her than simply those facts. Phyllis had not lived a blessed life. Nor had her sister always been the strong, confident woman who'd stood before her class all these weeks.

And then something dawned on Caroline. All the time she'd spent searching the Internet for the birth family she hadn't known might finally come to good use.

"I know a little about searching for people on the Internet," she said slowly. It wasn't as if she'd ever done, or ever would do, anything illegal, but there were things a lot of people didn't know about using the Internet. Ways to find out all kinds of information about almost anybody.

"I might be able to find out if your ex-husband is in his home state." There were several good services for tracking people, some of them free of charge. She belonged to a couple. "You don't happen to know his social security number, do you?"

Phyllis looked directly at her for the first time since the search had begun and rattled off the number. "It was on all our accounts all the years I paid the bills." She added, "You think you can find him?"

Caroline shrugged. "Depends on what he's been up to. Give me some time at home," she called, turning to walk away. "I'll be back."

"We probably won't be here," Phyllis called back. "Come by the house when you find something. We're in the phone book."

Heart full, Caroline walked home as quickly as she could. Phyllis was indulging in wishful thinking if she thought Calvin was suddenly going to turn up. But anything was possible.

She could have asked for a ride, but didn't want to pull anyone off duty and figured that by the time she'd waited she could've made it home, anyway. If she had to go to Phyllis's, if she hadn't received word that the little nephew she'd never met had been found, she'd borrow Mrs. Howard's car.

A BOUT OF NAUSEA just as she arrived home slowed Caroline a bit. She dashed to her bathroom upstairs. When she came out, Mrs. Howard was standing there with a tray of food and a pot of tea.

"I heard you were out searching. You missed your dinner," the older woman said. "Not a good thing to do in your condition."

She met Caroline's eye, her expression kind.

With a hand on the doorjamb, Caroline asked, "How long have you known?"

"Not long enough," Mrs. Howard said. "We should be eating more nutritiously than we have been," she continued. "And we will, starting now." With a pointed look, the woman motioned toward Caroline's door, following her in when Caroline had turned on a light.

"Does the father know?" the older woman asked as she set the tray on the desk.

She nodded. "He's here in Shelter Valley."

"Is he going to marry you?"

"We're…seeing each other," Caroline said.

"Good." Then, at the door, she asked, "Is he the young man who came visiting?"

"Yes."

Mrs. Howard nodded again, opened the door. "I liked him."

"I…I'm just home for a little while to look up something on the computer," Caroline offered, the sharing of her movements foreign to her. "I'll have to go back out when I'm done. May I borrow your car?"

"Of course," Bea Howard said. "As long as you're careful not to do anything to hurt that baby. If my feet would carry me, I'd be out there looking, too."

"I'll be careful," Caroline said, a sense of peace pushing its way in with all the turmoil swirling inside her. It felt good to have a mother caring for her again.

It was something she hadn't even known she'd liked while living in Grainville, but had been missing ever since she'd left.

SITTING IN MATT SHEFFIELD'S KITCHEN shortly after nine that last Thursday in March, John turned with everyone else when Caroline walked in through the living room. Phyllis and Tory had returned only moments before on the advice of Greg Richards, who'd said that at this point, they were considering Calvin abducted. His mother would be most needed at home. To answer phone calls, be present if the child was found and, though it wasn't said aloud, to receive any demands for ransom that might be presented.

"Her ex-husband's a crazy man." Matt was leaning against the counter, facing the men and women gathered there, but speaking primarily to one of them. Greg Richards, the sheriff of Shelter Valley. "I think that's where we should start."

Most of the friends who'd been with them all evening had gone home to get some rest. They'd all be needed to begin searching anew at the first sign of light if the boy still hadn't been found. Will and Becca were busy with their babies and the press. Which left Tory and her husband, Ben, Phyllis, John and the sheriff sitting around the table in Phyllis's new kitchen.

All eyes left Matt and turned to Caroline as she stumbled in.

"It's not Brad Langford," she said. "He's in jail in Virginia for unpaid traffic tickets. There's some other records there, too. His home has been foreclosed and he's filed for bankruptcy."

Greg perused the papers Caroline laid before him. She hadn't looked anywhere but at the sheriff. And the floor.

"Good work," Greg said. "How did you do this?"

"I'm a registered member of a couple of Internet search services. One in particular, a pay site, specializes in linking up all different kinds of records—banking, law enforcement, all sorts of things." At Greg's sharp glance, she stammered, "I, uh, used it to track down a missing family member." That, at least was the truth. "Anyway, having his social security number made it easy."

"So it's not Brad." Phyllis's statement fell into the air. Her eyes were intent on Greg and the pages in front of him.

"No."

Her chin trembled. "Thank God." With tears in her eyes, she stood silently, moved over to Caroline and held on. Caroline hugged her back, but John could see her discomfort.

Glancing at the papers, John was astounded—and slightly horrified. He'd had no idea it was possible to find so much information. It made him want to close all his accounts, unplug his computer and its IP address, pay his bills by money order and disconnect his phone. And why in hell did Caroline subscribe to those services, anyway? What "family member" was she tracking down? Her birth parents? She'd never said.

"This is impressive work." Matt was looking at Caroline's results and then at her. "I don't believe we've met."

"She's that student I was telling you about," Phyllis said, her smile weary but obviously sincere. "With the perfect test scores."

Lowering the pages, Matt held out a hand. "I'm very glad to meet you."

Caroline shook his hand briefly, murmured something and stepped back while the others continued to talk about what she'd managed to do in a very short period of time.

And through it all, she just stood there, never smiling. Saying nothing. John wanted to get up and shake her. It was obvious that she had no idea of the value of what she'd been able to do. It had been easy for her, so it must be easy for everyone. And her reaction made him a little angry.

What was it going to take to change this woman's view of herself? To give her the confidence she lacked?

"So…" Phyllis sat back down next to Tory. "If it's not Brad, who is it?"

"Could be anyone," Greg told her. The FBI had been called in, bulletins sent out. "Calvin might very well have wandered off like we thought and, if he *was* picked up, it happened later. Maybe not even here in town."

Face drawn, Matt Sheffield watched the sheriff and nodded. Phyllis did the same. Ever since Phyllis's return, the couple had been avoiding each other. John had a feeling it was the only way either one of them could cope.

"A woman desperate to have a baby of her own sees a toddler standing alone, probably crying, and decides she can make him happy. That type of situation happens far more than we like to think."

"What about that guy who was hanging around the day care a couple of years ago? Shane something-or-other. Is he still institutionalized?"

"No," Tory said. "Bonnie told me the other day that he's living in a halfway house for mentally challenged people."

"Well, there you…" Matt started, pushing away from the counter.

Greg shook his head. "Nope. I already checked him out. He's been home sick and under supervision all day."

Talk continued, possibilities suggested. At ten, Beth, the sheriff's wife, called, saying that Clarissa had fallen asleep with their son and she was putting them both to bed at her house. After hanging up, Matt finally slid in beside Phyllis on the built-in bench by their corner table. She leaned her head against him, tears trickling slowly down her face.

It was as if, with their daughter safe out for the night and Calvin missing, there was nothing more for her to do, nothing holding her together.

Her son's disappearance had stripped her of confidence, of strength, leaving her weak and helpless.

John recognized that feeling. It was all too familiar.

And it was a risk that always accompanied deep love. A risk he couldn't take again.

How would he ever survive having a child of his own?

CAROLINE STOOD by the far kitchen wall, listening to the talk around her, not speaking at all. Wishing she could talk to John. He looked about as sick as she felt. She had no idea what he could say to her that would take away the sting of the day's events. Or what she could possibly say to him to ease the fear he felt so deeply. She just needed to talk to him.

"Okay." Greg grabbed a pad and pen from his pocket. "Let's go through a list of everyone either of you has ever known," he said. "Anyone you can think of who might have a grudge, deserved or not. Anyone who just plain didn't like you for some reason."

He gestured to Phyllis. "Let's start with you."

Caroline knew she should probably just go.

Other than her ex-husband, Phyllis wasn't aware of any enemies. A woman whose job she'd taken in Boston, maybe. A student she'd failed the previous semester.

Caroline wasn't surprised to hear that the list was so small. Phyllis was the kind of person people just naturally liked. Perhaps because she seemed to genuinely like everyone herself.

Then it was Matt's turn. Caroline didn't know how to leave without interrupting, drawing attention to herself. No one seemed to remember she was there. Except maybe John. He'd looked at her a time or two. Motioned for her to slide onto the end of a bench, but she'd shaken her head, declining his suggestion. She didn't belong there.

"What about the woman you went to jail for?" Tory asked as his list drew to a close.

"Shelly Monroe?" Matt asked.

"She hated you enough to send you to prison."

Matt and Phyllis both disagreed. "He writes her a check every month," Phyllis said. "He'd be at the top of her fan list."

"He does?" Tory asked. And then, looking at Matt, "You do?"

Running a hand lightly over Phyllis's head, tangling his fingers in her hair, Matt said wearily, "She's not a bad kid. She just had rotten luck. My intention has been to help her. I can afford it. And she deserves the break."

"Deserves it for stealing years of your life with her lies?"

Tory asked. Phyllis sent her friend a shake of the head so imperceptible that Caroline guessed she was the only one who'd even noticed. Admittedly, she was paying more attention to Phyllis than anyone else would. Probably more than she'd ever paid to any other person in her life. But if paying attention to the little things was the only way she was going to know her sister, she needed to notice every detail she could file away.

"She was a desperate kid, trying to hold on," Phyllis was saying. "I don't begrudge her the money. It saw her through college and it's giving her son a chance at a better life than she had."

Her sister's eyes were completely devoid of makeup, swollen and without their usual spark of energy.

Matt, too, seemed drained to the core.

They'd both been through so much, and now they were facing such unspeakable horrors….

"Have you heard from her lately?" Ben asked, a hand on Tory's thigh.

"I never hear from her," Matt said. "Except by way of the endorsed check in my bank statement at the end of each month. Truly, she's not a problem. She graduated from college and is teaching school someplace in Utah."

"No, she's not." Caroline straightened, her heart suddenly pumping so fast she was light-headed.

Or maybe it was the stress, combined with the baby growing inside her, that brought about the roaring in her ears.

"What do you mean?" Greg Richards spoke, but everyone was staring at her. For once Caroline didn't care.

"She's not in Utah." Finally, she had the answer that had been plaguing her on and off for weeks.

Unfortunately, she was afraid she'd really screwed up. She'd made the connection too late.

"Caroline?" John stood and approached her, his hand on the small of her back, a steady force, helping her focus.

Oh, my God. She looked around her. What if she was too late?

"She was in Phoenix the first day of Ellen's trial…" She stopped, giving her heart time to slow to its normal speed.

"The day Randi and Zack's son was taken," Greg said quietly.

"In the photo of you outside the court building, Matt was holding Randi's son, right?" Caroline continued. "I saw a picture on the Internet news that night."

Everyone stood at once, as though ready to run out the door. "She thought Billy was Calvin," Tory said.

"We have no way of knowing if she's even in Arizona," Greg cautioned, but he'd unclipped the phone from his belt.

"She is," Caroline said, feeling cold all over. "I just saw her again—outside the Psychology building." She turned to Phyllis. And started to cry. "I'm so sorry," she said. "I couldn't remember who she was. Until now, listening to Matt. I remembered seeing her photo in an old article about Matt's trial…."

Greg was on the phone, giving orders. Caroline could hear him. Was aware of the urgency in everyone's movements. But all she could see was her sister.

"Don't be sorry, Caroline," Phyllis said, tears in her own eyes as she gave her a hug. "You might just have saved Calvin's life."

Or lost it for him, Caroline added to herself, afraid to look at John, to see confirmation of her worst fears.

On that one, only time would tell.

CHAPTER SEVENTEEN

JOHN FOLLOWED Caroline to Mrs. Howard's place to drop off her car. Then, with the older woman's blessing, he took Caroline home for the night. Whether news came or not, he didn't want her left alone. Regardless of what anyone said, she was eaten up with guilt. She'd been through too much lately, was asking too much of herself for a woman who was pregnant and on her own. She didn't look well.

"Really, I'm okay," she insisted. "I can stay in my room." But he knew it was a lie, because she was sitting in his car, on the way to his house, before she voiced that argument.

John didn't bother to answer.

Once home, he led her straight to his room. It was the only one with sheets on the bed.

"I shouldn't stay here," she said, standing in the doorway with drooping shoulders and a halfhearted wariness.

"The bed's made," he said from right behind her. "And you're exhausted."

Caroline nodded, picked up her toiletries and asked if she could use the bathroom.

John pointed to the arch on the opposite side of the room. It opened into a bathroom suite the likes of which she'd probably never seen before. What had seemed commonplace when he'd showed his friends around his new house a couple of years before was now an opulent embarrassment to him. Why on earth had he thought he needed a jetted tub? He took showers; he hadn't taken a bath since he was ten.

He was suddenly picturing Caroline in there with bubbles foaming around her swollen breasts, her legs falling open…

No, he wasn't going to do that.

Especially not tonight. What kind of sick pervert was he? Lusting after a woman who was exhausted, sick with worry, pregnant.

He wasn't only not going to do that *tonight*, he wasn't going to do it ever. Not with Caroline. She couldn't be a momentary fling. Or a six-month fling. Or even a year's fling. She was his daughter's mother. A fling with his daughter's mother would be far too complicated.

Besides he…

"You have metal things sticking out of your tub."

"They're jets."

She nodded, as if she'd known that all along. "I saw a whirlpool once, last winter, when I went to Frankfort."

The weekend they'd met.

"The jets didn't seem to protrude quite so much."

He'd seen the spa by the pool on her floor that next morning, when he'd left her room just after dawn. "Those were plastic, not chrome."

A little boy was missing. They were two damaged human beings who were going to have a baby. And they were talking about spa jets.

"Well," Caroline said, standing there in her jeans and white top. "One thing's for sure. If Sara and I ever find ourselves homeless, we can camp out in your bathroom and have enough space for every single one of our possessions."

Her grin was weary, but still a grin. John almost hugged her.

Until he remembered that he didn't want to. And that she didn't want him to.

"I'm just going down the hall to my office to check e-mail. You get into bed. I'll be back later to check on you," he said.

"You'll keep your cell phone on, right?" she asked. It was the number Phyllis had said she'd call.

"Of course."

"Okay. Good night."

She hadn't asked where he was going to sleep.

John closed the door softly behind him and walked slowly down the hall. Did that mean she expected him to climb in beside her at some point? After she was asleep?

Or did she expect him to make up a bed in one of the guest rooms on the other side of the house?

He could go back and ask. Or he could just wait until later and figure it out for himself. Once he knew what he wanted the answer to be.

If he ever knew.

John tended to his e-mail. He drank his beer. Watched a rerun of his favorite law show. He checked on Caroline. Checked his cell phone. Changed from slacks to sweatpants and an old T-shirt.

And eventually, when he was too tired to think anymore, he lay down beside the mother of his child and fell asleep.

THE RINGING OF THE TELEPHONE woke them. Recognizing the ring as he rose to consciousness, John was confused. Who was his arm around?

"John?" Caroline's voice brought it all back to him. He jumped out of bed, away from her, and grabbed the phone.

Calvin had been found. He'd been thrown from a car as his abductor attempted to elude capture by off-roading up the side of a mountain outside town, where they'd been hiding in a cave. He was hurt, but the extent of his injuries wasn't known. He was being transported to the Shelter Valley clinic, where the town's emergency trauma team would be waiting, and if necessary, he'd be flown by helicopter to Phoenix. Everyone was gathering at the clinic to offer Matt and Phyllis support.

John told Tory he'd bring Caroline and hung up. If anyone was alert enough to wonder why he suddenly seemed to know Phyllis's student more personally than any of the rest of them did, they certainly weren't going to say. At the moment, anything but Calvin's life was inconsequential.

"HE'S LOST A LOT OF BLOOD" were the first words Caroline heard as she and John arrived at the clinic at five after six in the morning. She'd changed her clothes, but neither she nor John had taken time to shower. An intern was there speaking with a shocked-looking Phyllis and Matt. Both were still dressed in the clothes they had on the day before. Caroline had a feeling neither one of them had slept.

"We've alerted the blood bank in Phoenix."

Having come in in the middle of the conversation, Caroline caught only enough to know that her nephew was being flown out, which meant that he was critical. And without warning tears sprang to her eyes. She'd never met the little guy and she loved him as if he were her own.

Medical staff were coming in and out of an open door halfway down the hall, obviously where they had Calvin. She still didn't know the extent of his injuries.

Glancing back, Caroline saw Phyllis staring straight at her, noticing her tears. She needed to hug her so desperately, but after that one look, Phyllis was gone, surrounded by her family and friends as they ushered her in to see her son. Caroline stood for a moment and then, with a quick but insistent word to John to call her as soon as he knew anything, left the hospital and walked home.

From there she called Jesse and begged him to pray for his cousin's recovery.

"HEY, BUDDY, I didn't know you were still here."

John glanced up as Will Parsons, the lines around his eyes more pronounced than he'd ever seen them, approached the clinic's deserted waiting room.

"Yep." It wasn't much of an answer but was all John had.

Shortly after Phyllis and Matt had left for Phoenix, the others had all filed out. John had every intention of following them to the parking lot. He'd just never gotten around to standing up.

A couple of orderlies were still around, probably cleaning up from the morning's ordeal before locking up the trauma unit that was open only when needed.

Will dropped down into the seat next to him, long legs stretched out. John studied his friend, noticing that the silver in Will's temples was spreading. Most days, when Will was his usual commanding self at school or a star athlete on the golf course, it was hard to remember that he was pushing fifty.

"Tough morning." Will peered toward a scrub-covered young man with a mop, backing from the hall into the room that had held little Calvin Sheffield less than an hour before.

"Yeah." John's vocabulary seemed to be on hiatus with the rest of his functional skills.

"I just got off the phone with the *Arizona Republic*," Will said, almost conversationally. "Giving them the scoop. That student of Phyllis's was absolutely right. Shelly Monroe had him."

Though no one had said, mostly because all energy had been focused on saving Calvin's life, John had suspected as much.

"A couple of months ago, her twelve-year-old son was killed in a drive-by gang shooting outside their apartment complex," Will continued. "Out of her mind with grief, she came to Shelter Valley to look for Matt and found him married with a couple of kids. Apparently she's been shadowing them and somehow determined that Matt owed her a replacement for what she'd lost...."

John fully understood being out of one's mind with grief. He couldn't imagine committing a crime because of it, though. Because he hadn't suffered enough? Could that be in his future?

Or had there been something already askew in the young woman's life that had allowed her to behave so criminally?

"Looks like she'll be the one going to prison this time." Will shrugged. "Or at least a mental hospital if she's deemed to be insane."

John nodded, wondering how someone developed such a sense of entitlement that she could rationalize stealing someone else's kid. Wondered what horrible things might have happened to her as a child. If anything *had* happened to her.

"You need a ride?" Will's question was as offhand as the quick look he sent John.

"No."

"Didn't think so."

John nodded a second time. Rested his elbows on his knees with his hands clasped between them. Will wouldn't push him for explanations. It wasn't their way.

"How do you do it?" he asked.

Will frowned. "Do what?"

"You know, the whole love business. If you stick with it long enough, it's a sure loss. If it doesn't get you one way, it gets you another."

Will didn't say anything at first. When he finally spoke, he seemed to be agreeing with John. "If you make it through the car accidents and diseases and crimes and divorce, old age'll do it to you."

The tile beneath her feet, laid in twelve-inch squares, was a low-grade ceramic, probably over cement. "Right," John muttered.

"So then don't do it, don't love anyone, don't risk anything—what've you got?" Will sounded as though he was analyzing which club to use on a long-shot drive.

"Peace of mind."

"I don't find it particularly peaceful to think of facing the next thirty or forty years coming home to an empty house."

"And there's no guarantee you won't be doing just that," John said, unable to find a way past that truth. He'd *lived* it, dammit. Was still living it. He needed some kind of guarantee. "Look how close you were to losing Becca a few years ago."

Will sighed, crossed one leg over the other. "You're right."

They sat in silence, watching the orderly drag his mop bucket down the hall, into another room.

"So back to my original question," John said when he started to fear that Will was going to sit there until they'd solved this. Or at least until he was satisfied that John was satisfied. "How do you do it?"

"It's simple," Will told him, sitting forward to meet him eye-to-eye. "I have no choice. Love is there."

It wasn't the guarantee John needed.

A WEEK TO THE DAY after Calvin had disappeared, Phyllis Langford was back in class. Dressed in a bright yellow suit with her makeup impeccable and her auburn hair newly styled, you'd never have known that she'd just spent a week living in hell.

Her son had been released from the hospital a couple of days before, she told the roomful of students who'd been offering support to her and her family. As it turned out, there were no internal injuries and as soon as the doctors had stitched him up and placed a cast on his left arm, he'd begun to rally immediately.

The lecture was short that day, and Caroline heard very little of it, wondering instead if Phyllis would talk to her afterward, or in any way acknowledge that they'd progressed beyond student and teacher. In some ways she hoped not. She had her hands full trying to figure out what to do about John.

Or rather, her growing obsession with the man's phone calls. And his tangible reluctance to commit himself to anything beyond a surface reality.

Then, just as class was being dismissed and she'd have her answer as far as her sister was concerned, Caroline's cell phone vibrated from the pocket of her new drawstring black cotton capri pants. A quick glance told her Jesse was calling, and Caroline hurried from the room.

"Jesse? What is it? Is something wrong?" She could hardly breathe as she erupted out into the blinding sunshine of an eighty-five-degree day.

"Nah. You worry too much, Ma." Probably.

"I'm just calling to let you know I've thought it all through."

He'd told her he needed time. "Okay."

"And I've made my decision," he went on as though she hadn't spoken.

Dear God, could she hope this was just a dramatic offer of forgiveness to her for being his mother and getting "knocked up?" "What decision?"

"If you're going to insist on having this baby without marrying her father, I'm quitting school and coming out there…."

"No!" After a curious glance from a passing student, she lowered her voice, moving slowly away from the Psychology building where she'd been standing. "No, you're not, Jess. You're going to stay there, get fabulous grades and graduate from Harvard."

"In some ways, I wasn't like Dad at all, Ma, but in this I am his son. It's my duty to take care of you and I don't really care what you say. There's nothing you can do to stop me. It's what I have to do."

God in heaven, please help. "Listen, Jess—"

"I'm not going to listen, Ma. I've made up my mind. I've got to get to class now…"

"Jess!" she called urgently, afraid her son had already hung up.

"Yeah?"

"I won't try to change your mind, I promise."

"Okay. Thanks."

"Just promise me that you'll wait until this summer to make any final decisions." She scrambled for words, for coherent thoughts, to buy her some time. "Sara's not going to be here until August anyway."

"I'll think about it."

How could the sky be so blue, the sun so bright, when her world was threatening to crash down around her knees?

"Will you at least call me before you do anything?"

"Yes."

"You promise?"

"Yes."

It was the best she was going to get. Caroline hung up, entertaining a desperate notion—get John to pretend to marry her, just long enough to convince her son she didn't need him. For her children, she was ready to do anything.

"CAROLINE!"

The voice shot through Caroline's ears to her heart as she closed her phone and turned.

"I was hoping to catch you in class, but you'd already left," Phyllis said, hurrying toward her. "Got a minute?"

It was what she'd been hoping for. And dreading. A sign that she and Phyllis had progressed beyond the student/teacher level.

"Sure."

Carrying her satchel over one shoulder, Phyllis indicated a deserted and shady cement-mounted swing off in the distance. She didn't say anything more as she led the way through the grass, her heels traversing the hard desert ground without mishap.

John, where are you? Caroline had never been so unsure of herself. Birthing a breach calf in the middle of the night during a record-breaking winter storm she could handle. Making it through a conversation with her sister just might be too much.

Phyllis sat on one side of the bench, so she took the other, careful not to make it rock in case her sister didn't want to rock. Personally, Caroline loved rocking. She'd spent many, many difficult hours, her most difficult hours, rocking on that old swing back home.

She didn't know what to do with her bag, so she held it on her lap, and then felt self-conscious about its obviously homemade origins. At least her white three-quarter-sleeved blouse and pants and sandals were store-bought. And new.

"I just wanted to thank you," Phyllis said, her expression warm as she faced Caroline. "I'll never forget everything you did for us last week. From joining the search to figuring out that Shelly had to be the kidnapper…"

Tongue-tied, Caroline watched her sister, who didn't seem to have any problem with doing all the talking.

"And then…that work you did on Brad. Do you have any idea how much wasted effort you saved? He would've been our prime suspect and if we'd been looking for him, it would've given Shelly time to get out of town.…"

Caroline just smiled. Sort of. It was her best rendition at the moment.

Pausing, Phyllis blinked away the sheen of moisture in her eyes. "I knew for sure you were an angel sent from heaven when you spoke up about that girl. How on earth you noticed her in that picture, and then again, here, and put that together with a ten-year-old photo…"

Caroline had no answer for that. Except the truth.

"And as if that wasn't enough, the next day…"

Phyllis glanced off, the hands in her lap clenched so tightly her knuckles showed white. "I don't remember much about last Friday morning, but what I do remember is you being there, a virtual stranger, crying over my son's life." She turned back to Caroline. "All week long, I've been seeing that look on your face.…"

"It was nothing." Caroline finally found her voice long enough to defuse the situation before it exploded all over her. "Just a tough moment after a virtually sleepless night."

"In a very short time, you've proven to be a very good friend to me." Phyllis reached over, took Caroline's hand in her own, squeezed. And didn't let go.

With a chest expanding and contracting of its own accord, breath that designed its own rhythm, Caroline stared at those clasped hands. And noticed the opal ring on her sister's finger.

She couldn't do it anymore. Not any of it. She couldn't pretend. Couldn't hide. Couldn't hold on.

Tears filled her eyes—years' worth of tears. A lifetime of them. They were not small or graceful tears. They were big drops of water that fell from her eyes to the back of her sister's hand.

"What...?" Still holding Caroline's hand, Phyllis leaned forward, peering up at Caroline's bent head.

"What did I say?" she asked. "I didn't mean to hurt you, Caroline. I'd never do that."

"I...know." Her voice was as thick and wet and overflowing as the tears, making it almost impossible for her to speak.

"I don't think either of us is the type to allow an outside friendship to interfere with our teacher-student relationship," Phyllis said, as though she thought that might be what was causing Caroline concern. "I had Tory in class a couple of years ago and it worked out just fine. I taught Ben, too."

"I'm...not worried...about that." Caroline sniffed. And then again, inelegantly.

A tissue appeared and she took it. One-handedly blew her nose.

"So what's wrong?"

Lifting her head, she studied Phyllis's features and knew what she had to do.

With tears still falling, albeit more slowly, she said, "I'm going to tell you something. When I'm done, you might want me to quietly disappear. If that's the case, I will do so without a backward glance and you'll never hear from me again."

"There's nothing you could say that would make me want you to disappear." Phyllis's smile was full and generous, her eyes soft with an affection Caroline had dreamed of for months.

"You don't know that," Caroline said with a shuddering

breath, wondering if there was some way to make this easier. "You don't know anything about me."

Shaking her head, Phyllis gave her hand another squeeze. "I might not know the circumstances of your life," she said, "but I'm not the least bit worried about what you might have to—"

With a raised hand, Caroline silently asked Phyllis to stop. She couldn't listen to any more. Every word was going to be a nail in her heart if Phyllis needed her to go. And she had to be strong enough to keep her word and do as her sister asked if that should happen.

Phyllis's gaze was steadfast. The time had come. And Caroline couldn't find a single word.

Not knowing what else to do, she reached inside her blouse, found the chain nestled there and pulled. The hard, cool touch of the gold was familiar, a comfort. Holding out her palm, Caroline opened it, exposing the sapphire.

Phyllis frowned, watching her. She glanced at the ring and then at Caroline, her brows creased in confusion.

"This ring is supposed to tell me something about you that I'm not going to like?"

"No, not by itself." Life wasn't that easy. "My mother gave it to me." It was the truth. Twice. Grace had given it to her, having received it from Maureen Houseman.

"My mother gave me a ring, too," Phyllis said, holding out her right hand. "I wear it all the time."

Caroline nodded. And waited—simply because she had no idea what to do next. What to say.

"So, what are you telling me?" Phyllis finally asked. Her voice wasn't accusatory. Just confused.

"Your mother was Maureen Houseman."

The jerk of Phyllis's hand was slight but felt like an earthquake to Caroline. "How'd you know that?"

"I'm...um...related to her."

"You're related to my mother?" Ring hand suspended, Phyllis stared at her. "To *me?*"

Caroline nodded.

"How?"

In the end, it was simple. "We're sisters."

Phyllis didn't move. Didn't blink. Didn't smile. Nor did she jump up and run away.

"Older or younger?"

"You're older."

She shook her head. "No way. Even if I'd only been a year old, I'd have remembered my mother having a baby."

"You weren't a year old."

Phyllis stared, her heart in her eyes as a strange sort of recognition seemed to dawn—at least subconsciously. "How old was I?" Her voice was hoarse.

"Two minutes."

CHAPTER EIGHTEEN

"I'M SORRY." Phyllis wiped her tears, and her nose, with the back of her hand, staring at Caroline as though she'd never stop. And she hadn't. Not since she'd first heard the news. That had been over an hour ago.

"Don't be sorry," she whispered, touching her sister's hair, smoothing it away from her forehead. They'd said so much. And had so much more to say.

"But I am," Phyllis said, her brow creased with pain. "I feel so incredibly guilty. I got to know Mom and Dad. To be raised in a privileged upbringing, go to whatever college I chose...."

"And I have a mother who loves me as much as any mother ever loved her child," Caroline told her. "Even if she didn't particularly understand me."

"But..."

With a finger to Phyllis's lips, Caroline shushed her. "I can't live with regrets."

Phyllis pulled Caroline's ponytail around, running her fingers through the ends of it, smiling through her tears. "Your hair is so long...."

"Randy liked it that way."

"I do, too."

"I like yours short."

"I always hated the color of my hair."

"Really?" Caroline grinned at her twin. "I loved mine. It was different."

"And being different mattered?" Phyllis's eyes grew serious.

"I was already different," Caroline told her. "My hair was a difference I didn't have to hide."

"I HAVE A SON. His name's Jesse." They'd spent the past hour and a half talking about their childhoods and teenage years. Which, for Caroline, led to Jesse.

"A son?" Phyllis glanced around them as though, now that his name had been spoken, Jesse would magically appear. "Where is he?"

"He's seventeen and a student at Harvard."

"I have a nephew!" A huge smile accompanied Phyllis's words. "He's a genius and attending one of my old alma maters!" She sobered. "That's why you and Randy married so young."

Nodding, Caroline wondered when her worth was going to diminish in her twin's eyes. And how she was going to handle it.

"I CAN'T WAIT for you to meet Calvin and Clarissa. Wait until I tell him that it was his aunt who saved his life!"

"How do you think Matt's going to react?"

Phyllis gave her a hug, like the others she'd bestowed in the past hours, and Caroline soaked it up as though it were the first. She had a feeling every hug she received from her sister for as long as she lived would feel that way.

"Matt already loves you," she said softly in Caroline's ear. "Just as I do."

"So, YOU WANT TO TALK about twin studies?" Caroline asked sometime later when the first silence fell between them. She didn't know about Phyllis, but she was overwhelmed. With what had already happened, and all that was still to come.

"We have so much more to talk about," Phyllis said. "Not the least of which is this." She pointed down to Caroline's protruding stomach.

"I'm pregnant."

"I suspected as much. You don't have enough weight on you anywhere else for that to be the result of lazy living."

Caroline nodded, bent her head.

"You said your husband died last summer."

"That's right."

"So it's a pretty sure bet the baby isn't his."

Caroline wanted to die. Phyllis's reception of her had been more than she'd ever dared dream. And now, so soon, she had to step down in her sister's eyes.

"That's right."

She felt Phyllis's finger under her chin, lifting her face. "It's okay," Phyllis said. "This isn't some small Kentucky town stuck in the Dark Ages. This is the twenty-first century and unmarried women have babies all the time."

"It wasn't planned."

"That's what I figured."

"It was a one-night fling."

"Caroline." Phyllis smiled, raising her hand to kiss the back of it, holding it against her cheek. "In all that research you did about me, you must've missed something kind of important." She made a face. "Not that I'd want this particular information broadcast, you understand."

"What?"

"Calvin and Clarissa are the result of a one-time fling—on the sound board in the recording studio at Montford. I'd just met Matt that day…."

"You're kidding!" Caroline started to laugh. And to cry.

She had no idea where life would lead her, but she had a pretty good idea that wherever it was, she wouldn't be going there alone.

At least not in spirit.

THE LAST THING John expected when he pulled into his driveway Thursday at dinnertime was to see Caroline sitting on his front porch. He'd missed her truck parked across the street.

"What's up?" he called, leaving his car in the driveway.

"Just wanted to talk for a minute, if that's okay," she said, her usual timidity mixed with a glow he didn't recognize at all.

"Sure," he said, but his chest was tight as he led her inside. Something was going on and he was still trying to figure out how to deal with what he already knew. His discomfort was not diminished by the fact that he'd been thinking about calling her.

Or by the little spark of pleasure he'd felt when he'd first seen her sitting there, looking cute in a pair of black cotton pants and a white blouse. She still didn't wear makeup, but he was used to that now. He actually liked it.

As though from long habit, she took her seat at the counter in his kitchen while John poured her a glass of juice.

"I have some big news," she said.

"You're having twins." He was joking, of course, trying to introduce some levity.

His heart dropped when she didn't immediately express her horror at such a thought.

"No," she said. "That would've showed up on the ultrasound."

He'd forgotten about that.

"But, as a matter of fact, this does have to do with twins."

She seemed different. And that was making him nervous as hell. "What do you mean?"

"I am one."

"You're one what?"

"A twin."

"You said you were an only child."

"I also said I'm adopted."

True, she had.

He'd never seen her so full of energy. It was making him edgy. Either that or scaring him, and he preferred edgy.

"Maybe you should start at the beginning."

And when she did, John wished she hadn't. In a way, the story was too fantastic to believe. And in another, it all made perfect sense. A far-too-intelligent woman trapped in a life that was suffocating her, in some backwoods town, grieving and alone. That woman finding a new lease on life, a new identity and doing everything she could to learn about her new life. It explained her obsession with the computer. Her Internet research skills.

"That's why you came to Frankfort. On account of Phyllis." A part of him wanted her to deny it.

"Yes."

"You were using me to get to her." He didn't love Caroline Prater. Didn't feel anything for her, other than concern because she was pregnant with his child. Being used didn't matter.

The light that had been shining in her eyes since he'd first come home now dimmed. "John, it wasn't like that."

It seemed pretty clear to him that it was. And really, this wasn't a bad thing. He'd been worried about doing something ludicrous like starting to care for her. This nipped that little problem in the bud.

"Can you honestly tell me you didn't approach me with hopes of making some kind of contact, no matter how third-party, with your sister?"

Her eyes dropped and he knew he had her. He was free. He'd won.

So why didn't he feel like celebrating?

SHE SHOULD HAVE STAYED. Should have fought for herself. Fought harder for their friendship. All the way home, Caroline's inner self berated her.

And what could she have said? asked the woman who'd lived in Grainville all her life. He was right. She'd gone to him with one purpose in mind. To be close, however vicariously, to her sister.

She could've told him all that had changed at some point during their dinner together in Frankfort. Except then she'd be acknowledging her feelings toward him—attraction at least—and that wasn't their story about what had happened. They'd both been lonely, grieving, dreading the holidays. There'd been nothing personal. That was the version they'd recounted to each other and to anyone else they needed to tell.

So, this division between them was for the best. Life had been getting too complicated. She'd slept in his bed one night the week before and missed it every night since. She thought of things to tell him all day long. And dreamed about that one kiss they'd shared not long ago...

Pulling up in front of Mrs. Howard's, she laid a hand on her belly.

Sara would have her daddy. And Caroline would have her life. It was all working out just fine.

PHYLLIS CALLED a little after seven to invite Caroline over for dinner. And to move in with them.

Laughing, Caroline told her she had studying to do, but accepted an invitation to spend the weekend with her sister's family, giving them a chance to get to know each other before they made any other offers.

The second time the phone rang, she grabbed it instantly, hoping it was John.

"Caro?"

The bottom dropped out of her stomach when she heard the tears in her mother's voice. "Hi, Ma. What's wrong?"

"He's drinking again, Caro. Not just two or three like before you left, but all the time. He broke Gram's old rocker last night, stumbling to the table for supper."

While her mother loved that old rocker, she wouldn't have called just because of that. She wouldn't have spent money on a long-distance call unless something life-threatening had happened.

"He hit you today, didn't he?" she asked, her throat tight with anger. And fear.

She might be different from her adoptive mother, but she loved Grace with all her heart. And in spite of his illness, she loved her father, too.

"Y-y-yesss…"

Without any conscious awareness that she'd been considering it for weeks, Caroline made her decision.

"It's okay, Ma, I'll come home. You go over to Mrytle's and stay until I get there. And don't worry, we'll get help for Pop. He'll be okay again, just like before."

"I know you don't understand, Caro, but I love him so.…"

"I do understand, Ma," she said softly. "I love him, too."

And if she was going to be the type of woman her sister could admire, the type of woman *she* could admire, she'd have to listen to her heart and do what she knew was right.

With tears streaming down her face, Caroline pulled out her old bags and began filling them methodically. She'd go see Phyllis tonight; she couldn't bear to leave without one more hug. She'd tell Mrs. Howard in the morning, just before she left. And call Montford to withdraw from her classes. If she drove twelve hours a day, she could make it home by Monday. She hoped her father wouldn't go beating down Mrytle's door before then.

But if he was running true to form, he'd be on his best behavior for the next few days. He'd always been that way after he hit either one of them.

And then there was Jesse to consider. If she was home in Grainville, with her parents, and Randy's family, and all her friends who—once they'd recovered from their initial shock over what she'd done—would look after her, he'd stay in school.

Her family needed her. She had to be there for them. It was all she knew how to do. It was who she was. It was who her sister would expect her to be.

And if a small part of her was running away from a man who wanted for her what she'd always wanted for herself— to have the right to live the life she felt meant to live, to speak her mind and quit tempering her strengths—then so be it. John might want those things for her, but she was kidding herself if she thought he'd ever be available to insure that she got them. He wasn't going to join the living again.

When he'd buried his young wife, he'd dug his grave right beside Meredith's.

She had to get as far away from him as possible before she made the biggest mistake of her life and fell in love with a man who would never love her back.

HER FIRST MONTH HOME, Caroline ached so badly she wasn't sure she'd ever recover. The only joy in her life, other than the small flutters she was occasionally feeling, were her phone conversations with her sister. Phyllis called every other day. Without fail.

"John was shocked that you'd left," Phyllis had told her the first week. The night before she'd gone home, she'd confessed to Phyllis that John Strickland was Sara's father.

"Shocked that I left without telling him, maybe," Caroline had returned, an unusual bitterness entering her voice. Maybe she *had* gone to Frankfort to meet him that first time because of Phyllis, but she certainly hadn't made a baby to get close to her sister.

The jerk should have been able to figure that out.

After this particular conversation, Phyllis never mentioned John to her again.

Which didn't stop Caroline from thinking about him all the time. She'd thought they were friends. Real friends.

Friends didn't send checks in the mail to cover the expenses of having a baby. Friends attended doctor's appointments and made plans for childbirth classes.

But then, perhaps the fault was hers. In spite of all the warnings he'd given, all the protestations she herself had made, she'd begun to think of John as more than just a friend.

HE DIDN'T WANT TO GO. The annual end-of-term barbecue at the Parsons's home was something he'd looked forward to last year. He and Lauren had officially announced their wedding date that night. He'd supposed his coming marriage would bring him the peace and contentment his friends all seemed to feel. Instead, the announcement had only increased the sensation of a rope tightening around his throat.

One beer into this year's event, he stood out in Will's barbecue gazebo, where he'd wandered hoping for a few minutes of less frenetic energy. Keeping his friend company while he cooked, John glanced over at the redheaded woman who'd followed him, a determined glint in her eye.

"Her son is staying at Harvard for the summer session," she told him.

He nodded, hoping Phyllis would take the hint and go away. Caroline Prater's life was no business of his.

"Her father's still drinking."

"Maybe they should take him to AA."

"They have. It's taking longer this time, but she won't give up on him."

That sounded like her.

Docile on the surface she might have been, but underneath, Caroline Prater was made of steel.

"The doctor says the baby's growing just fine."

He nodded, already in possession of that information. Carolyn had written a short note when she'd first returned to Grainville, giving him both her contact information and that of her doctor. He'd figured it was her way of keeping their agreement to allow him involvement in his daughter's life.

In any case, he'd called the doctor immediately, and he did so after every appointment.

"She's hoping, after Sara's born, to enroll in a community college about fifty miles from the farm. She likes their daycare facility."

And would she be driving that old truck fifty miles each way through winter storms?

"She put an ad in a Louisville paper, trying to find someone to run the farm for her until she gets back on her feet."

John spun to the side, facing Phyllis directly. "What do you want from me?" The question was delivered more harshly than he'd intended.

His friend didn't flinch. "What do you want for yourself?" she asked, then turned and walked away.

Just like a damned psychologist, full of questions but offering no answers.

SHE'D HAD NO RIGHT to take his unborn child so far away from
him. About the only contact he could possibly have with his
daughter at this point was her heartbeat at the end of a stethoscope and she'd robbed him of that. She'd had no right. Sara
was as much his child as hers.

She had no right to take his unborn child away....

The litany got John to the airport, down the jetway to his
seat, through the car rental line and down the long, deserted
country road into Grainville. He drove through the town and
back out the other side to take another long, deserted country road to the address she'd given him more than four weeks
before.

She had no right to take his unborn child away propelled
him down the dirt path that served as her driveway, out of his
car and up the rickety wood steps to her peeling front door.

He raised his hand to knock. Hesitated.

She had no right to take—

"John?"

He swung around. Dressed in the flower-stitched denim
outfit he'd seen her wearing the day she'd come from shopping in Phoenix, with her hair up in its usual ponytail, Caroline was sitting on an old porch swing that looked like it
might break at any moment.

"You had no right to take my unborn child so far away
from me."

Smooth, Strickland.

"I know. I probably wouldn't have done it, but my family
needed me."

And he didn't. And her family came first. He understood
both facts.

"I let you down." It was hard for him to admit.

"No, you didn't."

"Yes, I did. I took the first out you gave me."

"You were honest with me from the beginning."

The Kentucky air was cool compared to Arizona, yet it felt oppressively warm.

"I told you what I needed to believe at the time. I don't know anymore if it was right."

He wanted to sit down. To ask for a glass of iced tea. Or a piece of pie. The place called for it—and for all the other things that he was sure had gone on here for years and years. Family things. Bonding things. Real things.

Grainville was in the middle of nowhere. A backward town. Lacking money and success and class. But it was peaceful. There was a sense of life, of continuity, as though things didn't end, the way they did in his world. Even the dust held memories.

It seemed to remember the footsteps of her husband, the laughter of her son, the wail of a cow giving birth.

He was tired. Losing his mind.

"Can I get you some tea? I made some this morning. I got it out just as the sun was coming up so it's steeped just right."

"That sun tea you told me about? Yes, I'd like some, thank you."

He waited outside, standing there on her warped wood porch, an interloper, on the outside of something he couldn't see into. Something bigger than he'd ever known before.

The glass was an old gas station giveaway with advertising on the side. And the tea, when he took a sip, was the best he'd ever tasted.

"Why are you here?" She was leaning against the rail—a rickety, splintered rail. He was ready to grab her if she started to fall.

"I don't know." He'd just flown across the country. That seemed to call for honesty, if nothing else.

"I have a guest room. You can stay there if you want."

"Thank you." Was he staying? Did he want to stay? He had no idea. Yet he was relieved to know there was a place for him.

He finished his tea. Asked about her father. About her last doctor's appointment. How she'd been feeling. If she'd been tired, like the doctor had predicted she might be.

He told her about a project he'd won in Denver. A signature building downtown.

"I wonder who that is." Caroline was looking toward the road. A car was approaching. He wouldn't have noticed, or considered that one might know or want to know every car that passed.

Apparently it was an unusual enough happening, or there was little enough going on here, that Caroline paid attention to passing cars.

A nondescript sedan turned into the driveway, pulled up and stopped.

"Phyllis?" Caroline ran down the steps so fast he was afraid she was going to trip. "What are you doing here?"

He could have reiterated the question, but it wouldn't have been in quite that delighted tone of voice.

He didn't hear Phyllis's initial response. The two women were hugging as though it had been years instead of weeks since they'd seen each other. But he got the gist of it a couple of minutes later when the three of them settled with glasses of tea in Caroline's old, but spotlessly clean, kitchen.

That was after his good friend had deposited her bags in Caroline's guest room. Which had been offered to him…

"I'm surprised to see you here." She didn't pull any punches as she settled across the table from him, a glass of cold tea in her hands.

"Same here."

She hadn't mentioned that she was coming.

But then, neither had he.

CHAPTER NINETEEN

PHYLLIS TURNED to Caroline. "You and I have a birthday to celebrate in another couple of weeks and since we missed the first thirty-four, I'm not missing this one. And I'm planning to be with you when you have that baby," she said. "If it's going to be here, fine. Matt's perfectly happy to bring the twins for a summer in Kentucky."

And where did Phyllis think they'd all fit? John wondered, a trifle sourly. It wasn't like there was a Hilton or even a Motel 6 anywhere close.

He was the one on the rescue mission here.

Even if it had taken him a damn sight too long to figure that out.

Thanks to Phyllis, he didn't have another chance to speak privately with Caroline before dinnertime. He'd hoped the Psychology professor would be tired and need to rest. Or at least go and unpack her bags.

Phyllis hadn't even excused herself to visit the bathroom.

He'd flown more than three-quarters of the way across the country, to a deserted little farm in Podunk, Kentucky, and couldn't find one second for a private word with the mother of his child.

Just before dinner, an engine roared in Caroline's driveway. John had been there long enough to figure out that if you heard a car, Caroline was having company.

What now? It was bad enough having Phyllis there without facing another human challenge in his path. Selfishly, he had preferred it when Caroline was in Shelter Valley, where he'd had her to himself.

Yet he had to acknowledge the reassurance of knowing so many people cared. Even if he let her down, she'd be okay.

She didn't need him.

Good for her.

He didn't like that.

"Carrrooollll Llllyynnn?" The bellow was deep, slurred and singsong with drunkenness. John's hackles rose.

No one moved as heavy steps sounded outside on the porch. Caroline flinched when the visitor stumbled. And continued up to the door.

"Carrrolllll…"

"I'm here, Pop."

John stiffened as he heard her call out to the obviously inebriated man. Her voice wasn't at all accusing, as his would have been, as he wanted hers to be. It was concerned. Worried, even. And filled with love.

She went to the front door, held it open and didn't even seem to notice as the unshaven man in stained overalls fell against her as she stepped over the threshold.

"Is that the pie from Ma?" she asked.

"Yeah." The old man looked down as though only just discovering that he was carrying something. "I believe it is."

"She sent you over with it three hours ago."

"Was it that long?" His voice, rising in question, had a tone of complete innocence.

"Yeah, Pop, it was that long ago. You stopped in town, didn't you?"

"I might've," the older man said, his booted foot catching on the edge of a throw rug in Caroline's tiny living room.

He righted himself with a grunt and a belch, barely managing to save the pie from becoming a floor decoration.

"But you promised you wouldn't do that, Pop," Caroline said patiently, taking hold of her father's arm to steady him as she guided him toward the kitchen. "You know how much it hurts Ma when you do that."

"Yeah," her father said, glancing down at her with remorseful eyes. "I don't wanna do that," he said, his voice slurred.

"I know you don't, Pop. So I'm going to ask you stay here for a while, have some coffee, sober up before you go home to Ma, okay?"

"Okay," the old man said, his voice trusting and docile. He loved his daughter, John saw.

And he loved his wife.

This man who, at times in his life, had beaten them both.

"I had a little drinnnk…" the man said. Looking sideways at Caroline he teetered. She reached for the pie, but was too late. It tipped. He tried to catch it, but his clumsy moves only sent the plate to the floor, where it splattered all over, a splash of glass and blueberry and flour crust, spraying her floor, her walls and even the side of the old tweed couch at the edge of her living room.

"Damn!" the man said, lurching. John jumped up, reaching out an arm as the man missed his step. But he was too far away.

"Pop!" Caroline's voice rang loudly and she did as John did, reaching out to the old man. Caroline was closer, her shoulder breaking her father's downward descent, and he righted himself.

She staggered a few steps and a second later, John was there, taking her father's weight. Ready to curse the old man to hell for the damage his foolishness could easily have done to his daughter and her unborn child.

But something held him back. An awareness, maybe. Of what, he didn't know. Or maybe he did. Caroline's dad was ill. But he was a good man. A loving man. He needed help. And Caroline needed to give it to him. And to believe in him.

John wanted to do the same.

"Let's get a rag to clean this up." Phyllis was already down on the floor, picking the biggest pieces of glass out of the mess. As John led Caroline's father to a chair at the table, Caroline moved toward the kitchen sink.

"Did I do that, Caro?"

"Yeah, Pop, but it's okay. We'll clean it up in no time."

"Don' tell your ma, girl. She'd be right mad with me. And I jus' get so upset when she does that."

"I know. I won't tell her, Pop."

She soaked a rag. Wrung it out. But before she could kneel down beside Phyllis, another car came down the driveway.

"That's Jesse's truck," Caroline said before she was anywhere near a door or window to have seen the vehicle.

"My grandson's home!" her father chortled. "Hallelujah!"

By the time Caroline had sidestepped the blueberry fiasco to make it to the front door, John could hear strong steps running up to the porch.

"Jesse? What are you doing here?" Caroline might have meant to sound reproving about her son's unexpected appearance, but her voice expressed only delight.

Even John could tell she'd missed her son unbearably. Almost embarrassed by the fervor with which she threw her arms around the six-foot-tall teenager as he came through the door, John tried to look away, to give Caroline privacy for this emotional reunion with her son. He couldn't do it.

Mesmerized by the obvious depth of love they shared, he stared as Jesse, instead of pushing his mother aside like most teenagers his age might have done, returned his mother's hug with the same intensity. The young man wrapped his arms closely around her and his words of greeting were muffled by their embrace.

The boy's dark hair was cut short, and he was easily twice the weight of his pregnant mother. Lean. Just big. John had a hard time accepting that this young man was Caroline's son. It didn't seem to fit.

And for the first time, he had a clearer idea of the man she'd loved and lived with for more than eighteen years. If his son was anything to go by, Randy had been a big man. One a woman could either feel immensely safe with—or scared to death of.

He knew which it had been with Caroline. She'd felt safe.

Jesse opened his eyes, spotting John over his mom's shoulder. He straightened. "Who's that?" he demanded, his shoulders back.

"Jesse!" Caroline's voice was full of warmth, love, happiness and a hint of reprimand. "Mind your manners."

"Sorry." The boy hung his head.

"Jesse." Caroline drew him forward. "This is John Strickland."

Hearing John's name, the boy's entire demeanor changed. Still defensive, his stance now also revealed a machismo that seemed entirely unnatural.

John held out a hand. "Hi, Jesse, it's good to finally meet you," he said. "Your mother's told me a lot about you."

Jesse ignored his hand. "You gonna marry my mom or not?" the boy asked.

"Jesse Randall Prater!" The voice was deep, not the least bit slurred and completely disapproving. "That is not our way."

"Sorry, Papa." Jesse's manner changed immediately as he turned back to John. "It's nice to meet you Mr. Strickland."

John almost preferred the belligerence. At least it was honest.

Before John could do more than nod, Caroline had her arm looped through Jesse's. "There's someone else I want you to meet," she said, urging Jesse toward Phyllis.

"Jesse, this is your aunt Phyllis. Phyllis, my son, Jesse."

"No kidding!" Jesse said, his smile huge and warm and obviously genuine as he stared at the red-haired woman who stood before him.

Phyllis's smile was easily as full as his. "You don't look much like your mom," she said.

"You do!" Jesse replied, coming forward to give Phyllis a hug. "Wow, this is so random!"

John wasn't sure what random meant, exactly, but it must be good.

"I have an aunt who graduated from Harvard, is a Psychology professor and even looks like my ma."

"You also have an uncle and a couple of cousins to meet," Phyllis said. She spent most of dinner regaling Jesse with tales of his two-and-a-half-year-old twin cousins while Caroline kept jumping up to make sure everyone had the food and condiments they wanted. John managed to keep Ed Prater's coffee cup full. Caroline had said earlier that she'd told Jesse about his grandfather's drinking—when she'd called to tell him she was moving home. He'd been sympathetic and had called her every day, but she'd been uncertain of her son's reaction if Ed hadn't dried out by the time Jesse came home. She needn't have worried. The young man had treated his grandfather with respect. Because he'd had practice with a father who drank?

"Won't your wife be missing you for dinner?" John asked Ed.

"Nah," the older man said. "I'm sure Caro called her and told her I'm here. She always does when I screw up. She never lets me leave until I'm sober enough so I don't screw up again when I get home."

And who, John wondered, protected Caroline while he was here? Did the man never "screw up" with her?

It was something he had to find out.

"What do you think of Phyllis?" John asked the older man after dessert, when he walked him out to his truck.

"I understand she's a friend of yours," Ed said.

"Yes," John nodded. "One of the best." Phyllis might have given him a kick in the butt that night at Will and Becca's party, but only the best of friends would have bothered to do so.

"She seems a good sort," Ed said, climbing into a truck as old and dilapidated as Caroline's. "Just hope she doesn't put such highfalutin ideas in Caro's head that she ain't happy here with us no more."

"That'll never happen," John said. It was the first thing he'd been completely sure of all evening.

By the time John was back inside, Caroline had gone back to have a bath and go to bed. Without even telling him goodnight.

"She was exhausted," Phyllis explained. "One unexpected guest is a big deal here, and she had three. Plus her father to deal with."

John nodded and glanced around, feeling awkward now that Caroline was gone. Jesse came in from the barn, where he'd gone to reacquaint himself with the place.

"At least Papa's done a decent job out there," he announced to no one in particular. "The stalls are all clean and in good repair. The used tractor he bought Ma last fall's been started recently."

John didn't know the first thing about working a farm. And he'd never been to Harvard, either.

"You can have my room, Mr. Strickland," Jesse said. "I'll sleep out in the barn."

"That won't be necessary." John didn't want to give the kid any more reason to resent him.

"No, really," Jesse said, grabbing a blanket and pillow from a hall cupboard. "Ma would kill me if I didn't and, believe me, a night in the barn is preferable to having her mad."

Intrigued, John was almost tempted to pursue the conversation further. Caroline mad was something he'd yet to see.

But he'd caused enough damage in this family for one lifetime. With a nod to Phyllis and Jesse, John retreated for the night, to a room filled with football and rodeo mementos. And pictures of a man and a woman—and a child in various stages of growing—that kept him up long into the night.

"I CAN'T BELIEVE IT" was Caroline's first thought as she sat up the next morning. It was after ten. She hadn't slept so late in years. Hadn't been able to sleep more than a couple of hours at a time since Randy died.

Dressing quickly in faded maternity jeans from her pregnancy with Jesse and an oversize yellow smock that, at sixteen, had been her favorite, she stepped into a pair of old and comfortably familiar boots, pulling her hair into its ponytail as she headed for the bathroom. Two minutes later, washed and brushed, she made it to the front room in time to cheer Phyllis on in a game of backgammon with Jesse. Aunt and nephew were carrying on as though they'd been family all their lives. And when Jesse won, John took the hot seat, giving her son a couple of games before winning the next three in a row.

Caroline hadn't been so happy in this house in years. She didn't kid herself that it was going to last. This was a time out of time. Everyone in that room, other than her, had other lives to get back to. They'd all be leaving, just as they'd all come. The three extra vehicles in the yard were testimony to that.

Still, as she sat on the sofa and laughed so hard her sides hurt, she couldn't help offering thanks.

That night, after a completely full day, including a long and wonderful visit with her parents but no time for a private conversation with John, Caroline said good-night and went to bed. Her parents had gone home, John was in Jesse's room, Jesse in the barn again and Phyllis was in the guest room. Her house—and heart—were full.

Which was why it made no sense that she couldn't find peace. Couldn't sleep. Her body was singing a tune she hardly recognized. A tune she'd only heard once before. One winter night in Frankfort. A night that had led her deep into trouble.

All day long it had been singing. Ever since she'd sat in the shadows on the porch swing the day before and watched the man she'd been thinking of appear before her eyes, almost as if she'd summoned him there.

Now, with him here in her house, the song was so loud she couldn't hear anything else.

After an hour of tossing and turning, she finally gave up, pulled on her favorite old sweats and a T-shirt and went out to the porch, to curl up on the swing that had always been a sacred place to her.

It wasn't empty. Caroline was halfway across the porch when she saw the shadow of a body there—and the old wood gently swinging.

"I'm sorry I took your place." His voice whispered through the night, increasing the tempo of the song inside her. It was driving her crazy.

"That's okay. It's a good spot. Most every trouble I ever had found its way there."

"Join me?"

She knew it was dangerous—not so much for the two of them, since they had plenty of chaperones. But for her, the heart inside her that was beginning to open and flower for the first time since she was seven years old.

"We need to talk," John said, "and with this houseful of people, we aren't going to get too many opportunities."

He was right. Though they could talk just as well with her perched on the porch rail. Or the step.

"I won't bite."

"I know." Rather than make a big deal out of nothing, Caroline joined him on the swing. Or at least, she told herself that was why she'd given in.

With a foot pushing gently against the uneven porch boards, John rocked them slowly. There was nothing quite like Kentucky night air in the spring. Chilly enough to cool heated skin, warm enough to be peaceful. It was too early in the season for lightning bugs, but also too early for mosquitoes. May had always been one of Caroline's favorite months.

"You must be finding all of this hard to take," she said, spreading her arms.

"I'm finding it different than anything I've ever known." A nice way of agreeing with her?

"You'd hate the slow pace."

"It's peaceful."

"And backward."

He pushed against the ground, his knee brushing her thigh, a touch Caroline felt all the way through her.

"Do you ever think about that night we made love?"

The question threw her completely off guard. "All the time." It was the truth, even if she'd never intended to share it with him. She wondered if he thought about it. Ever.

And wondered why he was there. How long he was planning to stay. If she'd see him again before Sara was born. Or after.

With one arm along the back of the swing, and the other resting easily by his side, John could have been the most relaxed man on earth. Caroline was so tense her muscles were hurting with the effort it took her to stay still. She braced herself, a hand on either side of her legs on the swing, and waited.

"I think we should get married."

She knew he'd said the words. She'd heard them. She just couldn't comprehend them. Or understand why he'd said them.

"It's an obvious and logical solution."

Not to her it wasn't. She wasn't ever going to marry again. And if she did, it would be to a man who was down on his knees with love for her, not one who was calmly swinging without so much as a hand on her shoulder.

What kind of marriage would that be?

"Say something."

"When Randy and I first got married, he was the strong one, the savior, the one with all the answers," she said slowly. "Then Jesse started to read when he was four. By the time he was ten, he was jumping grades in school. And I got my GED. Jesse would go to Randy for help with problems and Randy wouldn't know the answers. Jesse would come to me and I'd be able to help him. Jesse went to Randy for help less and less. And more and more Randy started to feel inferior. And the more insecure he felt, the more he used his physical strength, in voice, through intimidation, to show us he was still the head of the family. Eventually he gave up even that. By the time Jesse was sixteen, Randy kept to himself. And he drank. A lot." She stopped, remembering the number of times she'd sat on that very swing, crying, as she heard her sweet husband stumbling around lost and drunk in the house.

She could have gone to him, but her presence only seemed to hurt him.

"Why are you telling me this now?" John asked, his voice low.

"Because people from different classes, different backgrounds—different kinds of intelligence—can't merge." The words were hard to say. Because she knew them to be true. "Eventually their differences only tear them apart."

"Everyone's different," John said. "If we only married people just like us, think how boring life would be."

He had a point. But...

"It depends on the people and what they do with those differences," he continued. "That's something I've learned during these months with you."

She'd taught him something? "I had the impression that I irritated the heck out of you."

"I think I was more irritated by the fact that I thought about you far too often when I'd expressly decided not to."

Her heart started to beat faster. *He'd thought of her.* Like she'd thought of him? Anywhere close to that?

"At first I assumed your quiet ways were a sign of weakness, but now I see in them a strength that's beyond what most people are ever lucky enough to possess. You loved a man who was loyal to you and who loved you every day of his life. Even when you couldn't reach him anymore, you had the courage and strength to love him."

She'd had no choice. Randy was her husband, she his wife. She'd married him for better or worse. And she'd loved him. Where was the courage and strength in that?

"In a backwater town that puts more emphasis on how to grow crops and raise cattle than it does on book learning, you raised a son who won a full scholarship to Harvard. You followed your convictions to get an education when there wasn't one readily available. You have the citizens of two towns in love with you."

"Two small towns," she mumbled.

"And when you found out you had a twin sister, you—a shy country girl—found the courage to meet a big-city architect, just for the chance to make contact with someone who knew her sister."

She turned her head, glancing at him. Though her eyes had adjusted to the darkness, she couldn't make out his shadowed expression. "You were angry that I'd used you."

"I was desperate for an excuse to put some distance between us."

Facing forward again, Caroline gripped the edge of the swing so tightly she was sure she was getting splinters.

"Your heart is closed," she said. "You can't commit yourself because you're afraid to risk loss." These were all things they'd been over before. How could he possibly suggest marriage? It wasn't possible for the people they were.

"There's not much peace in going home to an empty house for the next forty or fifty years." He paused. "That's what my friend Will said."

Glancing over again, she whispered, "There's no guarantee you won't be."

"And that," he murmured, "is what I said. But Will was right."

She couldn't do this. Couldn't hope, or allow the song inside her to break free. She had a family to think about. A life ahead of her. A son. A new baby to raise. She had to keep her heart intact.

And if she listened to this man, believed him, she'd be giving her heart to him to break. He was so shut off, so scared of losing again, he wouldn't be capable of doing anything else.

"I think there are guarantees."

His words shocked her. "What?" She already knew there weren't. Tragedies happened. Illness happened. It was all part of life. That knowledge didn't stop her from living. In a way, it added significance to life and to love because she appreciated every single day, but there were no guarantees that the next day would be just as good, just as full.

"Look at this house," John said. "It's small and old and certainly not valuable by the world's standards, but there's more life here than in any place I've ever lived. Even when you were here alone."

Maybe.

"But more than that, look at it now. Busting at the seams with people who love and support you. You lost Randy. Jesse moved away. I let you down. And your house is still full of people who're determined to be there for you."

Tears burned her eyes, tightened her throat.

John lowered his arm from the back of the swing, slid his fingers beneath her hand, prying her grip from the edge. "Loved ones die," he said, his voice no less intense for its softness, "but the guarantee is that love doesn't. It lives on in our hearts for those who are gone, and it lives on in our lives through those who are left."

Her chest was so full Caroline couldn't say a word. She could hardly think past the sentiment he was expressing, the truth of which rang more true to her than anything she'd ever heard.

"Look at all the traumas we've been witness to in the past couple of months," he continued, his conviction clearly so much more solid than any doubts he'd ever uttered. "Ellen's trial. James's death. Calvin's disappearance. Your coming home. But no one was alone. Everyone was surrounded by a love that gave them the strength to take one more breath, one more step, and get to the next, better day."

She squeezed his hand. He was a good man. A great man. One who had the courage to face his fears. And maybe even find a way beyond them.

"We don't love each other." She couldn't marry him. As much as she wanted to, she couldn't do that. If her life with Randy had taught her nothing else, it had taught her that love was the most important ingredient in any relationship. When all else had failed with them, the love had kept her going.

"Don't we?"

Well, she loved him, of course. Ridiculously. Madly. But...

"Do we?" She was still staring straight ahead.

With one finger, John turned her face toward him. "I love you, Caroline Prater, enough to turn me inside out."

"Me, too," she whispered, tears dripping slowly down her cheeks.

John's hand curved around the back of her head as his face came closer. "I need to hear you say the words," he whispered against her lips.

"I love you, John Strickland, enough to turn my whole self inside ou—"

His lips covered hers and the world really did evaporate around her. Sweet peace settled in Caroline's heart, spreading in a circle that grew larger and larger, filling up every part of her.

Opening her mouth to him, she taunted and teased, expressed her hunger openly, honestly, begging him for all the things she'd been denied all these months. And just as she was about to beg for more, she felt a jab where her waist used to be.

"What was that?" John asked, pulling away from her.

She grabbed his hand, laid it on her expanded belly. And waited.

"Oh, my God…" The awe in his voice brought tears to her eyes again. Ecstatic tears. Tears that, for as long as she lived, would never fully dry.

She'd found John. She'd found love. She'd found her guarantee.

EPILOGUE

SHELTER VALLEY MAYOR Becca Parsons stood in her living room on the third Friday night in June, feeling a bit nostalgic, somewhat subdued and honestly happy.

Her sister-in-law Randi and Randi's husband, Zack, were deep in conversation with Sam and Cassie Montford about something. Probably pets. Randi had taken over the university's pet-therapy club and had expansion ideas.

"The cake and presents are all set up in the sunroom," Martha Marks whispered behind her. Martha seemed so much lighter these days, now that the trial was behind them— Ellen's rapist convicted and in prison.

Becca nodded her thanks, watching as Caroline Prater and John Strickland, hand in hand, slowly traversed the large room, stopping to speak with everyone they passed. Currently they were with the Nielsons and Greg and Beth Richards. Looking fabulous in navy evening dress, they were there for a combination wedding and baby shower before their wedding the next day.

Or so Caroline thought.

"He's going to be happy." Martha's next words were spoken beside her.

"I think so, too," Becca said, and then looked at her closest friend. "I was really disappointed when it didn't work out for the two of you."

"I know." Martha smiled, looking radiant in her black cocktail dress as she watched the soon-to-be-married couple. "Me, too. But now…"

Martha had found her magic in David—the untraditional preacher they'd all grown to adore.

The wedding couple were speaking with the bride's parents, two of the most sincere people Becca had ever met. She'd heard they'd had quite a time in Phoenix the day before picking out the new dress and suit they were wearing.

"Funny how life works, isn't it?" Martha said now. "You think you know what you want, you try to make it happen, and you resent fate when things don't work out the way you planned. Then, after you give up trying to be in control, fate gives you something better than you'd ever dreamed was out there."

"Good to know there's a force that's stronger than us watching out for everyone, huh?" Becca half teased her friend who, until a year ago, had considered herself a woman without faith of any kind.

Martha nudged her and Becca had to go to the door again, this time to welcome Phyllis and Matt Sheffield and Tory and Ben Sanders, all looking splendid in party attire. Tory and Phyllis both wore floor-length navy gowns, though Tory's was tighter than Phyllis's.

"I thought you'd be the first ones here," Becca said, leaning forward to give Phyllis a hug. Phyllis had recently cashed in the stocks from her divorce settlement and bought a small cottage in Kentucky, not too far from Caroline's farm.

"I wanted to give her time to make her own way among her new friends," Phyllis said. "But don't worry, Tory and I will be in place in a couple of minutes."

Dressed in black slacks and a white shirt with the sleeves

rolled up, Will joined Becca at the door. "I think we're set." His hand slid into hers.

Becca stole a second to smile up at him. "Five years ago I never would've believed…"

"Shh," Will said, placing a finger gently against her lips. "We're blessed, Becca. We needed the hard times to fully appreciate the good times. To really value what we have. Just think what a waste it would've been to go through life and not feel this gratitude every single day…."

She smiled, almost unaware of the noise and conversations and well wishes all around them as she turned to her husband. "I love you, Will Parsons," she whispered, and couldn't quite hold back the tears that sprang to her eyes.

"And I love you, Becca."

"Okay, if you two are ready, I think everything's—oh, sorry," David Marks came from the room behind them. "Didn't mean to interrupt."

Becca moved into the throng in the living room, searching for her comrades in arms, the sound of Will's laughter ringing behind her.

"Ladies and gentlemen, may we have your attention, please?" she called a couple of minutes later in her most mayoral voice. "If you'd all move into the next room, we have a surprise for you."

She sought out Phyllis and Tory, who nodded, and then watched as Caroline and John walked together into the middle of the crowd. John turned, caught Becca's eye with a grateful look, then smiled and turned back just as the music started.

And Caroline stopped.

"It's the 'Wedding March,'" she said as the entire room fell silent, waiting for her to catch up with the rest of them.

"We didn't want you to settle for a short ceremony in a judge's chamber," John told his wife-to-be. "Look."

They were standing at the door to the formal dining room, which had been turned into a beautiful wedding chapel complete with six pews, steps, an altar and more flowers than Becca had had at her own wedding.

"Ma? May I do the honors?" Caroline's son Jesse appeared at her side, dressed in a dark brown suit, offering his elbow.

Caroline gazed at the circle of people around her, then slid her arm through her son's and walked regally up the aisle to become one of them.

Becca had a feeling that the backwoods farm girl had finally caught a glimpse of herself as the princess she'd always been.

"They've got it made," Will said softly beside her. "Summers in Kentucky, the rest of the year here..."

"We all have it made," Becca whispered back as David Marks stood at the pulpit in front of them. "Shelter Valley has known its share of heartache, but it always comes down to this, doesn't it?"

"Comes down to what?" Will asked, leading her to their seats in the last pew.

"The union of hearts," Becca told him.

Holding her husband's hand, she silently repeated the wedding vows they'd taken more than twenty-five years before, reflecting on what had been, and on what was still to come.

And when the ceremony was finished and Caroline walked radiantly down the aisle, Becca was the first to step forward and welcome the newest member of the Shelter Valley Heroines.

They were women who knew what mattered most in life. Women who weren't afraid to fight for what they wanted, or give up what they didn't want. Women who were loyal, who'd known their share of fear and who didn't quit.

No matter what life handed them, they'd survive.
Because love was stronger than life.
And the heroines of Shelter Valley knew that.

* * * * *

If you enjoyed SOMEBODY'S BABY,
you'll love HIDDEN,
Tara Taylor Quinn's new novel
from MIRA Books. HIDDEN
is available in July 2005.

Turn the page for an excerpt from HIDDEN,
an exciting and emotionally involving
story about a woman who goes into hiding
to protect herself—and her little boy.

1

San Francisco Gazette
Tuesday, April 5, 2005.
Page 1

Single Socialite Disappears.

Leah Montgomery, one of the country's most sought-after and elusive heiresses, was reported missing by her brother, San Francisco attorney, Adam Montgomery, and sister, Carley Winchester, in San Francisco last night after she failed to attend the two-hundred-dollar-a-plate orphaned children's fundraiser she'd spent the past six months organizing. The thirty-one-year-old was last seen yesterday at 3:20 p.m. leaving Madiras where, according to the upscale salon's owner, Samantha Ramirez, Montgomery received her weekly massage and manicure and had her hair cut and styled, in preparation for that evening's event.

Again according to Ramirez, Montgomery had been planning to wear a black satin gown with red lace trim. Late last night, when police searched Montgomery's penthouse and condominium, they found a dress matching that description hanging from one of the two showerheads in the woman's shower. Montgomery's white Mercedes convertible is also missing.

There are no leads in the case, though police are rumored to be questioning California's newest state senator, attorney Thomas Whitehead, who was to have been Montgomery's escort at last night's fundraiser. Whitehead was elected to the Senate last fall, just fourteen months after his seven-months'-pregnant, fashion-designer wife, Kate Whitehead, disappeared without a trace. Before her disappearance, Mrs. Whitehead was frequently seen in the company of her longtime best friend, Leah Montgomery.

"Mama! Mamama!"

Shaking, heart pounding so hard she could feel its beat in her ears, Tricia Campbell lowered the newspaper enough to peer over the top at her eighteen-month-old son. She could see him sitting there in his scarred wooden high chair in their modest San Diego home, pajamas covered with crumbs from the breakfast he'd long since finished, wispy dark curls sticking to the sides of his head. Could smell the plum jam he'd smeared all over his plump chin, cheeks and fingers. And she could definitely hear him....

"Mamamama! Down!" The baby, pounding his clenched fists on the stained tray of his chair, was working up to a frustrated squall.

The paper fell to Tricia's lap. She stared at her son, seeing him as though from afar—as though he belonged to someone else. The little boy was almost the entire sum of her existence—certainly the basis of every conscious decision she'd made in the past two years—and she couldn't connect. Not even with him. Not right now.

"Maamaa?" The little voice dropped as though in question.

Wordlessly, she glanced down at her lap, staring at the small, grainy picture that accompanied the article. It must've been pulled from the files in a hurry. The likeness was old, an image captured more than two years before. Taken at yet another of Leah's constant stream of charity events—a Monte Carlo night with proceeds to offer relief to recent hurricane victims.

Tricia recognized the dress Leah was wearing. The smile on her face. The picture. She'd been standing right beside her when that photo was snapped. Had posed for one herself. After all, they'd both been wearing gowns from the latest Kate Whitehead collection—gowns that were to have their own showing later that year.

"Mama! Down! Mama! Down!" The loud banging, a result of her son's tennis shoe kicking back against the foothold on his chair, caught her attention.

With a trembling hand, she pushed a strand of her now-mousy-brown hair toward the ponytail band that was supposed to have been holding it in place, watching as the toddler screwed up his face into the series of creases and curves that indicated a full-blown tantrum. And felt as though the expression was her own. Grief. Anger. Confusion. Leah was missing. Leah—her best friend. A piece of her heart.

Leah, whose memory afforded her a secret inner hold on sanity in a life that was nothing but secrets and insanity.

"Down!" The squeal of fear in her son's voice catapulted Tricia out of her seat, across the foot and a half of cheap linoleum to his secondhand chair. In no time, she had him unstrapped, and clutched his strong little body tight, cheek to cheek, the tears streaming down her face mingling with his.

She was shaking harder than he was.

"...Engine Eleven respond, overturned traffic..."

"Let's go!" Captain Scott McCall dropped his sponge into

the bucket of water he'd been using to clean the windows in the station's kitchen and ran for the door. An overturned vehicle on the freeway couldn't be good.

A flurry of heavy footsteps hitting cement rang through the station. Silent men, focused on the moments ahead, or perhaps the pizza they'd just ordered and would now have to eat cold, if ever—all doing the jobs they'd been trained to do. Street boots off, Scott pulled on the heat resistant pants with attached boots that he'd thrown over the side of the engine when they'd returned from a Dumpster fire that morning. He grabbed his jacket off the side mirror and jumped aboard, scooping up the helmet he'd left in the passenger seat.

Cliff Ralen, his engineer, already had the rig in motion. They traveled silently, as usual, having worked together so long they had no need for words. Scott was the captain, but he rarely had to give orders to any of the three men riding with him. They were well-trained, as firemen and as co-workers. He was damned lucky to have a group of guys who shared a sixth sense when it came to getting the job done.

The engine couldn't get to the freeway quickly enough for Scott. Was it a multiple-car accident? Someone could be trapped inside. More than one someone. It was interstate. A second engine would be called. Police would be on-site.

With a rollover accident, there was a greater possibility of explosion.

And a greater possibility of severe injury—or death.

Sweating, impatient, Scott clenched his fists, waiting. This was always the worst part for him. The waiting. Patience wasn't his strongest suit.

He knew what it was like to be on the other side, helpless, feeling time slip away while you waited for help to arrive....

He tapped a foot against the floorboard. *He* was help. He

and his men. The guys would secure the area. Check for signs of fire danger. Rip car doors from their jambs. Break through back windows.

And Scott, as the engine's paramedic, would...

Do whatever needed to be done. He always did. He wouldn't think about the people. He wouldn't feel. They didn't pay him to think too much. Or to feel.

Feeling weakened a man. Got in the way. Could make the one-second difference between saving a life and losing it.

Scott wasn't going to lose a life. Not if there was anything humanly possible he could do to save it.

He wasn't going to witness another life fading away while he stood helplessly by and watched.

Period.

With his door open even before Cliff pulled to a halt, Scott jumped out. Sweating, he took in the entire scene at a glance—the circle of tragedy, with bystanders on the periphery and his men moving forward checking for fuel leaks, other signs of explosion danger, trapped victims.

Engine Eleven was the first on site. Goddamn, it was ugly. A pickup truck, the mangled cap several yards away. Off to the other side, also several yards from the smashed vehicle, was a trailer hauling a late-model Corvette. Whoever had been driving that truck had been going too fast, jackknifed the trailer, lost control. Judging by the roof flattened clear down to the door frame, the truck had rolled more than once.

Whoever had been driving the truck was nowhere in sight. He hoped it was a man. Or an old woman who'd lived a full life. *Please God, don't let it be a young woman.*

"She's trapped inside!" Joe Valentine called out. He'd worked with Scott for six of Scott's eleven years with the department.

If she's young, let her be okay, he demanded silently as he grabbed his black bag and approached the truck. *She's just trapped. Between the steel frame of the truck, the air bags and seat belt, the vehicle might have protected her.* Cliff took a crowbar to the upside-down driver's door. Metal on metal, screeching over raw nerves. *He'd treat her for shock. Rail at her about the reason for speed limits. Make sure she understood how lucky she was to have escaped serious injury.*

It was half an hour before Scott had his mind to himself again. He'd filled out his report. *Tuesday, April 5, 2005. 11:45 a.m. Responded to call at...*

Kelsey Stuart, the young woman who'd borrowed her boyfriend's truck to pull her recently deceased father's car to her apartment in San Diego, had been pronounced dead at the scene fifteen minutes before.

By the time she heard Scott's black Chevy pickup in the drive shortly after eight on Wednesday morning, Tricia had had twenty-four hours to think about Leah's disappearance, to work herself into an inner frenzy and an outer state of complete calm. Much of her life had been spent learning things she'd never use. But little had she known, growing up the daughter of a wealthy San Franciscan couple, that the ability to keep up appearances had also equipped her with the skills to lead a double life.

"Hi, babe!" Even after almost two years of living with this man, sharing his bed and his life, she still felt that little leap in her belly every time he walked into a room.

She was in the kitchen and plunged her hands into the sink of dirty dishwater to keep from flinging them around Scott. He wouldn't recognize the needy, clinging woman.

"Hi, yourself!"

He'd been gone four nights—part of the four-on, four-off rotation that made up most of his schedule, broken only once or twice a month with a one- or two-day on/off turn. She could have justified a hug. *If* she'd been able to trust herself not to fall apart the moment she felt his arms slide around her.

"Daaadeee!" Taylor squirmed in his high chair, seemingly unaware of the toast crumbs smeared across his plump cheeks and up into his hair. His breakfast was a daily prebath ritual.

"Mornin', squirt!" Scott rubbed the baby's head and bent down to kiss his cheek, as though he was spotlessly clean. "Were you a good boy for your mama?"

"Good boy." Taylor nodded. And then, "Down!"

He lifted his arms up to the man he called Daddy. Someday Taylor would have to know that Scott wasn't actually his biological father, but maybe by then Scott would have adopted him and—

She abruptly yanked the plug from the bottom of the sink, watching as the greyish water and the residue of bubbles washed away. She couldn't think about the future. It was one of her nonnegotiable rules.

Unless things changed drastically, there would be no future for her. Only the day-to-day life she had now. Only the moment.

Hearing her son squeal, followed by silence from the man who usually made as much or more noise than the little boy when the two were playing together, Tricia glanced over her shoulder.

"Scott?" She dried her hands, moved slowly behind the man she'd duped—yes, duped—into taking her in. She'd played the part of a destitute homeless woman, and then grown to love Scott more than she'd ever believed possible. Face buried in Taylor's neck, he was holding on to the boy.

Almost as she had the day before…

"Is something wrong?" she asked, the terror that was never far from the surface tightening her throat around the words. Had he had enough of them? Was this going to be goodbye?

Could she handle another loss right now?

He didn't look up right away, and Tricia focused on breathing. Life had come down to this a few times in the past couple of years—reduced to its most basic level. Getting each breath to follow the one before. Clearing her mind of all thought, all worry, her heart of all fear, so that she could breathe.

"You want us to leave?" she made herself ask when she could. Probably only seconds had passed. They seemed like minutes. Her arrangement with Scott wasn't permanent. She'd known that. Insisted on it.

The back pockets of her worn, department-store jeans were a good place for hands that were noticeably trembling.

"Can we put him in his playpen with Blue?" Scott asked.

Taylor's addiction to Blue's Clues could easily buy half an hour of uninterrupted time.

"I need to talk to you."

It was bad, then.

He wouldn't look her in the eye. Hadn't answered her question about leaving. And his thick brown hair was messier than usual—as though he'd been running his hand through it all morning.

Scott had a habit of doing that when he was working through things that upset him.

She wanted to speak. To tell him that amusing Taylor with Blue while they talked was fine with her. That she was happy to hear whatever was on his mind.

She just didn't have it in her. She'd hardly slept. Was having trouble staying focused. Jumping at every innocuous click, bump or whoosh of air. She'd even dropped Taylor's spoon earlier when the refrigerator had clicked on behind her.

With a jerky nod, she followed him into the living room, where one entire corner was taken up with Taylor's playpen, toys and sundry other toddler possessions. She would've moved the changing table someplace else now that he was older and it was easier to have him climb onto the couch rather than lifting his almost twenty pounds up to the table for a diaper change, but they didn't have anyplace to put it, so it was still there, being used to store toys and videos. Scott's house, as was the case with most of the homes in the older San Diego South Park neighborhood, didn't have a garage.

And the crib and dresser in Taylor's small room left no space for anything else. Which made the fact that they had little else less noticeable.

"What's up?" They were in Scott's room—their room for now—with the door open so she could hear Taylor.

He paced at the end of the king-size bed, staring down at the hardwood floor. Sitting in the old wooden rocker that had become a haven to her, Tricia hugged a throw pillow to her belly and waited.

Scott stopped. Glanced over at her. He sat on the end of the bed she'd made only an hour before. With hands clasped between his knees, he looked over at her.

"I haven't been completely honest with you."

Her breath whooshed out, but her lungs didn't immediately expand to allow any entry of air.

He opened his mouth to speak, then shook his head.

"What?" Her voice was low, partly because she was having trouble saying anything at all. Partly because of Taylor in the next room. But also because, as she saw him sitting there, she watched—felt—the struggle inside him.

She knew. Oh, not his secret, obviously. But she knew all about the dark pain associated with keeping secrets.

"I shouldn't have lied, and I'm sorry." The conversation was getting more and more ominous. Tricia wanted to scream at him for lying to her. She'd been lied to enough. Couldn't take any more.

But how could she be upset with him for something she

was doing herself? No one was guiltier of hiding things than
Tricia Campbell—name chosen from the Campbell's soup
can she'd seen on his counter when, the morning after the first
time they'd had sex, he'd asked her full name.

"Why…" she coughed. "Why don't you tell me what this
is about?" If she had to find another place to live, she'd need
as much of the day as she could get. Taylor had to be in bed
by seven or he'd be too tired to sleep.

Still hugging the pillow, Tricia tried her hardest to ignore
the far-too-familiar sense of impending darkness, the dread
and panic that she could never seem to escape. She thought
of the blue sky outside. Of the beach in Coronado, there for
her to walk any time of the day or night. She thought of cuddling up to her small son for a long afternoon nap.

"I'm—I haven't always lived…this way." He gestured to
the room.

"What? I'm keeping the place too clean? I don't mean to,
I just…"

"No!" He grinned at her and Tricia's heart lightened. That
quickly. It was why she'd been drawn to the man in the first
place. There was something special about him and something deep in her recognized it. Even if, consciously, she had
no idea what it was.

"I love everything you've done to the place. The curtains
and pillows, the rugs. I love having meals I don't have to fix
myself, and having help with the dishes. I love always being
able to find what I need because it has a place, so I know
where to look for it."

Good. Okay, then. She wasn't just using him. She was giving him a valuable service.

"Have you ever heard of McCall faucets?"

The question threw her. "Of course. They're top-of-the-line.
In custom homes all over the country. They do shower fixtures,
too."

"And toilet hardware," he added.

"So?" She frowned, pushed against the floor with one bare foot to set the chair in motion. "You want to replace the kitchen faucet?"

He shook his head.

She hadn't really thought so.

"The shower?" Please let it just be that.

"No, Trish. I want to tell you that my family *is* McCall faucets. *I* am McCall faucets."

She was going to wake up now and find out that this was a twisted dream, another way her psyche had dreamed up to torment her. She was going to wake up and find out that it was really only one in the morning and she had a whole night to get through before she could rise out of bed and feel the promise of sunshine on her skin. Seven and a half hours to go before Scott got home from his shift at the station.

"Say something." He was still sitting there, dressed in his blue uniform pants and blue T-shirt with the San Diego fire insignia on it, hands clasped. She hadn't woken up.

"I'm confused." It was a relief to tell the complete truth for once.

"My grandfather is the original designer and patent holder of McCall faucets. The company now belongs to my parents. My younger brother, Jason, has an MBA in business and will probably take over the vice presidency from my uncle when he retires in a couple of years."

Wake up. Wake up. Please, wake up.

"Do you have a large family?" That seemed the smart thing to concentrate on until she could get herself out of this crazy nightmare.

Scott was one of those people? The kind whose wealth and privilege instilled the belief that they were above the law? One of those people who made mistakes and knew that society wouldn't dare *not* look the other way?

Scott was coming clean? When it was more important than ever that she continue with her lies?

He'd said something—about his family she presumed—and was now awaiting her response.

"I'm sorry, I missed that. I was listening to Taylor." The lies slid out of her mouth so easily these days.

His mouth curved in the half grin that often made her stomach turn over. It didn't move today—except maybe to tense in pain. Someday she was going to miss that grin.

"I said that I have numerous aunts, uncles and cousins, both of my maternal grandparents and both parents. But Jason in my only sibling."

"No sisters?" The ridiculous question, considering what he was telling her, proved to her that this was only a dream. Reassured her.

Scott shook his head. "Just a bevy of female cousins."

She felt a brief curiosity about them. Would probably have liked them. If she could've met Scott sooner, in college maybe, before she'd made the one critical choice that had ruined the rest of her life.

Staring at the braided rug in the middle of the floor, between the rocker, bed and dresser, she didn't realize Scott had stood until she felt the warmth of his hand prying the pillow from her fingers. With gentle pressure, he pulled at her hand. Tricia didn't resist. In his arms she came alive.

She knew her attempt at escape through fantasies of nightmares for the lie it was.

Everything Scott had just told her was true. All true.

And everything about her—including her mousy-brown hair—was false.

HARLEQUIN *Super*ROMANCE

COLD CASES: L.A.

A *new* mystery/suspense miniseries from

Linda Style,

**author of The Witness
and The Man in the Photograph**

His Case, Her Child
(Superromance #1281)

He's a by-the-book detective determined to find his
niece's missing child. She's a youth advocate equally
determined to protect the abandoned boy in her charge.
Together, Rico Santini and Macy Capshaw form an uneasy
alliance to investigate the child's past and, in the process,
unearth a black-market adoption ring at a shelter for
unwed mothers. The same shelter where years earlier
Macy had given birth to a stillborn son. At least,
that's what she was told....

Available in June 2005 wherever Harlequin books are sold.

If you enjoyed what you just read,
then we've got an offer you can't resist!

Take 2 bestselling love stories FREE!

Plus get a FREE surprise gift!

Clip this page and mail it to Harlequin Reader Service®

IN U.S.A.
3010 Walden Ave.
P.O. Box 1867
Buffalo, N.Y. 14240-1867

IN CANADA
P.O. Box 609
Fort Erie, Ontario
L2A 5X3

YES! Please send me 2 free Harlequin Superromance® novels and my free surprise gift. After receiving them, if I don't wish to receive anymore, I can return the shipping statement marked cancel. If I don't cancel, I will receive 6 brand-new novels every month, before they're available in stores. In the U.S.A., bill me at the bargain price of $4.69 plus 25¢ shipping and handling per book and applicable sales tax, if any*. In Canada, bill me at the bargain price of $5.24 plus 25¢ shipping and handling per book and applicable taxes**. That's the complete price, and a savings of at least 10% off the cover prices—what a great deal! I understand that accepting the 2 free books and gift places me under no obligation ever to buy any books. I can always return a shipment and cancel at any time. Even if I never buy another book from Harlequin, the 2 free books and gift are mine to keep forever.

135 HDN DZ7W
336 HDN DZ7X

Name	(PLEASE PRINT)	
Address	Apt.#	
City	State/Prov.	Zip/Postal Code

Not valid to current Harlequin Superromance® subscribers.

Want to try two free books from another series?
Call 1-800-873-8635 or visit www.morefreebooks.com.

* Terms and prices subject to change without notice. Sales tax applicable in N.Y.
** Canadian residents will be charged applicable provincial taxes and GST.
   All orders subject to approval. Offer limited to one per household.
   ® are registered trademarks owned and used by the trademark owner and or its licensee.

SUP04R   ©2004 Harlequin Enterprises Limited

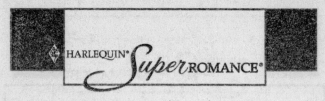

COMING NEXT MONTH

#1278 STRANGER IN TOWN • Brenda Novak
A Dundee, Idaho, book

Hannah Russell almost killed Gabe Holbrook in a car accident. Gabe's been in a wheelchair ever since, his athletic career ended. He's a recluse, living in a cabin some distance from Dundee, and Hannah can't get over her guilt. But one of her sons is on the high school football team and when Gabe—reluctantly—becomes the coach, she finds herself facing him again....

#1279 HIS REAL FATHER • Debra Salonen
Twins

Lisa never had trouble telling the Kelly brothers apart. Even though they were twins, they were nothing alike. Joe was quiet, and Patrick the life of the party. Each was important to her. But only one was the father of her son.

#1280 A FAMILY FOR DANIEL • Anna DeStefano
You, Me & the Kids

Josh White is trying to care for his late sister's son, but Daniel's hurting so much nothing seems to reach him. The only person the boy responds to is Amy Loar, Josh's childhood friend. Amy has her own problems, but she does her best to help. Then Daniel's father shows up and threatens to sue for custody, and the two old friends have to figure out how to make a family for Daniel.

#1281 HIS CASE, HER CHILD • Linda Style
Cold Cases: L.A.

He's a by-the-book detective determined to find his niece's missing child. She's a youth advocate equally determined to protect an abandoned boy in her charge. Together, Rico Santini and Macy Capshaw form an uneasy alliance to investigate the child's past, and in the process they unearth a black-market adoption ring at a shelter for unwed mothers. The same shelter where years earlier Macy had given birth to a stillborn son. At least, that's what she was told....

#1282 THE DAUGHTER'S RETURN • Rebecca Winters
Lost & Found

Maggie McFarland's little sister was kidnapped twenty-six years ago, but Maggie has never given up hope of finding Kathryn. Now Jake Halsey has a new lead for her, and it looks as if she's finally closing in on the truth. The trouble is, it doesn't look as if Jake has told her the truth about *himself.*

#1283 PREGNANT PROTECTOR • Anne Marie Duquette
9 Months Later

The stick said positive. She was pregnant. Lara Nelson couldn't believe it. How had she, a normally levelheaded cop, let this happen—especially since the soon-to-be father was the man she was sworn to protect?